She Should Have Called Him Siegfried

Regina Glei

ISBN: 1-4775-4368-6
ISBN-13: 9781477543689

Part 1

chapter 1

SUNDAY, 5TH OF September

Never before had Hagen Patterson allowed a potion client to see his cellar. Alissa sat opposite him, watching him from between test tubes, Bunsen burners, and vials that crowded his massive ceramic-tiled workbench.

"What if I called the police and told them that you have a chemical plant and plenty of illegal substances hidden in your cellar?" she asked, smiling at him.

He wiped his sweaty, cold hands at his lab coat.

"Then you wouldn't get potions for Benjamin anymore."

Her smile deepened and brought out the laugh lines under her green eyes. "Why are you showing me your cellar, Hagen?"

"To intensify our relationship."

"To what end?"

"We are much alike, you and I."

"Are we?"

He tried to ignore the hint of scorn in her voice.

"Yes, we have the same goal."

"Oh really?"

She put one nylon-covered leg over the other. He caught a glimpse of knee from where he stood opposite her and stared at the hem of her business suit skirt. It had been a while since a woman had him sweating like that.

"I'll be frank with you, and I hope you'll appreciate that. I do have a few clients, but not many and you are my only love potion client. It's very fortunate that we met. I have a special interest in love potions and with your and Benjamin's help, I'll be able to refine the formula and make it more effective."

She nodded. "Yes, I already suspected that you don't really know what you're doing."

He frowned. "I do know what I'm doing."

She tugged blond hair behind her right ear and her smile deepened once more, revealing her very white teeth.

"I'm sorry, Hagen; I appreciate your help, really. I also appreciate that you admit that you're using me, or better to say Benjamin, as a test subject. That solves some unasked questions and underlying mistrust."

He nodded, noticed he was clutching his lab coat, and released it. He turned to his hundreds of test tubes and vials.

Not one of them contained the same liquid or powder and they transformed his alchemist's workbench into a display of all colors of the visual spectrum.

He took up a vial containing a sky-blue liquid.

"Then let me brew your potion."

"What's her name?" Alissa asked after a short silence.

"Excuse me?"

"The woman you want to brew a potion for."

"Why should I tell you?"

"That trust you spoke of. You know the name of my object of desire; why shouldn't I know her name?"

"Juliana," he said, reluctantly.

Alissa smoothed the skirt covering her thighs.

"Juliana and Benjamin. My, if those two knew what we're doing down here," she said.

Hagen chuckled.

"Do I hear a little bit of bad conscience in that chuckle?" She grinned at him.

"Not bad conscience, thrill."

She nodded and that lock fell into her face again. She tucked it back behind her ear. Her ears resembled Juliana's precious lobes. Evenly formed, they clung flat and smoothly to her head.

Hagen poured a few drops of the sky-blue liquid into a test tube containing a base of milky white slime and then added a small dose of a gray powder. After stirring the mix with a glass rod, he lifted the test tube with metal tongs and heated the potion over a Bunsen burner until it boiled and turned a grayish blue. He killed the flame and poured the liquid into a waiting vial half filled with a pink fluid.

He smiled to himself as Alissa gasped when the gray-blue and pink liquids swirled together and became crimson, dark as blood. He slipped the used test tube into a rack, where others that awaited cleaning were lined up, and set down the metal tongs. The mix lost its color while it cooled down and gave way to a water-like transparency.

Hagen reveled in the sight. *I brew for the view.* He grinned at the silly rhyme. He drew in the acidic scent of the potion, a bit like fresh limes.

"So amazing," she said.

"Now we have to let it finish cooling down."

An awkward silence filled the cellar whose naked brick walls made it look cold and damp. Hagen looked up from the potion that he had just brewed and into Alissa's eyes. She stared back, openly, expectantly. Should he dare? If he did, she'd assume that he had brought her down into his cellar just for that. Had he? Well, yes.

"How old are you?" Hagen asked.

She arched an elegant brow. "How rude."

"No, not at all, you're very attractive. I'm wondering how you managed to stay that attractive."

A smile curled her lips. "I'm forty-two, and thanks. If I had a secret for how I stay attractive, would you want to make a potion out of it?"

"If I could."

They grinned at each other.

"How old are you, Hagen?"

"I'm thirty-one and damned happy that I finally left my twenties behind me. You don't gain respect in my profession before you've reached a certain age."

Alissa crossed her arms in front of her chest. "And what do we do until my potion, or better to say Benjamin's, has cooled down?"

"Oh, I have an idea."

"Now I'm thrilled."

"We could retire to my study and console each other." He pointed at a wooden door to his left. "Only until Benjamin and Juliana give themselves to us, of course." He waited for her answer, barely daring to breathe.

She considered his proposal for an awfully long time. Finally, she smiled, got up, and walked in her high heels towards his study. He followed her, hands getting sweaty again, and inhaled the heavy scent of her expensive perfume. He watched how her hips, framed by her tight skirt, weaved in the rhythm that her high heels demanded. In those shoes, she was taller than he was. Taller women aroused him without fail.

Emma Patterson never grew tired of watching her only son. He just raised a fork and shoved a slice of meat into his mouth. He chewed while he looked at his mashed potatoes. He lacked Hollywood star qualities, his hairline had already receded, and traces of gray peeked through the cropped brown hair. He had a snub nose, which softened his face, and he possessed Emma's well-formed, sensual lips.

As so many times before, Emma decided that her son's eyes were the source of his charm. Those dark brown eyes, bottomless, hiding secrets, one look and some women melted away, Emma included.

He had hidden in his apartment downstairs the entire Sunday. That woman had been with him, Alissa—Emma didn't know her surname. She had started to visit him regularly two months ago but that afternoon had been the first time she had stayed for several hours.

Emma got up to get another bottle of wine from the small wine rack next to her fridge. As she passed him, she sniffed the air around him. Yes, the heavy, sweet stench of woman rose from him. Emma shuddered. Alissa was at least ten years older than Hagen was. What the hell did he find appealing about her?

Don't be so envious; that's humiliating, a deep, pleasant, but invidious, male voice said. Emma heard the voice of Hagen's father in her head since the night of Hagen's conception.

I'm lonely; I haven't had sex for ages. I can be as envious as I wanna be, she thought back.

The voice in her head chuckled like an old geezer.

She didn't know his name. He had never bothered telling her. She called him Alberich or Al.

Oh, let me please you, darling.

Fuck yourself in the knee.

Alberich snickered.

That vicious snicker made her want to bang her head against the wall to make him stop. Instead, Emma uncorked the wine and poured a glass for Hagen.

"Oh, thanks."

He looked up at her and smiled. Sometimes, when he smiled, all of that mystery and depth vanished from his eyes and naked kindness remained behind, like now. Emma loved him as her son again in such moments and not as a man.

She poured herself a glass as well, wishing those "son moments" happened more often.

She Should Have Called Him Siegfried

Yes, I concur; your erotic fantasies are really embarrassing, Alberich said.

Shut up.

She sipped from her wine and stared over Hagen's head at her favorite *The Ring of Nibelung* poster, the one from the Bayreuth Festival performance of 1983, conducted by Georg Solti. Yes, she had made the right choice to move this poster from the living room, which Hagen rarely entered, to the kitchen. It soothed her to see the two things that she loved most together now.

Your son a thing? You're learning, my dear. That's a good way to prepare yourself for the time when I must leave you to join him.

I won't let you have him, Emma thought and drank more wine to Alberich's chuckle in her head.

Hagen cleaned his plate of sauce with a piece of broccoli.

Emma wondered whether this Alissa woman received a potion from Hagen.

I'll bet it's some sort of love potion.

It could be anything, Al.

Nah, I'm sure it's a sex drug, he said.

Alissa fell under the category that Emma called "vamp."

Exactly, Alberich said.

Actually, Emma hadn't spoken to Alissa yet, but the way she moved, walked, talked, and poised her head and body said enough.

It does; she's gorgeous.

Alissa was a passionate and dangerous woman, jealous, moody, and driven.

Don't bash her like that.

Well, at least he had finally slept with someone again. Anything and anybody that got his mind off Juliana was good.

She smiled at her son. "I noticed that—"

Emma, don't.

"—Alissa stayed at your place the whole afternoon."

Hagen put his fork onto his empty plate and frowned at her. "Mom, stop spying on me."

"I'm not spying. I noticed her car; that's all."

Hagen stood abruptly. "Thanks for the dinner, Mom; see you."

"Sorry, Hagen, I didn't mean to—"

"Yeah, I know. Night, Mom."

Then he was gone and Alberich snickered in her head.

Downstairs in his apartment, Hagen took a long, hot shower. Damn his mother for spying on him.

He had reduced their number of dinners gradually over the years until they had settled on once a month on a Sunday. Hagen lived on the ground floor of his mother's old two-story brick house, had his separate entrance and, more importantly, exclusive use of the cellar.

Hagen would have liked to take a shower prior to the dinner, but Alissa had left only minutes before his appointment upstairs. Alissa…he was a little sad that the hot water washed away her scent. He'd phone her the next day. That little threat that she'd call the police had made being with her all the more exciting. He stretched comfortably as he dressed in his pajamas after the shower and entered his bedroom—his shrine.

Hagen's shrine was smaller than Emma's Richard Wagner collection, but much more personal. It consisted of seven pictures hanging on the wall to the right of his bed. He had arranged six of the pictures in a circle around the seventh and all of them depicted Juliana.

Hagen practiced his nightly ritual and stood in front of the blessed wall that carried Juliana's photographs.

"Good night, my love. One day you'll be mine."

After saying so, he concentrated on the seventh picture in the middle. On a good night, her portrait would seem to warp out of two dimensions to change her face from flatland into full form. Her pointed nose emerged first, her full lips next. Her high cheekbones, her noble forehead, and her chin emerged at the same time, then the hollows of her eyes, and last, but not least, her adorable ears.

Her face was oval, elegant, and highly symmetrical. He found that symmetry most pleasing, soothing and exciting at the same time. Her lips seemed to beg for his kisses; her smooth skin seemed to long for the caress of his fingers.

After the plasticity of the central picture faded because he stared too strongly, he looked down at the single framed photo that stood below the ring of seven on a hip-high cabinet. It depicted Juliana in a wedding dress, more beautiful than ever, but the lucky man beside her was not Hagen but Gabe, Gabriel Daniels, the man that she had married instead of him. Hagen let the image of Gabe sober him, before he sighed and turned around to go to bed.

chapter 2

I TASTE BITTERNESS. Not unpleasant, it is black and strong with a hint of chocolate in it. After a while, I understand that it's mocha. I smile; George has made it for me. He knows that I love mocha.

I try to focus, to see what is on the other side of my eyes. It hurts. Most of the time, the pain is so great that I cannot focus. I stay behind my eyes and don't even think; every thought is agony. But sometimes, when something special happens, like the sweet bitter smell and taste of a good mocha, I struggle to leave the fortress of my head for a while.

All of my thoughts, my memories, one after the other, disappear away. I have already lost so many. I can no longer remember the face of the baby that we lost.

He was born prematurely; he died five weeks after his birth. I had wanted to name him Carl. I had called him Carl for five weeks.

Pain explodes in my brain as I find George's face in the blur before me. He smiles at me.

"Helena, darling, are you trying to wake up?"

His voice is so gentle.

It's too difficult to speak yet. I smile instead and wait a moment, testing whether the pain will get worse or if it will stay confined to its current level. My head throbs; my brain fights with the thing that is destroying it.

The evil tumor. I forget so many things, but its grand sounding name is burned into the cells surrounding it: glioblastoma multiforme.

I can feel its knotty mass in my head, eating away at what is left of my brain. It festers and grows and spreads and I know that it'll kill me eventually. Though not yet. There's a certainty in me that I must do something; knowledge that I have a mission yet to fulfill before I can give in to the pain and let it win so I can be at peace.

The pain doesn't get worse for the moment; it lets me speak. "George?"

"Hi, honey, oh, bless you."

He smiles, then kisses my forehead. I feel the pressure of his lips soft against my skull. He kisses my lips and I manage to kiss him back.

"You're so sweet, George, thank you."

He beams at me.

The greater the misery, the happier you are with the little things. He wasn't happy before when I was awake. When something becomes rare, we treasure it and it gives us joy, even if that something is only a brief moment of lucidity.

"No, thank you for being awake. This is amazing. It's been only two days since you last spoke to me; you're getting better, love."

I'll only get worse although I cannot imagine what worse could be like. "I won't get better, George."

"Oh, don't say that, sweetie, you will get better. You will."

This is bad. I hear hope in his voice. I don't want him to hope. I don't want him to be hurt even more.

I feel the onslaught of headache nearing again and try to concentrate on what I have to say before the evil mass in my head buries it. Headache—what a weak word for the agony under my scalp.

"George, every day you're giving me something strange to drink. It tastes weird, not bad, but weird. What is that?"

"Oh, my God, you noticed? That's great, sweetheart. Don't be shocked. I think it really helps you. You didn't have clear moments before you drank this stuff. The mix comes from Hagen. It's a secret, but he's a healer, honey."

"Hagen…" I fall silent.

The pain is too great and my vision blurs. The colors in front of my eyes blend into each other and become a pulsing gray. George says something else but I cannot hear him anymore. His voice mingles with the other sounds around me: the cars driving by outside, the birds and the wind, and the hum of our refrigerator down in the kitchen. How can I hear it from up here in our bedroom? My thoughts float into the center of pain and lose coherence.

Hagen…how befitting that he brews potions and how strange that they help. I've never believed in supernatural things before the tumor. However, now I do, because I can feel them beyond the prison of my mind, sleeping in the shadow of my eyes. I feel them coming, events on the verge of existence, waiting for a chance and a way to hammer themselves into reality.

chapter 3

MONDAY, 6TH OF September

Hagen usually ate his lunch in the cafeteria of the chemical plant he worked for but preferred to sit alone. Recently though, a new colleague, Cindy, had started to eye him quite obviously. She was young, around 25, Hagen presumed, fresh from university, and far from being classy like Juliana or Alissa.

He smirked at Cindy's inner fight whether to invite herself to his table or not. She had hesitated for an entire week but apparently she had stiffened her resolve over the weekend and boldly approached him with her tray.

"Hi, Pat, can I sit here?"

"Sure." He graced her with his smile. People at work called him Pat, short for Patterson.

Cindy beamed and sat down opposite him. She was a tiny bit cross-eyed and had short, dark hair. A boyish girl, trying to hold her own in a male dominated job, doubly difficult at barely five foot two.

"How was your weekend?" she asked, cheeks flushed.

"Oh, nice and quiet."

Nobody had told her yet that he strictly separated his working life from his private life. He had to…if any of his colleagues knew what he brewed in his cellar….

"I've been surfing a bit over the weekend. Is your mother Emma Patterson?"

For a second, he thought she meant surfing the ocean, but net-surfing befitted Cindy much better.

"Yep, that's my mom."

"Wow, that's so cool. I wish I had a mom like that. My mom is so boring, only knitting sweaters'n stuff. You know, I'm a big classics fan, too, especially Wagner. I'm ravenously envious that your mother managed to see the real thing in Bayreuth. And her webpage is gorgeous."

Her speech came out quick and fluent, she had clearly rehearsed it. How pathetic.

"Oh really, you should e-mail her."

"Yes, I might do that. You like Wagner, too?"

"No, I hate classical music and especially him. I prefer heavy metal."

She started to fidget in her seat. He had to stifle a grin and felt almost sorry for her.

"Oh…um." She smiled sheepishly. "I've never listened to metal much."

"You should; it's liberating."

"Yes, I might."

They ate in silence. Cindy's hands were cramped around her knife and fork. Hagen waited, highly amused by her plight.

"You don't like Wagner because of your name?" she finally asked.

His grin broadened. "No. I don't like my mother. *She* gave me that name. It's not Wagner's fault, is it?"

Her eyes widened in shock. "You don't like your mother?"

"Not overwhelmingly, no. She could never quite hide that she loved her operas more than she loved me. Her choice of name never encouraged me either." He made a pause. He just had to test her. "Do you really like opera? Who's Hagen, how was he conceived and who's his father?"

"Um, what?"

"Can you answer the questions or not?"

"Sure I can. Hagen is the bad guy, the one who kills Siegfried, his father is the dwarf Alberich and well...his mother was a prostitute."

"I think it was called whore back then," Hagen said and grinned. "And yes, you're right, seems you do like opera."

"Of course I do, why wouldn't I?"

"Maybe you were just looking for a reason to talk to me and Googled my name."

Cindy blushed so much he could have fried eggs on her cheeks.

"Anyway, back to Hagen. So, not exactly great prospects for the boy, destined to be evil," he said.

"It's just an opera."

"It seems to be more than that in my case. I don't know my father, Cindy. My mother has never bothered to tell me who he is."

She stared at him with her mouth open. Either his saucy talk would scare her off or it would make her crazy about him. He hoped for the latter. She'd become a pain in the neck in that case, but he longed for play. He had long reached a dead end with Juliana. She had just celebrated her third wedding anniversary. Every day, he waited in fear for the news that Gabriel had finally gotten her pregnant.

Hagen smiled that vicious smile that he used consciously ever since Emma had made the mistake to tell him about it. He slightly lowered his head so that he looked at Cindy as if over the rim of glasses. That angle accentuated the depth of his eyes.

Cindy smiled shyly. "You don't know who your father is?"

Ah, she didn't know yet which way she wanted to go. He granted her a little slack.

"No, I don't. Considering the time I was born though, it must've happened during my mom's infamous visit to Bayreuth. So maybe my father is German. Dreadful thought, they're such a stiff and serious people."

"Not necessarily, the Bayreuth Festival is a pretty international event."

"Yeah, maybe another fan or maybe someone important, one of the singers perhaps, someone from the orchestra…who knows?"

Cindy's eyes glowed. Yes, he'd have her to play with for a while. He'd tease her, entice her, and then he'd crush her heart between his fingers.

"That's exciting. I'll bet he's someone famous, otherwise your mom would've told you, wouldn't she?"

She Should Have Called Him Siegfried

Their lunch chime rang out and she looked disappointed that they had to stop their conversation.

They returned their used trays and walked down the hallway to their chemistry labs. She waved at him before she vanished into hers. Hagen merely nodded, not waving back. He had run out of zinc. He'd have to smuggle some out of the company tonight.

They only did petty stuff here at the company, industrial appliances, normal affairs, nothing surprising. Nevertheless, he had wanted it that way; he had passed on research jobs in order to be where nobody would notice if tiny bits of ingredients went missing for the real research that happened in his cellar.

Home from work, Hagen sat down on the stool that Alissa had used the previous day. He took a vial with zinc powder out of his bag and marveled at it for a moment. He put it down onto his workbench and flipped his cell phone open to call Alissa.

"Hi, it's Hagen."

"Oh, hi...everything all right?" she asked, sounding astonished that he had called.

"Yes. Have you administered?"

"No chance today. Tomorrow."

"Let me know the result."

"Sure."

Her voice was cold and impatient.

"You know, I liked what happened yesterday and would be glad to repeat it," he said.

"Oh..."

Silence followed. Hagen played with the zinc vial for a few moments before speaking again. "You didn't like it?" He had thought she had.

"I can't talk right now. I'll call you later." She hung up the phone.

He took his cell phone from his ear and stared at it. "Whew..."

He sighed. It would've been nice to fool around with Alissa, but he could live without her.

He got up to store the zinc in his repository, a huge and heavy wooden closet. On his workbench, chaos seemed to prevail though Hagen knew the exact location and quantity of every ingredient on the table. In his cabinets, meticulous order ruled. On the left hand side of the main closet, hundreds of same-sized jars contained powdery ingredients, neatly labeled with stickers he had printed out. On the right hand side of the closet stood hundreds of same-sized bottles that contained labeled liquids. A giant industrial refrigerator for perishable ingredients stood between the closet and an open rack, which housed his collection: all kinds of samples in formaldehyde. He had acquired most of them for their looks, not their practical value. He had not yet needed a pig's heart for his experiments, or a cancer-infested lung. But how could he be a reputable alchemist if he didn't have a deformed monkey fetus in his collection?

As he opened the closet, his gaze fell upon his favorite object among the formaldehyde bins: the hand of death. It was an old woman's hand, gnarled and deformed by an extreme case of gout. The hand barely resembled that of a human anymore. It had something alien and abhorrent about it and yet, with the way the crooked fingers were posed inside the yellowish liquid, it looked elegant.

Juliana had smoked for a while. Luckily, she had given up on it, but Hagen would forever remember how her hand had held a cigarette. The pose had once given him an erection. The gout hand in formaldehyde bore an aftertaste of such sensuality and elegance, made all the more morbid by the illness that had deformed it. One look at that hand and one knew that it must have hurt terribly.

Hagen poured the purloined zinc into the big, nearly empty zinc jar. Then he went about his routine checklist of identifying what he had run out of and making plans for what he could and should steal next.

☙❧

Regina Glei

Report No. 8 from Agent 9836B12
Subject: Hagen Patterson (HP)
Status: Results remain inconclusive.
Next action: Further investigation.
Details of current status:

1) Following up on several rumors concerning HP distributing illegal substances.
2) 75% certain that HP doesn't distribute massively.
3) Credit card check negative. No unaccounted for surplus money on known accounts.
4) Sources for raw material unconfirmed. Company HP works for is a possible candidate, also his connection to Ivan Fuller, surgeon, HP's school friend. Both sources await confirmation.
5) Recipients of illegal substances remain unconfirmed. Ivan Fuller is a possible candidate. Erratic behavior reported on several occasions.

chapter 4

Hagen's cell phone rang and ripped him out of his cataloguing. His heart rate increased as he fumbled in the pocket of his lab coat. Did Alissa call him back? He frowned at the display that read "Ivan."

"Hi, Ivan."

"Hey, man, what's up?"

"Nothing special."

"You gotta come over and it's gotta be right now. I've got something for you." Ivan's voice dripped with wicked anticipation.

"Where?"

"The hospital, back entrance as usual."

"It's pretty late."

"Come on, man. And bring me a new round, will ya?"

Ivan hung up without waiting for a reply. Hagen sighed at his phone, then took a bottle of milky-white Ivan-mix from the fridge.

Still wearing his lab coat, Hagen drove to Ivan's hospital in his fifteen-year-old Toyota. He parked a block away and walked towards the huge hospital castle. This was the place where his potion client Helena had almost died. This was where, day by day, life ended and began in pain.

Years ago, Ivan had made Hagen a fake ID, and Hagen opened the delivery entrance door with it. Hagen checked his watch as he entered, eleven p.m. He yawned and walked through the corridors towards the hospital's archive, careful to avoid the security cameras.

Hagen used his ID card to get into the archive and the lights flickered on automatically. Ceiling-high racks filled with patients' files from the days before computers slumbered here. Hagen reached the far end of the archive and knocked on a supply closet's door, two—pause—three, and Ivan opened.

"Ah, finally," Ivan said as he grabbed Hagen's arm and pulled him inside the room.

Ivan, a young Gregory Peck in blond, had an angular, male, yet soft face with deep blue eyes that gave him a Hamlet-like air of tragic melancholy. His eyes had a slight feverish glow to them and dilated pupils. Ivan suffered from constantly elevated body temperature—a side effect of the potion that Hagen brewed for him.

"Got something for me?" Ivan asked and let himself fall into the farther of the two plastic armchairs in the supply closet. A small table stood between the chairs. Nothing more would fit into the tiny room. It had no window, only white bleached walls and always stale air.

"Sure," Hagen said. He produced the Ivan-mix bottle from his pocket and put it onto the table.

"Are you getting enough sleep?" Hagen asked.

"Sleep's for losers." Ivan grinned.

"Is that so…Every time I give you a new dosage, I understand less why you're taking this stuff. You know that it's not good for you."

"Doctor's habit and forbidden stuff is the best. I really don't get it. How can you manage not to take any of this precious, heavenly stuff that you brew?"

"Occupational hazard. If I took it, I wouldn't know what I'm mixing anymore."

"You don't know what you're missing, man." Ivan unscrewed the bottle's cap and took a sip. "Argh, although you could improve the taste of this shit."

"I'll put in a little strawberry flavor next time. And I do know what I'm missing, a strong hallucinogen that fries a few million brain cells every time you take it."

Ivan chuckled.

"You all right? Seriously, you look awful, man."

"I love you, Hagen; you're the only person who ever tells me that."

Ivan giggled and Hagen grinned.

"I'm fine, but I need an anti-love potion. There's this nurse who I did a few times; she thinks that she's in love with me. She's the worst groupie I've ever had. I've got to get rid of her. I'm serious, man; I need you to brew me something for or, more correctly, against her."

"I have a potion like that. It's pretty strong though, invokes depression."

"I don't fucking care. I have to get rid of that broad; she's killing me."

"Okay, next time we meet."

"Thanks, man."

Ivan giggled again. The potion started to work and his eyes became unfocused. His left hand jerked, spastically, and a moan slipped from his lips. Hagen watched with morbid fascination.

"What do you see?" he asked.

"Colors, they're blending into each other…" Ivan's speech was slurred.

"What else?"

"A house in the woods, a villa, there's a guy who's holding a girl captive. He's abusing her. She's so young… Oh, my God…"

"Stop that. A story like that was just in the news."

Ivan laughed out loud; drugged, stoned, and pleased. He suffered a laughing fit and couldn't stop for a while. Hagen waited. As he did so often, he wondered why he didn't want to experience anything like that himself.

You know why, Hagen; if you took that stuff, you'd lose control and you dread nothing more than that. He frowned.

"What's wrong?" Ivan asked.

Impressive, Ivan registered and interpreted facial expressions even under the influence of the potion.

"Nothing. Why did you want me to come here today, only to give you your next dosage? Selfish bastard," Hagen said affectionately.

Ivan raised a finger into the air. "Nope. Got something for you, too. The supplies you asked for and something else…Hehe."

Ivan reached under his chair and produced a plastic box where he kept his stash of stolen drugs. Hagen smiled. They were a formidable team. The things that you could do with a combined stash of chemicals and medicines were divine.

Ivan opened the box and took out a small plastic bag. He threw it to Hagen, who dropped the bag into a pocket of his lab coat.

Next, Ivan took an object wrapped in white linen, a part of a torn bed sheet, from behind his chair. He placed the thing onto the table between them with exaggerated care, and with drug-slowed fingers, he revealed a new piece for Hagen's formaldehyde collection.

Hagen gasped and Ivan chuckled with satisfaction.

"Ha, I knew you'd like it." Ivan fidgeted in his seat like a kid who had given his mom the perfect present.

Hagen stared at a woman's hand inside a large glass jar. The hand had been severed an inch above the wrist, a hint of slender arm still attached. The woman had been in her prime. It was hard to guess from the hand but she had been under forty for sure. Fire had burnt and marred the little and ring fingers and the side of the hand, but the two other fingers and the thumb were intact and hovered in the yellow fluid with such elegance that it made Hagen squirm. The slight bend of the fingers, crowned by still lacquered, long, elaborately manicured fingernails, sent a tingle into his own hands and a sting through his privates.

He turned the jar around and around on the table to look at this emblem of female sensuality from all angles. The sight of the burns intensified the tingle in his fingers, a sweet sting of lustful pain, paling before the wounded beauty.

"How did you get this? And what happened to her?" Hagen asked.

"Some house fire in town a few days ago; it was also in the news. A couple and two kids burnt, only one child survived. She," Ivan pointed at the hand in formaldehyde, "was still alive when they brought her here. I haven't seen her though, wasn't on duty. She had third and fourth degree burns to over seventy percent of her body and died hours later. She had an organ donor card. They took her apart and the rest landed in the morgue so I took the hand just before the remains were taken to the crematory; nobody noticed." Ivan beamed proudly.

Hagen held his breath for a moment. "You took the hand yourself?"

"Sure. Sawed it off." Ivan giggled.

"You're mad."

"No, I'm a surgeon; she wasn't the first corpse that I've worked on."

"Have you stolen body parts before?"

"No, that was a first, and, man, it was exhilerating!"

"Why did you do this?" Hagen asked, still completely baffled.

"Whew, you don't like it?"

"No, no, I love it. This is fantastic; it's totally perverted, but my greatest present ever." He laughed, embarrassed. "But why, why did you do this?"

"I thought you'd like it. Why else?" Ivan said, half beaming, half not understanding Hagen's question.

"Ivan, this is crazy; this is necrophilia, desecration of a dead body. This is a crime, and it's gross. And you did that to do me a favor?"

"Oh, come on, she was dead. They burned her body to ashes an hour later. It didn't hurt her. They had totally cannibalized her body. She was empty. She was thirty-eight and in brilliant shape. They harvested all of her organs. Now how gross is that? Why not take her hand? Why not put it in formaldehyde and give it to someone who'd cherish it and hold it dear? That way a part of her stays alive. Sort of…"

Hagen stared at his friend. He tried to take his mind off the image of a harvested human female body with a pried open rib cage, without a heart, kidneys, liver…he didn't know what else they would take.

"Well, I don't know what to say…thank you. I'll cherish that hand, I promise…What was her name?"

Ivan giggled in his doped state. "Man, you should hear yourself talking. You act as if that hand was holy. It's just a hand of a dead housewife-chick who had the bad luck to die from a fire."

Hagen squirmed. Ivan's words hurt worse than a beating.

"Ah, ah, I can see it. Your obsessive streak is coming through. You're nuts, Hagen. How do you do that? How can you elevate things like that? Like your slut Juliana. She doesn't want you, man. She's spitting into your face; forget her. What you need is a good fuck and…"

"Shut up!" Hagen shouted so loud that Ivan jumped.

Then Ivan chuckled, his pretty face distorted by the potion, his left eyelid fluttered, the well-formed blond brow above it twitched. "Oops, sorry…"

"Damn it, nothing is holy for you. You pull everything and everybody around you into the dirt. You're a monster," Hagen said, calm again, stating facts.

Ivan's grin looked insecure and defensive. "We should stop analyzing each other. We always fight when we do that."

"Agreed. Well, thanks for the present."

Hagen wrapped the cloth around the glass jar again. He had to hide the sight of this divine hand from the profane man in front of it.

"What was her name?" Hagen asked again.

"I'm not sure if it's wise to tell you."

"She's dead, Ivan. Without a name, this is just a hand. I need a name and you will tell me her name."

Hagen stared fiercely at his friend. Ivan looked at his hands, kneading them. The fire, the scorn and the mockery vanished from his eyes.

"Colleen Hardwood, her husband was John Hardwood. Her two kids who died were called Irene and Malcolm. Her daughter Lana survived. She's ten years old and is now living with the grandparents."

Hagen took a deep breath to calm himself, so terribly aware of his power over Ivan. To be loved means to have power over the one who loves you, like Juliana had power over him. Well, he, in a way, loved Ivan too. So what did that mean in terms of power?

"Thank you, Ivan; really, this is a great present. I really appreciate it." Hagen smiled at him.

Ivan visibly relaxed and grinned back in his drugged state. "Glad you like it. I knew you'd like it."

She Should Have Called Him Siegfried

With the tension gone and under the influence of the potion, Ivan fell asleep in his chair ten minutes later. Hagen spread Ivan's body as comfortably as possible over the table and the two chairs and covered him with an old blanket that lay behind Ivan's chair. Then Hagen tiptoed out of the hospital with the severed hand of Colleen Hardwood under his arm.

chapter 5

SNOWFLAKES DANCE IN my mind. Each is different and every one contains a thought. I try to grab them, to hold them, but they immediately melt on the palms of my hands and the thought is lost forever.

Carl, my baby, he is still there, even though I cannot remember his face. I had wanted Carl to play with Emma's child. We were pregnant at the same time. She got her baby, Hagen…but Carl died.

A part of me is happy that I cannot remember Carl's face anymore. It had been shriveled, ugly, yes, ugly. Had he lived, maybe he would've become a pretty child. But he died, a tiny mass of fragile skin and flesh and bone.

George wanted a child so much, even more than I did, to carry on his name, to teach him baseball in our garden. I don't know if George knows that I secretly took the pill after Carl's death. I couldn't stand to go through all that pain and suffering again. I didn't want to risk another hell of hope and pain. What if the second child died too…?

This is my greatest sin: I've never told George why he remained childless. Could he forgive me if he knew? I will ask him, maybe, right before the end. And yes, I am grateful that I don't remember Carl's ugly little face anymore. It haunted me for so many years.

Other snowflakes are melting at this very moment. That monster in my brain, my other child, eats them all.

A new snowflake dances through my mind. It is big and strong, and it refuses to melt. The drink that I'm drinking every day, that Hagen brews. I know now what it is. It's magic; it's a potion. I felt that all along. It's keeping the alien at bay. I don't know how it does that, but the alien's growth has slowed down, allowing what is left of my brain to rest a bit, to adopt and adjust. That's why I'm able to think at all….

Hagen, the son that I didn't have, the son without a father. I know him.

No, I don't.

When we say we know someone, it's a lie. Nobody truly understands another. I know George well, but not entirely. He doesn't know me either; he is not aware that I refused him the child for whom he wished.

I need to see Hagen; I have to thank him and to tell him that I can see things, feel things of great importance on the verge of my mind. I must reveal to him that I can see a light around George. Something shines beneath his skin, as if his soul manifested itself through his skin and eyes. I must tell Hagen.

I have to keep that snowflake in the air, away from the alien thing that will burn it to oblivion. The alien roars; it consumes me. It hurts…it hurts so bad….

chapter 6

EMMA HATED MONDAYS, when everyone at the office was irritable and frustrated that a new workweek had begun, just like her. After she returned home, she did the only thing that helped: playing *The Valkyrie, Act 3*.

A formidable piece, oh yes, Alberich said.

She ignored him.

The music cannonaded through the entire second floor of her house. It generated from the center of her shrine, the living room; she called it music room. It was clustered with pictures of Ring Cycle performances, CDs, LPs, DVDs, Blu-rays, and VHS tapes neatly arranged in an open rack, much as her son's despicable things in formaldehyde.

Despicable? I love his collection.

Of course, you do, you perverted idiot.

She had decorated all other rooms of her second floor with posters of *Nibelung* performances as well, but the music room was the centerpiece of Emma's extensive collection.

She sat in her kitchen, letting the music and the sight of her favorite poster from *The Ring* performance of 1983 purge the bitterness and the fatigue from her veins. She was now fifty-nine years old, beyond good and evil, as she used to say.

Nah, not yet, Emma, not yet, not as long as I'm with you.

She prayed for her retirement goal of sixty-two to come closer. Another three years, then she'd quit. She actually could already afford to quit, but she wanted to work for another three years to finance at least one more trip to Bayreuth.

Oh yes, back home!

Asshole.

Alberich snickered.

Emma was, again, on the seven-year-long waiting list for tickets to the Bayreuth Festival, and hoped that she would get tickets when she was sixty-three. The thought put a smile on her face. Yes, she'd work the last three years before retirement for *The Ring.*

For me.

Emma didn't comment; she didn't want him to upset her tonight. Her thoughts strayed this way and that and ended where they did most of the time: on her son.

Our son, Emma, my son, and one day he'll be worthy of me, and I will take him over.

No, you won't.

Alberich chuckled. *He won't stop brewing, Emma. If you had told him about me ten years ago, maybe, but now he's too far down the road. You failed, honey.*

We'll see. I won't argue about this tonight.

Too bad, well, but then again, you hardly do that anymore because you know that you've lost.

Dream on.

He laughed.

Her subconscious registered a revolting sound that didn't belong in the third act of *The Valkyrie.*

Ah, ah, phone.

Yes, I hear it.

Emma rushed for the handset that lay on the small table, where she prepared food, next to the wine rack.

"Yes?" She hurried into the music room to quiet the heavenly notes.

"Hello, Aunt Emma," Juliana said.

"Oh, hi, Julie, wait, let me switch that off..."

Jeez, what could the chick want? Alberich asked.

Emma pushed the pause button on her stereo. The abrupt silence came as a heavy shock.

"Sorry to disturb you," Juliana said.

"Oh, you're not disturbing. How are you?"

"Actually...not so well."

"Oh my, why?" Emma stared worriedly at the poster of the 1970 performance of *The Ring* at Bayreuth that hung on the wall over her stereo.

What has she done now? That girl is trouble, Emma; she always has been, Alberich said.

She was the child of the wife of Emma's brother. The girl had been a product from the sister-in-law's first, unhappy marriage. Emma had known Juliana since the child was four years old and Hagen was five. The children had played doctor and nurse back then.

That's where it started, Emma. I'll bet she asked him to show her his willie.

"I…is Hagen there?" Juliana asked.

"Sure he is, downstairs."

"Do you think he'd notice if I came over?"

"No, he's in his cellar, I think."

"Can I come over? I'd be there in half an hour."

"Sure you can, but you're making me worry."

"Oh, I'm fine. It's about Gabe. He's fine too, but…I have to talk to someone," Juliana said.

Gabe. I agree with Hagen. Why the hell did she marry that wimp? Alberich said.

"All right, I'll be waiting for you."

"Thank you, Aunt Emma, see you soon."

Juliana hung up the phone.

Emma sighed deeply. Trouble was brewing, big trouble.

I understand why Hagen fell for her back then, but it's time he finally got over her. Once I'm with him, I'll help him with that.

⇌⇋

Half an hour later, a fidgeting Juliana sat in front of Emma. One year younger than Hagen, Juliana had turned thirty this year and yes, she was a beauty.

In contrast to the vamp Alissa, Juliana looked like an incarnation of the suffering and virtuous lady. Alissa the whore and Juliana the nun, Emma couldn't fight those two images as she watched Juliana from across the kitchen table. Juliana's long, straight brown hair fell into her face and her fingers knitted at a handkerchief.

She Should Have Called Him Siegfried

The tendency, yes, but she's not a nun, Emma. You know that, I know that, and Hagen knows that as well. She's a wolf in sheep's clothing, to use that old image.

Just like you.

Emma had to stifle a chuckle. In the beginning, when Alberich had first joined her, she had had great difficulty hiding his existence in her head. More than once, she had answered him aloud and many people had thought her crazy.

Yes, those were fun times, too bad that you don't do that anymore.

"I can't talk to my mom about this, Aunt Emma," Juliana said. "She'd go crazy and offer five hundred different versions of well-meant advice. I just need someone to listen to the problem."

"Sure, what's up?"

Now, I'm thrilled, Alberich said.

"It's Gabe...he's infertile. His sperm is underdeveloped, almost non-existent. We've been to six doctors; nobody can help."

I knew it, Alberich cried in Emma's head. *I knew that guy was a sissy.*

"We've been seeing doctors for a year now," Juliana said, "and Gabe is tired of it. He's given up. He's talking about adoption, but I don't want that. I want a child of my own, with my DNA and my genes in it. Oh, damn it, Aunt Emma, I don't know what to do anymore."

Juliana sniffed loudly, still tearing at her handkerchief, and avoided Emma's eyes. Emma's entire body had stiffened, not wanting to know such intimate details about Juliana's and Gabe's married life.

Well, this isn't sexy, no, Alberich said.

"My God, Julie…that's awful," Emma said. "Is there really nothing that can be done? Take one of your eggs and his sperm and do it in the lab and then you get the egg implanted again or stuff like that?"

"No, we discussed this and a hundred other methods. His sperm is just not good enough, not even for the in vitro fertilization that you're talking about."

Oh, disgusting, Alberich said.

Juliana shook her head. "Really, we've exhausted the tricks and possibilities of modern medicine. There's nothing left but magic or a miracle or maybe alchemy…"

Juliana looked up at Emma for the first time since she had revealed that Gabriel was infertile.

Holy shit, Alberich shouted so loud in her head that Emma jumped.

She gasped. "You can't be serious."

"I'm desperate, Aunt Emma; I want a baby."

What a bitch. I told you…a wolf, a predator…she's a man-eating predator.

"Julie, no. No way. First of all, it would be much too dangerous for Gabriel and second, you cannot do that to Hagen. What the hell are you thinking? He's still crazy for you. You cannot walk up to him and say, 'Hagen, dear, my husband can't make me babies; please brew him a potion that changes that.'"

How gross…We gotta protect our boy from this beast.

"I know, Aunt Emma; I know…but…I thought maybe you could tell him that it's for someone else, a colleague at your office who's desperate about having a child, or something like that."

"No. I won't lie for you; that's out of the question."

Rare, but I totally agree with you.

The earnest, suffering nun vanished. "Look at it as a form of compensation for all of the pain and trouble that he has caused me," Juliana hissed.

Careful now, careful…Women like her go up in flames faster than tinder and she'll leave a massacre behind.

"Your pain and trouble? What about his pain and trouble?" Emma asked, desperately trying to stay calm.

"Ha! He raped me and got me pregnant!"

"We've gone over that at least a thousand times. He didn't rape you. I was there at that damned party and many other people were as well. We all saw how you teased him and how you got knowingly and willfully drunk. *You* let him kiss you and *you* led him upstairs."

Yes, she seduced him; I saw that too. But we don't know what happened in that bedroom, Emma.

Emma ignored him. "And it was ten years ago. I thought we had long left this story behind us. Don't bring it up whenever it's convenient for you."

"But he spiked my drink with his potion shit to make me willing."

"You have no evidence of that. It could have just as well been your imagination or the pot you were smoking. Get that out of your head, Juliana. Hagen did not rape you and you devastated him when you accused him of that.

"You ruined his reputation. Do you have the faintest idea of what you did to him with your lax talk about rape? He apologized to you a thousand times and yet, even after ten years, you want to use that against him as a weapon. Shame on you.

"And, if I may remind you, you had the abortion without consulting anyone. Hagen wanted to marry you and he wanted the child. You walked out on him and had that abortion. And no, I won't lie to him. I owe you nothing, Juliana, and Hagen doesn't owe you either. If anything, you owe him."

Juliana scoffed and looked away from Emma. Once again, she focused on her handkerchief.

Well said, Emma, well said.

All of a sudden, Juliana crumbled. "But I want a baby…and I want Gabe's baby. I…" she sobbed.

Emma sighed and shook her head. This was madness.

Far from it, Emma, this is as real as life gets.

Spare me your platitudes, Al.

Emma turned to Juliana. "I'm sorry but I won't lie for you. And, by the way, if the doctors cannot help you, why do you think that Hagen's hocus-pocus could? It's not science that he does in his cellar and it could make Gabe sick. Does Gabe even know that you're here?"

"No, of course not, but…Hagen's stuff seems to work. Helena, she should've been dead for a year but she isn't. Hagen's potions have kept her alive."

"You know about that?" Emma asked, fighting a sting of worry.

"Yes, I spoke to George."

Emma shook her head. "I have to tell George not to advertise this."

They remained quiet for a moment.

She Should Have Called Him Siegfried

That is where we don't agree, Emma. It's Hagen's destiny to brew potions. That's what you've born him for. That's what I've made you pregnant for.

Shut the fuck up, Al.

Emma stood and poured Juliana and herself glasses of wine. Oh, how much she wanted to throw her out instead, but Juliana was her brother's stepdaughter. Juliana sipped her wine and struggled to dry her tears.

"I want a baby, Aunt Emma."

"Go to a donor clinic, get some anonymous sperm, and raise the kid together with Gabe."

"But I want it to have his genes too."

Emma couldn't resist the temptation. "Apparently his genes aren't good enough."

Juliana gasped but said nothing.

"I might not believe in alchemy, but I do believe in nature. Nature has decided that Gabe shouldn't procreate. There's a reason for this."

Harsh things to say about a man, Alberich said.

Juliana scoffed again and downed her wine with two big gulps. She was still a beauty, despite her tear-smeared face and the swollen nose and eyes.

"Thanks for the wine," Juliana said, getting up.

Emma nodded at her. "Think about the anonymous donor clinic, Julie. If Gabe wants to adopt, he'll surely be fine with this idea as well."

"But I'm not fine with it," Juliana said and let herself out the house.

Emma stared after her. Yes, women could be fierce when it came to babies, and the nun-type was surely fiercer in that department than the vamp-type.

Oh, most certainly. Alberich giggled.

That Juliana wanted to go as far as asking Hagen for help…Emma could only call that cruel.

It's not cruel; it's evil, Emma, and selfish to a monstrous degree. She's great; she could be my daughter.

Emma dearly hoped that Juliana feared Hagen too much to ask him such an outrageous thing herself.

I wouldn't be so sure, Emma.

No, Al, come on, she's too afraid of him.

She pretends to be afraid of him, but if there really wasn't even the tiniest hint of rape going on in that bedroom ten years ago, then she's not afraid of him.

Emma shuddered. Her brother's stepdaughter or not, why did she still see Juliana and talk to her?

Yeah, why, Emma?

After all the trouble *she* had caused, not Hagen. Brothers and sisters have quit seeing each other over less. Emma shook her head again and decided to take a closer look at Alissa. Vamp or not, ten years older than Hagen or not, anything and anybody that got his mind off Juliana would be good.

chapter 7

Hagen ate his lunch alone in the cafeteria at work the next day. He poked at his food, frustrated that Alissa hadn't called him back yet. Well, he had a new centerpiece in his formaldehyde collection: the hand of Colleen Hardwood. He had been marveling at it until two in the morning.

Oh dear, he had forgotten about the mere existence of Cindy. She approached him balancing her tray.

"Hi, Pat, may I?" she asked, smiling hopefully.

"Sure," he said and, beaming, she sat down across from him.

"How are you today?" she asked.

"Fine, fine."

"So what kind of metal bands do you like?"

"Even if I told you their names, they wouldn't tell you anything. Don't bother."

Her countenance crumbled. This girl was far too easy to read.

"Well, I thought you could recommend some bands to me and I could try them out."

"Music finds you, not the other way round, and your favorite music has already found you," Hagen said.

"Oh, that's interesting, I've never thought about it that way. How about movies, do they find you too?"

"Look, Cindy, I'm not in the mood for this pubertal shit of what's your favorite color, movie, band, and ice cream flavor."

She almost dropped her spoon. Her eyes widened and her nostrils flared.

"Then…what would you like to talk about?" she asked.

"You're very easy to read, Cindy; that's not good. People immediately know what you think about them. They'll be seeking to take advantage of that. Let me guess. The kids in school asked you whether they could borrow your homework and you let them. You thought they were your friends, only to realize painfully that they copied your stuff, presented it as their own, and made you the bad girl, right?"

She looked like she'd burst into tears. "How do you know that? Just from looking at me?" she asked, her voice quivering.

"I'm right?"

"Yeah."

"Yes, just from looking at you."

She swallowed her tears and resumed eating. He felt a bit sorry for her.

"You have to hide your feelings from people," Hagen said. "If you don't, you invite them to hurt you and be assured they will, for people are inherently evil."

"Some are evil, yes, but not all and I think that, in general, humans are inherently good."

"They're not, Cindy; if they were, would there be so much crime and pain and suffering and war?"

"Oh, come on, Pat, that's lame."

"Ah, good. You have the seed of protest in you. That's good. I have hopes for you." He grinned broadly at her.

They continued eating in oppressing silence. What a relief it was when the lunch-time-over-get-back-to-work chime sounded. Being a teacher was tiring but he humbly accepted his mission: educating Cindy and showing her evil. The girl offered a whole universe of opportunity for this. It'd be fun to toy around with her.

Back at home Hagen waited for a call from Alissa. Should he phone her again? No, he had told her frankly that he wanted to repeat their sexual encounter. To do so twice would be too humiliating.

He refilled his magnesium jar with what he had stolen that day from the factory and stared at his workbench. No, he wouldn't work on Alissa's potion tonight. He wanted to know the result of the next administration before that. Instead, he went into his study next to the lab and threw a wistful glance at the sofa where he had made love to Alissa two days ago.

Except for the sofa and his desk, the only other furniture was bookracks that occupied all the wall space of his study. They housed his extensive collection of books on the occult, magic, alchemy, and potions. None of these books contained real secrets though; he had bought them in bookstores and read only a fraction of them. The library served as a cover-up for the one book of importance, an inconspicuous folder that contained a photocopy of *the* book: *The Book of Potions*, compiled by Sandra Stockard, Hagen's teacher. He took it out of its hiding place behind a bunch of books on herbs.

Tomorrow, George would come by for the potion for Helena. Hagen sighed. If only Juliana finally realized and accepted what Hagen had to offer her. He'd care for her like George cared for Helena. Gabe would let her die at a hospital if Juliana ever came down with a tumor. Hagen wouldn't.

He read the instructions for Helena's potion once more. He knew every potion in Sandra's book by heart, but read them anyway as he always did.

Back at his workbench, Hagen started to mix and boil and stir Helena's potion with that inner peace he had come to love. He had been born for this: mixing and stirring. He created life and death and truth and lies with powders and liquids. He mixed the elements of the world in ways that no one had ever thought of before to create something new—wonders and terrors, relief and pain.

He could think of nothing more creative than taking what was there and renewing creation itself with it. He had no doubt that Richard Wagner had done the same. He had mixed and stirred what he had loved, musical notes, until something had come out that touched people's hearts and made them weep and laugh even a hundred and thirty years later.

After he had brewed Helena's potion, he experimented with that amnesia potion he dreamed of making.

The ring of the doorbell upstairs made him jump. He checked the antique clock at the wall opposite his workbench: eleven p.m. Who could that be so late in the evening? Ivan?

He walked upstairs and peered through the peephole. His stomach made a jolt.

He opened the door and grinned at Alissa. "Hey, I hadn't expected to see you tonight," he said.

What a difference she was from that mousy, no make-up wearing Cindy-girl in a lab coat. Alissa wore a business suit with a sexily short skirt, nylons, high heels, as usual, and an elegant blouse. Add to that discreet, professional make-up, large golden earrings, and well-styled blond hair that screamed to be ruffled and stirred by a man's hand. She had the entire package that Cindy could never even hope to achieve.

"Hi, Hagen, I'm sorry that I was so rude on the phone yesterday." She beamed at him, radiant and excited, eager to break good news.

"Never mind, what happened?" he asked.

"Oh, nothing special, except that the object of my desire was present during your call."

"Oops, sorry."

"We had trouble at the reception with a notorious guest who had wanted to see the manager. It was nothing important though and not my fault. Then today, during lunchtime, I found a way to administer and I think it has worked a bit. He smiled at me tonight when he left; he usually never does that."

Her smile lit her entire face. She was working at the reception desk of a big five star hotel and Benjamin Morrow was one of the managers higher up in the hierarchy. That's all Hagen knew and he didn't need or want to know any more, except that Benjamin was happily married. Alissa was divorced and Benjamin was all she ever thought about these days.

"Hey, that's good. I'm happy to hear that."

"I think we should continue with the current potion and heighten the dosage."

Hagen shook his head. "We must be patient, Alissa. I know it's difficult, but patience is the alpha and omega of alchemy. The change must happen gradually, without the subject ever noticing he is being manipulated."

She moaned impatiently and Hagen had the sudden urge to put his arm around her hip. He drew her towards him and kissed her. She kissed him back greedily. The little success must have excited her.

Hagen's bedroom was too far away so they landed on the sofa of his living room, the closest comfortable place from the front door. There they urgently made love. He ruffled her hair and the way she bent her head when she came caused him immense pleasure. How her head moved, how her throat stretched, how the sinews and muscles played beneath her skin. Those movements possessed elegance, like the pose of his gout hand in formaldehyde and the slight bend of Colleen Hardwood's index finger. How amazing that throats could exert the same elegance. He found himself licking and kissing every square inch of Alissa's throat.

Afterwards, they lay exhausted and wrapped around each other on his sofa. They listened to the deep silence of the night that only the comfortable ticking of Hagen's big antique wall clock interrupted.

"I like your place," Alissa said. "You live your profession. Are the antiques real?"

"Thank you, and most of them, yes."

"Old stuff fits to alchemy, doesn't it? Do you have a big, antique four poster bed, too?"

"Big and antique yes, but no tester," he said and grinned.

She chuckled. "I'd like to test it next time."

"Sure, if we manage to make it that far."

She kissed his nose.

"How many different men are you seeing at the moment?" he asked, flinching, knowing immediately that it had been a bad question.

"That's none of your business, Hagen, and rest assured, the minute I have Benjamin in my bed, you're history."

Good, her voice sounded calm and bemused.

"Completely and totally understood. It's the same for me, by the way; the moment I have Juliana, I'll be true to her until the end."

"Why don't you give her your potions?" she asked.

"I have not had much opportunity to administer them. I don't see her that often. Sorry for being so business-like but I'm very glad that I've found you. Together with you, I can refine the potion until it'll be just right."

"Is that why you don't take money for the stuff?"

"I don't take money for any of my potions."

"Why not?"

"That would be profane. I'm seeking to create per-fection. I'm looking for keys to the secrets of the human mind, heart, and body. I'm glad for every test subject that believes and volunteers to contribute to the pursuit of a higher purpose."

"You definitely have a poetic and romantic streak, Hagen. I like that," she said and kissed his lips. Then she struggled to get up.

"You won't spend the night?"

"No. I have to work tomorrow." She started slipping back into her clothes.

"Do you want to take a shower?"

"No, I'll do that at home. See you soon, Hagen," she said and a moment later, she was gone.

Hagen remained lying naked on his sofa. That had been good. What a relief that she had found nothing wrong with their first time and wanted more.

He got up, took a shower, then stared at the photos of Juliana next to his bed. That night the central photo didn't do him the favor of becoming three-dimensional. Her face remained cold and distant. It did that some-times; it had nothing to do with Alissa. Some nights that picture seemed to hate him more than it did other nights.

He knelt down in front of the pictures and grief climbed up from his stomach to his throat. He put the one that depicted her with Gabriel face down and stared up at his shrine.

"Why do you hate me? Why? What have I done to you? Why do you prefer that boring idiot Gabe to me? Why? I hate you, my love; I hate you."

His knees felt heavy as he got up and climbed into his opulent bed. He lay awake for hours and for the thousandth time, he asked himself whether he should give her up. But what would be left of him if he did that? For ten years, he had focused on getting Juliana. They'd be worth crap if he gave up on her. Yes, he had made significant progress in his self-chosen profession, but other people had gotten over their first loves and married new ones.

No, he couldn't give her up, not now, not when he was so close to finding the ultimate potion. Actually, he still hoped to win Juliana without the help of potions. But if no other option remained, he wanted to have that ace up his sleeve: the potion to make her his.

chapter 8

WEDNESDAY, 8TH OF September

I don't know where George is. I'm sure he'll come back soon, but I dread every minute of his absence. A nurse is here instead. I don't even know her name.

George never leaves me by myself. When he's gone, someone else is in the house, a nurse usually, or sometimes Karen, our neighbor. Tonight, it's the nurse.

Oh, now I remember where George is. He has gone to see Hagen Patterson to get more potion. I had wanted to ask George something because of Hagen. What was it? I remember snowflakes, each of them a memory melting in the fire of my brain. The alien thing that sits in my head is hot and it melts all the snow around it.

Ah, I had wanted to ask George to bring Hagen to me or me to him. Because I have to talk to him. But I've forgotten about what. Did I ever know what I wanted to ask him?

The nurse makes strange noises. The way she walks and the way her clothes rustle are different from George's sounds.

Oh…the alien in my head sends out a pulse. It calls home to the planet from which it came, an altogether ugly place where everything is knotted and twisted. The pain buries me under all the hideous growth. The knot has a mouth in it; it bites into the brain tissue around it. It hurts!

George, where are you? I need you. Hold my hand, please…please. Don't leave me alone. It burns! It burns, like Colleen Hardwood has burnt. Who is that? I don't know that name. George, please….

She Should Have Called Him Siegfried

Report No. 9 from Agent 9836B12
Subject: Hagen Patterson (HP)
Status: Results remain inconclusive.
Next action: Further investigation.
Details of current status:

1) Found out that HP is administering an unknown substance to a woman named Helena Sears. She suffers from glioblastoma multiforme and doctors have given up on her over a year ago, giving her mere weeks to live. She is still alive though and in relatively stable condition. Her husband, George Sears, seems convinced that HP's "medication" helps her.

2) The nature of the illegal substance for Helena Sears confirms that our suspicions are correct. HP is not a simple hobby-chemist or drug producer. He might indeed be an apprentice of the trade. I will seek to confirm that beyond doubt as soon as possible.

3) It seems more and more likely that HP doesn't take money for his illegal substances.

4) Ivan Fuller is yet unconfirmed as a receiver of illegal substances.

Punctually at eight p.m., Wednesday night, after dinner, Hagen ushered George into his living room and made him sit on one of his armchairs. To put George onto the sofa where Alissa and Hagen had made love not yet twenty-four hours ago felt inappropriate. Hagen provided them with drinks and Helena's potion.

"Hagen, it's amazing. She's had three lucid moments in the past week, that's a first since I took her home. She's getting a tiny bit better. I'm so grateful to you."

"It's great that Helena is coherent more often, but please be careful. I've heard that, very often, terminally ill patients suddenly seem to get better before the final decline."

"Yes, yes, I know; I shouldn't hope. But it's been great, she spoke to me, even kissed me back."

George's blue eyes shone like beacons in his white, wrinkly face that even whiter hair and a white beard framed. He and Helena were both sixty-five. A content and happy man, especially that day, who lived at the side of the woman he loved. Hagen frowned at the sting of jealousy in his chest.

"No matter how long she'll hold on, I...we...owe this time to you. I don't know how to thank you for this."

"You're thanking me at every visit, George. I really admire the two of you. Neither of you ever lamented about the cancer or gave up. I wouldn't have been able to do that."

George waved his hand modestly. "There's hope as long as she's still breathing."

Hagen smiled broadly at him. "You're also thanking me by being so happy."

"But that's not enough. Let me give you something, anything. I've tried too often to give you money, but I want to express my gratitude somehow."

"I'll think of something."

"Yes, please do, anything."

"Don't say that too loud; you might not like the answer."

George raised an astonished brow.

"Once Helena is gone, one day, I hope it won't be for many years to come, but once she's gone and you'll be free of responsibility, I might ask you to become one of my test subjects. Don't worry, nothing painful or harmful. Maybe I'll be working on a longevity potion by then," Hagen said, trying to make his request sound harmless.

"Oh." George chuckled nervously. "Of course, but please something other than longevity. I don't plan on being around much longer than Helena."

He said so with a smile on his lips and equally trying to make it sound harmless, but the expression on his face was pained.

Hagen drew in his breath. "You love her that much…"

"Yes."

"What is it that you love so much about her, even after forty years of marriage?"

"Oh, we had our ups and downs, of course, but she's a good soul and she always cared. One day we were beyond all the daily knickknacks, quarrels, likes and dislikes. And not long after that, she fell ill…and…it may sound weird, but that illness has knitted us even closer together. It's hard to express that in words."

Hagen nodded. "I'm sure it is."

George stared at the bottle of thick brownish liquid for Helena that stood on the living room table.

"If we increase the dosage, would she get better?" George asked.

"We raised the dosage about a month ago. If her condition doesn't deteriorate, we can strengthen the dosage again next month. This strategy has worked over the past year, George; we shouldn't change it. And we also don't want her doctors to notice that she's taking more than prescription drugs, right?"

George sighed. "Yes, Hagen, you're absolutely right, sorry."

"No problem at all. I know how you feel; I really do."

George smiled at him and put the precious bottle into a bag he had brought with him.

"Thank you, Hagen, and I volunteer for whatever potion you come up with once Helena is gone," George said as he got up to leave.

Satisfied, Hagen returned to his cellar after George had left and did some good work on the next potion for Alissa, or, more correctly, for Benjamin Morrow.

She Should Have Called Him Siegfried

What kind of man did Alissa crave? What did Morrow look like? Hagen didn't even know how old he was.

He put Benjamin's potion into the fridge and closed its door. His gaze fell upon the hand of Colleen Hardwood. He had placed it next to the gout hand. Two human hands, two female hands, and yet entire worlds lay between them. He imagined Colleen's hand, those long, delicate fingers with the hard lacquered fingernails, caressing the crotch of her husband John. Hagen felt his best part hardening. He turned away and yelped as his doorbell rang obtrusively.

His heart leapt and his pants bulged further, maybe that was Alissa? How'd she react if she found him like this? He hurried upstairs, dropped his lab coat onto the floor, and threw open the door without checking who had rung the doorbell.

"Hey, man! Come here," Ivan said as he flung his arms around Hagen's neck and kissed him on the mouth.

Hagen yelped and pushed him away or at least tried to avoid Ivan.

"What the fuck are you doing?" Hagen shouted.

Ivan giggled and ran towards his car, pulling Hagen behind him.

"Wait!"

Too late, the door closed shut and it had an auto lock. Great, Hagen was now locked out. How embarrassing, he'd have to ask Emma to let him back in the house; she had another key.

"Ivan, what the hell—"

"Get in."

Hagen didn't have much choice so he got into Ivan's car. Ivan was a surgeon; he drove a Porsche. Ivan jumped in as well, pulled Hagen towards him by the collar and kissed him again.

Hagen fought him off. "Stop that!"

Ivan's eyes found Hagen's middle. "Man, are you having an—"

"It's not because of you," Hagen shouted.

Ivan stared at him for a moment and then burst out laughing.

"I said, 'it's not because of you!'" Hagen's ears felt hot and his cheeks were burning.

"All right, we come back to that later," Ivan said and hit the gas. The Porsche's engine whined comfortably as they sped down the street.

"What the fuck's going on, Ivan?"

"See that car behind us?"

Hagen turned around and spotted an old Ford that was trying to keep up with them.

"What about it?" Hagen asked.

"That's the bitch nurse I told you about, the one who's stalking me. I need that anti-love potion from you, man. I really need it."

"What was that kissing about?" Hagen couldn't help it, but he was still shouting.

"Show her that I'm engaged otherwise, that I also do men. I hope that'll turn her off."

"I don't do men! Don't kiss me again!"

Ivan chuckled wickedly. "Now what's the reason for your hard on, man?"

"That's none of your fucking business."

"Jerking off in front of your shrine?"

Hagen hit his own thighs with his fists. He had to exert a ridiculous amount of self-control in order not to let one of those fists fly into Ivan's face.

"If you weren't driving, I'd rip off your fucking dick."

Ivan chuckled. He drove much too fast.

"Slow down, damn it!"

Ivan laughed and drove even faster. He took a corner and the Porsche's tires squealed pathetically as centrifugal force threatened to get the better of them. Once around the corner, a long straight road lay ahead with not much traffic. Ivan stepped onto the gas pedal and the old Ford started to fall behind them.

"Yee-ha!" he shouted.

Ivan turned a few more corners at breakneck speed until he had outdistanced the Ford and then he slowed down to a more civilized driving speed.

Hagen said nothing. He even kept quiet when he noticed where Ivan headed. They were approaching their old playground, an abandoned factory where they had held parties and tried their first weed and potions.

"Honest, man, what did I interrupt?" Ivan asked.

"Nothing."

"Come on, I'm sorry."

"I won't tell you; you'll only tease and hurt me with it. That's why nobody loves you, Ivan, because you continue to tease when you shouldn't."

The very moment he spoke, Hagen knew that he had the upper hand again. Whenever Ivan apologized for something and went into the defensive, he lost; he always lost.

"Jeez, man, you're so fucking uptight," Ivan said but anything he would or could say now would bounce off Hagen; they both knew that.

"Seriously, man, that girl is stalking me. I need that anti-love potion. Give it to me when I drop you off at home."

"Then drive back. You locked me out of my house. I have to get the keys to my place from my mom. She goes to bed before midnight."

"Oh…sorry."

"Why are you driving to the factory?"

"You remember the way?"

"Of course, I do."

"Thought it'd be fun."

"We're not eighteen anymore, Ivan."

"So what?"

"Turn around and drive me home."

"The bitch might still be hanging out around there."

"Great…now she knows where I live. What's her name?" Hagen asked.

"Amanda Jablinsky or Kazinsky or something…"

"You did her a couple of times and don't even know her name?"

"So what?"

Ivan did him the favor and turned around at the next street corner, doubling back to take Hagen home.

"When's the last time you slept with Amanda?" Hagen asked.

"Oh, let me think…three weeks ago."

"What's wrong with her? Why don't you make her your permanent girlfriend?"

"Oh, Jeez, no."

"Why not?"

"She acts as if I was the best fuck she's ever had."

"You're afraid of her," Hagen said.

"What?"

"You're afraid of anyone who could be in danger of coming too close to you."

"Damn it, Hagen, why do you always have to start that analyzing shit?"

"Because you need it. Why don't you try to start a relationship with her, I mean a real relationship?"

"What do you know about real relationships, man?" Ivan said contemptuously.

"More than you, I think."

"Sometimes you really suck, Hagen."

"Likewise. And I won't give you that anti-love potion."

Ivan had to stop at a traffic light and looked sidewise at Hagen. "You're not serious, are you?"

"I'm deadly serious. Work things out with Amanda. I won't give you any potion."

"Fuck you! Get out of my car!"

"Gladly."

Hagen left Ivan's car. He was about ten blocks away from home; he could walk. He slammed the Porsche's door shut and walked to the sidewalk. The lights turned green and Ivan blasted off with screaming tires.

Hands in his pockets, the hard on long gone, Hagen walked down the dark streets. He had no jacket and it was chilly. He walked faster, trying to keep warm.

They were a couple of wrecks, Ivan and he, not physically or mentally, but emotionally challenged. Ivan was too beautiful. Too many people adored him. His looks were his curse and Hagen's curse had a name too, Juliana.

He flipped up the collar of his shirt and walked along the lonely residential area streets. He needed the better part of an hour to walk back to his house. By the time he rang Emma's doorbell, it was eleven thirty.

Emma opened the door, worry on her face. "What happened?"

"Hi, Mom, sorry, Ivan happened. I'm locked out. Can I borrow your keys?"

"Sure, come in for a moment. Jeez, you're freezing; let me get you a cup of tea."

Hagen soon sat in his mother's kitchen, telling her quite truthfully about the Amanda case. Emma shook her head as only mothers could.

"I know it sounds like a platitude, but Ivan will find a bad end, I'm sure," she said.

"Maybe," Hagen said and had to smile though he didn't really know why.

"That smile is scary, Hagen," Emma said with genuine concern in her voice.

Hagen stood after finishing his drink. "It's late, Mom. Thanks for the tea and the key, I'll give it back tomorrow."

"Sure, good night."

"Night, night," he said and left.

⇌

Emma looked at where Hagen had sat a moment ago, and yes, she was worried.

Women, they always worry too much, Alberich said.

Emma couldn't place a finger on what worried her exactly. However, this hunch that lingered in her guts since Juliana had begged her to ask Hagen for a fertility potion refused to leave.

Yes, that was awful, but don't make a bigger drama out of it than it is.

Before that question, there had been a balance of terror. Now that balance threatened to tip and no matter in which direction it would tip, disaster waited at either end.

Emma, it ain't that bad yet. Balance of terror…Jeez, cold war times are long past.

Ivan represented another unstable element in the equilibrium—a volatile element that threatened to go off and explode any time.

I like Ivan; he's crazy, which means he's interesting.

Ivan. Emma had never liked him. She had always thought Ivan to be bad company for Hagen, but the more she had protested, the more Hagen had hung out with him—typical rebellious teenager behavior.

They're not teenagers anymore, Emma; they're both over thirty.

Ivan scared her. He behaved like beauty dead set on destroying itself. Why could some people revel in their beauty and become actors and models while others suffered from it and didn't know how to deal with it?

Oh, fascinating aspect. I don't know either. Yes, he should've become an actor.

Emma sighed and started to prepare for bed, but she'd have a hard time sleeping that night.

I'll sing you to sleep, Emma, Alberich mocked.

Sometimes she could talk about or be talked to about Ivan and it wouldn't affect her, but not this night. Her personal Ivan horror story loomed huge and vivid before her mind's eye, as if it had happened yesterday.

Oh no. Not that one again.

Shortly after Ivan's eighteenth birthday, Hagen, one year his junior, hadn't come home one Saturday night and long past midnight, Emma had gotten into her car to look for him. She had known about the abandoned factory and had driven there. She had found the two boys inside, high on a cocktail of drugs and potions. Neither of them had been quite himself.

Yes, the boys were pretty stoned. Alberich snickered.

Hagen had been lying passively on a dirty old mattress, giggling from time to time, blissfully unaware of his own or Ivan's condition. Someone had chained Ivan to one of the concrete poles that supported the dilapidated roof of the empty factory hall. She presumed it had been Hagen.

Hagen seemed to have anticipated the unholy state in which she had found Ivan. Young Ivan had been sitting on the floor with his hands tied behind his back. A second rope had been slung around the first that held his hands together and tied him to the pole behind him. There had been a yard of play between the bound hands and the pole. Like a dog on a chain, Ivan could move, but only for a certain distance.

And a dog Ivan had been.

Woof-woof, Alberich barked in her head, then giggled.

As soon as Emma had entered the factory, Ivan had started to howl and cry. He hadn't exactly barked, but growled in a voice that Emma had never heard from a human being before that night. The closer that Emma had come, the more he had transformed into a beast. Ivan hadn't said a word; he had only growled in a deep and dark voice that hadn't been his own.

Yes, he saw a fun place that night, Emma, I'm sure. Alberich's voice changed; it became deeper, more seductive, and knowing.

Oh yes, I know a lot of things, my darling, more than you can imagine.

Dream on, she thought back.

Ivan had gone berserk in his chains. He had scrambled to his knees, though the bonds would have allowed him to get up, but he had stayed on his knees with his hands tied behind his back. As the second rope around the pole pulled tight, whirring under tension, he had growled at her and bared his teeth. Saliva had been drooling from the corners of his mouth. His blond hair had been disheveled and wild and his eyes...the look in his eyes was burnt into her memory. Ivan's pretty blue eyes had become inhuman.

A wild, animalistic stare had eaten away all intelligence and humanity and the creature behind those eyes had been utterly wild, angry, and evil. Emma had seen a glimpse of Ivan's soul. What she had seen had scared her more than anything ever had.

More than my awakening in you, Emma? Come on, I scared you more, didn't I?

If she had really seen Ivan's soul, it was tormented, twisted, and screaming with terror. Emma had tried to speak to him, had called his name—no reaction. She had tried to touch him, but he had snapped at her nearing fingers like a dog. So she had taken Hagen and brought him back home and had left Ivan in his bound state and in his madness alone in that factory hall, not daring to call Ivan's parents.

That was a good idea. His parents never would've understood.

Around noon the next day, when Hagen had sobered up, they had both driven back to the factory and had found Ivan peacefully sleeping, coiled up at the foot of the pole. They had untied him and brought him to Emma's house. Three hours later, Ivan had woken up without any recollection of what had happened the previous night.

At least, he claimed to have none. Emma was convinced that he had lied. Whenever Ivan looked at her after that night of horror, it had been with an air of knowing, as if he very well remembered that she had seen him with his soul laid bare.

He does remember, Emma. You can bet on it.

For a few months, the boys had kept their word, no more drug excesses. However, time corrupts all warnings and soon the boys had been back in the factory trying potions. Hagen had learned from the hellhound episode though. He let Ivan do the testing and stayed sober himself.

The hellhound episode had happened fourteen years ago and yet Emma still saw Ivan's wild, inhuman eyes hovering above her as she lay in bed and stared into the dark.

I can change your view, Emma. One word and I'll change it into whatever you like.

What would she have done if Hagen had looked like that? They had taken different potions that night, Hagen had confessed to her. Sometimes, a tiny part of her wished that Hagen had taken the hellhound potion. It might have cured her of her unholy love for him.

I can please you if you want me to, Emma.

Shut up!

What would it have looked like if she or Juliana had taken that potion? Possibly the hellhound potion did that to everyone. It didn't matter; she had seen Ivan under its influence and forever after, she had been afraid of Ivan the Terrible.

You're more a cat than a dog; you'd have become a tiger, I'll bet.

And it'd have made a snake out of you, Al, or a cockroach and I'd have squashed you under my feet.

Alberich chuckled wickedly in her head.

⌖

With Emma's key, Hagen opened the door to his ground floor. He felt like someone was watching him. He turned around and faced the darkness.

"Amanda?" he asked. A woman stepped out from behind the shadow of the giant oak tree that stood between Hagen's house and the street. "Please come in," Hagen said and entered his apartment, holding the door open for her.

Amanda was cute, blond, and in her late twenties. She was well proportioned and blue-eyed, like Ivan, though now a hurt, hunted, and accusing glare glinted in those pretty, blue eyes.

She walked up to him but didn't enter.

"Hi, I'm Hagen Patterson, a friend of Ivan, an old school friend in fact. I've known him for some twenty years and I'm not gay; I'm very straight. He pulled that stunt in order to scare you away and I think we should talk about that and him. Please come in."

Amanda looked baffled but nodded and entered. Hagen closed the door and pointed towards the living room.

"That way. What's your full name if I may ask?"

"Amanda Kablinsky, nice to meet you."

"Likewise, you want a coffee or something?"

"No, thank you, really…and thanks for seeing me."

"Not a problem. Please sit down."

She sat down on the sofa where Hagen and Alissa had made love exactly twenty-four hours ago. He sincerely hoped that Alissa wouldn't come to visit him right now. He had no idea how to explain to her that nothing was going on between him and this highly attractive young woman.

Hagen sat down opposite her in an armchair.

"So, you're Ivan's friend," she said.

"Yes, just friend, nothing more and I'm still shuddering in disgust from his kisses," Hagen said and smiled.

Her face remained stern. She clearly wasn't in the mood for smiles.

"How long have you been working at Ivan's hospital?"

"For half a year now and yes, I've been warned about him and yes, I do know that he, more or less, has had everyone worth having at the hospital. I ignored him but then he came after me."

"Ah, now I get it." Hagen nodded.

"Excuse me?"

"He was wondering why you refused him. That's why he came after you, not because you're special. Sorry to be so frank. Well, you were special until the moment you gave in to him. He conquered and moved on."

Her lower lip quivered and she twisted her hands in her lap.

"Amanda, I know you don't want to hear this, but I'm saying this for your own good. Give him up; forget about him. He's nuts. I've known him for twenty years and during his adult time of those years, he has had sex with hundreds of people, but he never had a single relationship. His sex partners change every month or so. There are some partners he has had sex with over a couple of years but he has not had a real relationship yet.

"I like him; he's my friend. He's a very smart and interesting guy, but he's nuts and he'll only make you unhappy. He has already made you unhappy. Whatever he said to you, that you're special, that it's never been that good for him, whatever, he said that only to fool around with you. He has no feelings for you and you're now nothing but a member of the long trail of broken hearts that he leaves behind him."

She lowered her head. "Why does he do that?" she asked in a trembling voice.

"The curse of beauty and a deep seated fear of someone touching his soul and showing him that it's empty. He wants it all and he wants it now, even though nobody knows what all is, him least of all."

Amanda looked up at him with wonder in her eyes.

"Yeah, a lot of people are telling me that I talk weird shit sometimes, don't worry," Hagen said.

"You don't talk weird shit. Well, maybe the truth is weird shit, but that sounded pretty much like the truth to me."

She was able to swallow her tears, as if Hagen's truth had sobered her up.

"Move on, Amanda, and forget him. He couldn't even remember your last name when I asked him for it. He isn't worth a single tear or one minute of your love and any mission you might venture on to help or cure him is doomed. Go home and get a good night's sleep and tomorrow you can start searching for a man worthy of you."

Silent but nodding, she got up and walked towards the door. Hagen followed her.

"I'll do that. Thank you very much for being so open with me, Hagen."

"No problem. Good night, Amanda."

At the door, she stared at him for a moment and he thought he saw respect and also some interest in her eyes. He smiled at her as innocently as he could.

"Good night," she said and left. Hagen closed the door behind her.

"No need for an anti-love potion here," Hagen said and turned to prepare for bed.

⌦⌫

George has returned. I can feel him lying next to me. It must be nighttime. I'm relieved that he's back. I knew he'd come back, but every time he leaves the house, he risks death. He could have a car accident, suffer a heart attack, or be killed by someone running amok. Life comes without guarantees.

Sure, the probability that anything like that happens is low, but every moment in life might be the last. Every breath we take brings us closer to death. That's the negative point of view. I always preferred: Every breath that I took and take lets me live a moment longer and brings me more experiences.

George is sleeping. I can hear his slow and steady breath. It has a hint of snoring in it that will gradually get louder.

Sleep is an extraordinary state. By imitating death, we live longer. I've been sleeping a lot recently. It is the best method to fight the alien in my head. When I sleep, the headache goes away.

I have stopped caring for day and night. They are planetary illusions anyway. Out in space, it's always night. Day, as we know it, is a rare phenomenon. I'm beyond that and I can now see in the dark.

I wonder where George has been…oh yes, I remember. He went to meet Hagen. I want to tell George that I have to see Hagen. But what's the message that I have for him? If I cannot remember the message, then I don't need to see him. The message…what was the message?

It's so difficult to keep a thought. The alien eats them all. It sits there in waiting, snapping at every bite it can get, getting fatter every day.

I have a name in my head, Colleen Hardwood. I'm sure that I've never known a woman by that name. Her name is not a snowflake but a snowball, like a beacon, bright and clear. Who is she? Who was she? Was? Yes…I know…I know that she's dead. She has died recently. I wonder of what.

What is happening? Many people have died recently. I don't know any of their names. Why do I know the name Colleen Hardwood? I must be patient, and I must try to remember her.

chapter 9

Thursday, 9th of September

From his usual table in the cafeteria, Hagen watched Cindy holding her tray and shuffling along. Jeez, even the way she walked looked unsexy and needed revision. She spotted him and their eyes met. He smiled at her and her face lit up like a lighthouse.

She approached him.

"Hi, sorry for yesterday, too busy," Hagen said and she smiled even broader and sat down at the table. The day before, he had eaten in a restaurant next to the company to avoid her, still too frustrated from his longing for Juliana.

"Oh, yes, I've been looking for you."

Hagen shoved food into his mouth. "So, let's talk some serious stuff here. You have no boyfriend at the moment, do you?"

She sipped from her glass of Coke and spilled a few drops onto her lab coat.

"Um, no...do you have a girlfriend?" she asked uneasily.

"Sorry to disappoint you, yes."

She swallowed air and avoided his eyes.

"Look, Cindy, you're not my type, but that doesn't mean that we can't be friends."

"What is your type?" she asked, fighting to keep her countenance calm.

"Ladies, elegant ladies, who look like queens in high heels and not like sluts. Women who have style and who know what they want and how to get it."

She poked her food. Hagen remained quiet and waited.

"You like to rub it in, huh," she said without looking at him.

Hagen smiled. "Good, be angry with me. That's the first step to leave that fancy you think to have for me behind you and to find a man who'd appreciate what you have to offer."

"I'm starting to understand why you're a loner. You're an asshole."

Hagen chuckled satisfied. "I always find it fascinating that people think I'm an asshole because I don't pretend and speak the truth."

Cindy grunted and ate a bite.

"Would you have preferred it if I played and pretended and gave you hope only to throw you away when I've had enough of the farce?"

"You're an egoistic, arrogant and self-complacent bastard," she said.

Hagen grinned. "Good, you're already starting to be cured of me. That was faster than I would've hoped."

80

She got up, took her tray, and sat down at an empty table a few rows away. Hagen watched her go while chuckling to himself. He truly didn't need to brew any anti-love potions. Grinning, he ate the rest of his food. That day the cafeteria meal tasted astonishingly good.

At home, Hagen was storing away the silicon he had stolen when his doorbell rang. This time he checked who was standing on the porch through the peephole before answering and he should've known—Ivan. Hagen opened the door and looked critically at his friend.

"Hi, I'm sorry for yesterday, man. Can I come in?"

Hagen stepped aside and let him enter.

Ivan's cheeks glowed and his eyes shone more than usual.

"What happened?" Hagen asked, leading the way to the living room.

"Oh, man, today was marvelous. I just came off my shift. Had to do a hair-raising operation. We all thought the girl was done for. Fifteen years old, monstrous car crash, and some metal bar impaled her. Wicked show, man, right between her breasts, missed the heart by a millimeter, but went right through a major artery. If we tried to pull the metal bar, she'd have bled to death within moments."

"Jeez, spare me the nasty details."

"The potion, Hagen, the potion! Do you know what it did? I could see through her, as if I had X-ray eyes. I saw what I had to do and when and how. I had a vision; it was prophetic. We opened her up and I pulled it off. I knew exactly where to pinch off the artery, where to stitch and how fast, and when to pull out the metal bar. We saved her, you and I; your potion and my hands and my vision saved her. She'll live; nobody thought she would, but she'll recover.

"The entire hospital is in an uproar. They're talking about a miracle and it was a miracle, in a way. Man, it was exhilarating, the best moment in my life! It was so awesome to see and to understand. I understood like never before how the human body works. It was unbelievable, man."

"Wow," Hagen said.

Ivan stared expectantly at him, glowing like a girl on her wedding day, and waited for him to say more.

"Today you pulled it off. Today the potion heightened your senses, but it won't always do that. Today you saved a life and congratulations, but tomorrow the same potion might blur your vision and you'll kill someone. I've never understood as much as I do now that you don't know what you're doing," Hagen said. Ivan had been lucky, nothing else.

"No, you have no idea! You brew these things, but you don't take them. You don't understand what it does to me. It makes me better, it takes me higher, and it makes me brilliant."

"Yes, it does now, but one day, sooner than you think, it'll destroy you. You're taking hard stuff, mind-enhancing stuff, and there's a price tag on it. One day your body will pay you back for what you're doing to it. One day you'll collapse and you'll have horror trips. It's great that you saved that girl. But now, at the height of things, you should start to reduce the dosage, gradually, slowly. If you start reducing now, you'll be okay. If you don't, today's success will be the beginning of the end, and the end will be horrible."

"Man, I hate you! I came here to celebrate with you. We performed a miracle. We played God today and all you can do is deconstruct it. Life's about taking risks and having fun, man. That's why you don't take your own shit, because you're afraid of the consequences."

"Someone needs to give a damn and that someone is most certainly not you," Hagen said dryly.

Ivan grunted and shook his head. He got up, went into the kitchen, and brought back two beers.

"You're low on beer," Ivan said and dropped onto the sofa again.

"Enjoy what you had today. Let them celebrate you at the hospital. But, as of today, start to reduce the amount of potion you take. You're a doctor; you of all people know that I'm right."

"Fuck you." Ivan drank half his bottle of beer.

"Well, luckily, I won't be there when her parents come to thank you in tears for having saved their daughter's life."

They both chuckled.

"Man, it was great, really. You should've heard the others, 'Doctor, you can't do this! We have to give her up.' And I said, 'No, that's her only chance; I know what I'm doing.' And then I pulled it off and they stared at me as if I was the reincarnation of Elvis Presley."

"Yeah, I'm sure you liked that part," Hagen said and they both laughed.

"By the way, Amanda looked so strangely serious at me today, despite all of the hero stuff."

"Oh, you can thank me for that. She waited for me here last night and I had a chat with her and cured her of you."

Ivan watched Hagen over the rim of his beer bottle. "How did you do that?"

"I told her that you're an asshole and that you're not worth her love and attention. It seems like I convinced her."

"Well, thanks."

"You're welcome."

"Bastard," Ivan said, grinning. "Come on, what did you really tell her about me?"

"The truth and I find it more and more fascinating how few people want to hear the truth or can bear the truth. Just at lunchtime, I had another truth issue with a new colleague of mine who—"

The doorbell interrupted them.

"Oh…" Hagen said and got up.

"A potion customer?" Ivan asked.

"Not that I know of."

Hagen walked towards the door, hoping it would be Alissa. He looked through the peephole and his mind went blank. He stood beside himself, suddenly, watching how his cool and his rational frame of mind disappeared; how instincts took over and naked fear.

His hand opened the door and he stared at his guest, no longer his own master, reduced to a cockroach beneath her feet.

She Should Have Called Him Siegfried

"Hi, Hagen, may I come in?" Juliana asked in her heavenly voice that was as high, innocent, and vulnerable as her looks.

His innards cringed. His breath became erratic and his heart started to race. She wore unobtrusive make-up, which subtly underlined her natural features. She had bound her hair into a ponytail, but one lock of brown silk hung into her face. Red lipstick graced her lips, her cheeks glowed rosily, and her brown eyes had that melancholy touch about them that made Hagen crazy for her.

She was tall. Like Alissa, she was taller than he was when she wore high heels, but that day she wore sneakers, jeans, and a black pullover with a golden cat, whose back was arched, stitched on it.

"Of course, I'm glad to see you," Hagen said, so self-aware that his countenance and his cool had crumbled away in her divine presence.

He stepped aside. She smiled and he shivered as she entered the house. She headed for the living room as if she lived there and only stopped, rather abruptly, when she became aware of Ivan.

"Oh, hello, Ivan."

"Now, that's a surprise. Hi, Juliana, how are you?"

"I'm fine. How're you?"

"Couldn't be better," Ivan said and grinned.

Hagen stood numbly in the doorway to his living room and felt the atmosphere in the room charging. Juliana and Ivan had never liked each other and they had never pretended otherwise. Fight lay in the air whenever these two shared the same space.

Ivan got up from the couch. "Well, I'll talk to you later, Hagen."

"Oh, please, I don't want to drive you away," Juliana said.

"That's perfectly all right, Julie. It's been nice seeing you. You lost a little weight, hm? Stress?" Ivan asked.

Juliana frowned. "No, diet."

"In that case, congratulations." He walked past her and patted Hagen, who was still standing behind them, on the shoulder.

Hagen felt like an alien in his own apartment, bereft of all power and free will, slave to her presence. He tried to follow the conversation. Juliana had lost weight? Hagen stared at her body and yes, she seemed thin under that pullover and in those jeans. Her body had been fuller in the past.

His innards screamed at the twist her body made as she sat down in the armchair. She immediately folded one long leg over the other. Had any woman ever sat down more elegantly?

He noticed out of the corner of his eye how Ivan shook his head with a smile of mockery on his lips. Hagen barely registered that Ivan left, barely heard how the front door closed shut behind him. He only snapped back to life when Juliana raised her head and looked at him.

"Um, can I get you something?" he asked.

Juliana pointed a long nailed finger at the beer bottles on the table. He wanted her to put that finger into his mouth.

"You got any beer left?"

She Should Have Called Him Siegfried

"I think so…" Hagen said and walked into his kitchen. Why had she come? She had never visited him previously. He saw her a few times each year at various family parties since his uncle was her stepfather. He knew that she sometimes visited Emma, though he didn't exactly know why. She constantly avoided being alone with him since that night.

That night…the one night she had given herself to him. Yes, she had been drunk and stoned; nevertheless, she had been his that night. Though she had denied it later, she had moaned and groaned for him that night, and she had come. For one night, Hagen had been in heaven.

He had been twenty-one, young, and foolish. He had had some adventures before her, but he had never loved those girls, always craving for Juliana. And it had hurt so much that she did nothing but tease and ridicule him.

Then that one night he thought he had won. She had kissed him, drunk and playful, and she had taken him to this very room where they had been alone. She had been the one to lock the door, not him.

Shyly, he had asked whether she would allow him to touch her breasts and she had pulled off her t-shirt and her bra and then one thing had led to another. She had more or less passed out after her orgasm, while he had continued making love to her the whole night. Had he known how this first night would end, he would've killed himself prior to dawn.

The next day she had stuck a knife in his heart, claiming he had raped her. He hadn't raped her! He had not! He hadn't spiked her drink with a potion either and that was the truth. Yes, she had been drunk and stoned, but he thought that she had known for whom she had taken off her bra, whom she had allowed to give her an orgasm.

Two months later, the second dagger had followed. When he thought that it couldn't get any worse, it had gotten worse. She had an abortion, claiming it had been his child.

Ivan had been right; he had run out of beer. He had only one bottle left, for her. Why did she want to drink beer? Beer was a drink for a woman like Cindy, not for a lady. Even his mother understood that and drank wine. He took the beer bottle and a soda for himself and poured both into glasses. It would be unbearable to see her drink from the bottle like a guy or a slut.

What did she want from him? It was unthinkable that she had come without a reason. He suddenly dreaded what she might want.

He returned to the living room, balancing the two glasses. He placed the beer in front of her onto the table and sat down on the sofa. Then he stared at her, waiting for her reasons for being there.

"Thanks," she said and smiled.

That smile hurt. It turned the knife embedded in his chest. Both knives still stuck in his body. The rape accusation was the knife in the front and the abortion was the one in the back.

"Still friends with Ivan?" she asked as she reached for her glass. The cat on her pullover moved with her and buckled over the curve of Juliana's left breast. Hagen gripped his soda glass firmer.

"Yeah, old habits never die," he said.

She smiled and sipped her beer. "No beer for you?"

"Ran out."

"Oh, sorry."

"Never mind," he said and waited some more. Did she expect him to ask her why she had come to visit him?

"You're looking good," she said.

"Thanks, you too."

"Heard you're helping poor Helena quite a lot with your potions."

"You heard that?" he asked, not enthused. As much as he liked George, the old man talked too much.

"Yes. George is very grateful and omits no opportunity to sing your praise."

"Oh really, I didn't know that."

Meek and vulnerable, he sat and waited for her to produce the whip that would lash him. Oh, what would he give to be able to make love to her on his sofa. What would he give for a single honest smile, her hand caressing his cheek, a kiss given willingly. He hated and despised the moment of odd clarity that he'd never get what he wanted, at least not without a little persuasion.

"You're probably asking yourself why I'm here," she said.

"Yes, I am."

Now the whip would come out. Hagen was so terribly aware of the hunched pose in which he sat on his sofa, awaiting the blow.

"It's been very difficult for me to come here. I fought with myself for months. But then I thought, it's about time that we leave the past behind us, isn't it?" she asked and looked expectantly at him, wanting an answer.

"Yes, it'd be great if we could do that."

"I'm sure we can." She smiled broadly at him.

She looked so beautiful when she did that. Her cheeks got these cute dimples when she smiled like that. Her smile turned that front knife in his heart a few more degrees.

"You see, I'm in trouble and I think you could help me."

"Sure, anything," he said, crouching further into the sofa.

"It involves potions."

"What kind of potion could you need?" he asked, trying to keep the tremble out of his voice.

"Hagen, I…" she trailed off.

How she said his name twisted the dagger one full round. Every single vocal and consonant felt like a whip-lash of its own. He wanted so badly for her to whisper his name while he was making love to her.

"I really don't know how to ask for this without offending you." She looked at her hands, which were resting in her lap.

"It's all right. Tell me, though I cannot imagine any kind of potion that you might need."

"Well, it wouldn't be for me; it would be for Gabe."

The whip lashed and it struck him over the crotch. He felt like he was kneeling naked before her. Although, the way she had said her husband's name had an awfully sobering effect.

"What kind of potion would he be in need of?" Hagen asked.

Juliana sat up, the cat on her pullover buckling some more over her breasts, making Hagen squirm.

She took a deep breath. "Gabe is infertile. His sperm is underdeveloped. We've been consulting with six different doctors the past year; nobody can help us. I just won't get pregnant and in vitro fertilization won't work either; we discussed all that. Gabe has given up and wants to adopt a child. But I think we have one last hope left, and that's you and your potions. I know this is very difficult for you, and I'm willing to offer compensation. We can negotiate about the compensation. You're my last hope, Hagen."

For a few moments, Hagen found it impossible to move. The whip had flayed off the skin from his entire body. He breathed; he could do nothing else. For a few seconds his mind, heart, and soul, everything, went blank.

She had dropped the whip and instead rammed the front dagger into his chest all the way to the hilt. He thought the dagger had been thrust in up to the hilt ten years ago, but he realized that only now, this very moment, had the stab been completed. Incredulity mixed with the shock.

"Let me get this straight," he heard himself say, astonished how down to earth and neutral his voice sounded.

"You want me, Hagen Patterson, the man who's already been craving you for forever, the man who'd do almost anything to make you love him, you want that man, me, to give your husband a potion so that his too weak sperm can fertilize you when he fucks you and make you a baby?"

"Hagen, please..." she started but he raised his hand to silence her and to his surprise, she adhered to the gesture and fell quiet.

With his hand still raised and his voice still calm Hagen continued. "And you would compensate me for this? How? By a round of charity sex? Is that what you had in mind?"

"If you say it like that then—"

"Quiet!" he shouted and she jumped. Hagen still had his hand in the air and it started to tremble. "I never would've thought, that I, Hagen Patterson, would say anything like this to you, Juliana, my love," he said, his voice quiet, but quivering. "But get up and leave my house. Now."

"Hagen, I—"

"Now!" he shouted and jumped to his feet, about to attack. "Get out!"

He didn't have to ask her a third time. She rushed towards the door. Once she had the front door in view and could be out faster than he could follow, she turned around and looked at him with tears in her eyes.

"You say that you love me, Hagen. If you really loved me, you'd want me to be happy. I'm sorry that I couldn't be happy with you, but that's the way things are. But we could be friends. I'd be eternally grateful if you could help Gabe and me. Please, Hagen, think about it, please."

"Leave!" he shouted so loud that he jerked. He hadn't known that his voice could be that loud.

Juliana sobbed. Then she rushed for the front door and out of the house. The door swung shut behind her with a bang.

Hagen stood in his living room, his body tense and trembling. Letting out a pained shout, he jumped over the table and grabbed her yet almost full beer glass and flung it against the wall. The glass smashed and left a dent in the wall.

Hagen jumped over the armchair and hammered his fists against that beer-streaked wall. His fists hurt, but he hit the wall again with so much force that the white finery crumbled off the partition. He beat the wall another time and hit hard brick.

Something cracked in his hand and pain raced through his whole arm. He fell to his knees yelping and sank to the floor in a sea of glass splinters and beer. He gasped for breath. The pain wouldn't let him breathe, not the pain in his hand, but the pain from the dagger in his heart that someone, that she, turned around and around and around.

He thought his heart had been broken ten years ago; he had been wrong. It broke now, this very moment. While he moaned and groaned, tears shot to his eyes. He sat helpless and powerless on the floor and cried his guts out. Never before had he cried like that, not even ten years ago when she had accused him of rape. He didn't want to cry, but he couldn't stop. Something inside him had been smashed, shattered, and it would never heal.

He cried for a while as he rummaged with his hands in the beer and the splinters. He had cut himself several times before he realized that he had to do something. He dragged himself into his bedroom and tore her pictures from the wall.

He threw one after the other of the six that framed the seventh picture into the farthest corner of his room, where their frames shattered and left more splinters. With an outcry, he threw the wedding photo of Gabe and Juliana after the ones he had already smashed. He took the last one, the central one, from the wall with his bleeding fingers and looked at it through his tears.

Howling and crying, he tried to throw it after the others, but he couldn't. He just couldn't. He sank onto his bed wailing, hugged the picture to his chest, and sobbed beyond help or control.

⚔

Pain lurks in the darkness beyond my mind. It is unfamiliar to me. It's different from the pain in my head. It's deep and cruel and complete. No physical pain is like that. This pain is more absolute. Physical pain has never started a war but that agony has. It has caused murder, countless murders. In its consequence, it's reaching so much farther than any physical pain ever can.

Physical pain is isolated, personal to one single body and not directed outwards. Physical pain can destroy only one spirit, the one belonging to the torment's owner, but that other pain, which I feel there now beyond the boundaries of my mind, is universal. It's outgoing, it's fierce, and it has destroyed empires. It is the pain of the broken heart.

I am happy. I've been spared that pain. I don't know it. Even my son's death hasn't caused me such pain. It's the pain of betrayal. My headache pales beside this rage and torment.

Whose agony is it? It's not George's. He's here with me, calm and content. I can feel him. He's just making me ready for bed. I'm sitting in my wheelchair beside the bed and he's fluffing up the pillows. It's not Colleen Hardwood's pain; she's dead.

I concentrate on the pain. Interesting, the monster in my head lets me do that without protest. I feel out at the corners of my mind. I feel, I sense, I touch, and I jerk my hand back in horror. It's the healer.

I leap into consciousness. I can open my eyes, and I see our bedroom before me more clearly than I have in ages. I see George. His hair has become even whiter. Has it been that long?

"George?" I whisper and he jumps and whirls around to me, joy on his face.

"Hey, bless you, my love. You're awake."

He kneels down next to my wheelchair and looks into my eyes. His pupils widen with astonishment and joy when he sees how awake I am.

"George, don't ask me how I know this, but Hagen Patterson is in trouble. He's in bad trouble. I have to see him, George; I have to tell him something. Please bring him here. You might have to bring him a few times. I don't know if I can manage to wake up when he's here, but I have to see him. I have to talk to him."

George is overwhelmed. I know why. He hasn't heard me speaking so many words and so coherently in a long time.

"Of course, honey, anything, but what's the message? Can't you tell me and I could tell him the message? Wouldn't that be easier?"

Oh, my smart George, yes, it would be easier if I but knew the message. "I don't know the message yet, George. I have to look into his eyes. It'll come to me when I do that. I know that; I feel it."

"Okay," George says, he seems confused.

"His potion. It does interesting things to me. It lets me see things that I've never seen before. He's helping me, and I can heal him too, maybe…"

I'm still feeling his pain. It's bad. And then I feel my own pain, paling in front of his, but bad it is nevertheless. I cannot help moaning and I have to close my eyes as it shoots through my head like a bullet.

"Hush, hush, my love, it's all right," I hear George say before the pain wipes out his voice. The monster in my head is angry that I defied it for a few moments.

<hr />

Hagen couldn't sleep. When the tears had dried, he dragged himself into his cellar, not knowing why. His cuts had stopped bleeding but the broken bone in his left hand hurt with every move.

He didn't know what he was looking for in his cellar until he stood before it. He had wanted to see something beautiful. He stood in front of the formaldehyde jar that contained Colleen Hardwood's hand. It still stood next to the gout hand of death. New tears shot to his eyes.

He took the jar with Colleen's hand and went into his study. He sat down on the sofa and cradled the jar. He looked at it from all angles and he cried for her, that she had died, that she had burned. He cried for the pain that she had endured.

He switched on his computer and Googled "Colleen Hardwood". She had kept a blog. He read through the blog the whole night, so terribly aware of her death and of her hand that stood in the jar next to the screen. He could see how her lacquered fingernails had typed that blog.

She wrote about her children, her husband, and how the kids nagged her and him to get them a dog. She talked about her occasional work at a nail salon, ah, thus the professionally manicured fingernails. She described a life that was so normal and fulfilling with a husband who had loved her and three wonderful kids. He found photos in the blog of herself, her husband, and their offspring. They had been beautiful people. And now nothing was left but the eldest daughter, the blog, and the hand.

Hagen cried for her and her family, cried bitter tears. He didn't know where his pain ended and theirs began or how much of his tears was naked envy for the life she had led. He was grateful though for one thing. Colleen took his mind off Juliana and the decisions that he needed to make now, decisions that would determine the rest of his life.

chapter 10

Friday, 10th of September

In the morning, Hagen took a shower, nursed and bandaged his hurt hands, and drove to work, ignoring that Emma called him on his cell phone several times. He didn't speak to anyone the whole morning. He hid behind his tubes and vials and worked quietly.

Without thinking, he went to the cafeteria when the lunch chime rang, because that was what he always did. Only when he arrived there did he realize that he would meet Cindy. With a moan, he lined up to get his food, hiding his bandaged hands as best as he could.

He sat down at his usual table facing the window. Moments later, without asking for permission, Cindy sat down opposite him. Her gaze wandered from his bandaged hand, which was trying to hold a fork, to his face.

"Actually, I'm still angry because of the things you said yesterday, but whew, you look like shit. What happened?"

"I don't want to talk about it," he said, startled at the scratchiness of his voice.

"Not as tough as you pretend to be, hm? Trouble with your girlfriend?"

Yes, it was only fair that she hacked back after the bashing he had done. He tried to ignore her and eat his food.

"I hope you didn't beat her," she said, pointing with her fork at his hands.

"I don't beat up women; I hit the wall instead."

"Good, I wished all men would do that."

He looked at her for a second. Damn, she still liked him, or maybe she'd started again after seeing that he was vulnerable too.

"Has a doctor checked your hand?" she asked.

He shook his head.

"You should get it checked; the little finger looks unhealthily blue to me. Doesn't it hurt?"

"It does," he said.

"Seriously, you should go see a doctor."

He nodded.

"You won't, right? What is it with you guys? Why is it so difficult for you to ask for help?"

He shrugged.

"Well, if there's anything I can do, let me know," she said. He stared her in the face, and she backed away a little.

"Cindy, I'm sorry that I've been such an asshole, really. You're a very sweet, smart, and nice girl. Don't waste your time with me. Look for some cute, uncomplicated guy, and make lots of babies with him. Don't waste another thought on me. I wouldn't be good for you."

He took his eyes off her baffled and frightened face and ate some more food, mechanically, without appetite. He felt her gaze on him the entire time.

"Wow, why wouldn't you be good for me?"

"Please, stop it. I'm tired and I don't wanna talk anymore."

"Okay."

They ate in silence until Hagen had finished. Then he got up, took his tray, and left the table without a word. He could still feel her eyes boring into his back. Why had he said that he wouldn't be good for her? The sentence had come out naturally.

He put the tray onto the conveyor belt that took it to the kitchen. He stared at all of the empty, dirty plates and at all of the people who were leaving the cafeteria with what had formerly been on those plates now in their stomachs, where acids now digested their food and converted it into energy. For a moment, he saw the mashed potatoes, salad, meat, and vegetables inside his stomach as a disgusting, stinking heap of organic material.

This was why he wasn't good for Cindy. She didn't have such thoughts. Alissa had. Alissa and Hagen were similar souls, hurt and corrupted and disillusioned. The pure and innocent Cindy was not. And up to yesterday, he had thought that Juliana had been pure and innocent, too. He quickly pushed the thought of Juliana aside and, hands in his pockets, walked grimly back to his lab. His cell phone rang. He fished it clumsily out of his lab coat. He moaned at the name on the display but answered.

"Yes, Mom?"

"Hi, are you all right?"

"Why shouldn't I be?"

"I heard stange noises last night from your apartment. Shouting, though I didn't understand anything, and what sounded like hammering and smashing."

"I told you a hundred times to stop spying on me, Mom, nothing happened, everything's fine."

"Hagen, I—"

He hung up the phone and stored it again in a pocket of his lab coat.

Decisions.

They knocked on his door mightily. There had been a cesura the previous day. It had divided his life into before and after Juliana's request. He would have to decide soon how to deal with the after.

He concentrated on his work throughout the afternoon and dreaded the coming evening, the entire weekend. It was Friday. How could he survive the following weekend?

He drove home in trance, a part of him wishing for a traffic accident that would catapult him out of his misery, but he arrived at home unharmed.

As he entered his house, the stench of the spilled beer made him cough and choke. He ran into the bathroom and threw up pathetically. Afterwards, he sat down on the cold tiles and flushed the toilet. He sat there for a while, doing nothing and thinking nothing, an empty shell of muscle and bone.

She Should Have Called Him Siegfried

His doorbell rang. Listlessly, he scrambled to his feet. As he approached the door, he wondered what he would do if it were Juliana. Kill her?

He peered through the peephole—Alissa stood on the porch. He opened the door for her and she slipped inside the house. She was beaming radiant, beautiful, heavy with perfume, and wonderfully styled.

"Hi, Hagen. Oh, today was so amazing. He spoke to me in our cafeteria at lunchtime. He talked to me. He's been ignoring me all this time but now he talks to me and…Gosh, you look awful, and what's that smell?"

Her hand flew to her nose, exposing her dark-red lacquered fingernails, like Colleen Hardwood's. He raised his hand to touch hers.

"Oh my, what happened?" she asked and gently took his bandaged hand.

He pulled her to him and hugged her as if she was a lifeline.

"Goodness, Hagen, what happened?"

He couldn't speak; he wanted to but he couldn't. He just hugged her for the moment. She seemed to understand, pushed him a tiny bit away and walked him to the living room.

"Come on, let's sit down first."

She led him on and inspected the living room. He followed her gaze to the wall and the floor where the beer glass lay shattered. Dried beer and blood surrounded the splinters on the floor. The spot where Hagen had broken the plaster from the bricks looked like a wound.

She towed him to the sofa and made him sit down. She sat down next to him, one hand on his shoulder, the other holding his bandaged fist.

"Tell me what happened," she said patiently, not urging him.

He listened into the silence, fixated on the armchair where Juliana had sat.

Finally, he spoke. "Juliana came to visit me yesterday. She has never done that before; she has never been here in my apartment before."

He panicked for a moment. What if Alissa found Juliana's request to be normal? His stomach revolted again; his saliva tasted sour.

"She knows that I crave her. We spent one night together, ten years ago. After that, she rejected me; it's all very complicated."

"That's all right; you don't have to explain," Alissa said.

"She knows that I want her, and although she knows that…"

Tears came just when he didn't want them. The misery came back, pain. He grunted in anger.

"She married this guy, Gabriel, three years ago. He's a business man, boring as hell. And she told me yesterday, to my face, that Gabe is infertile." His voice gradually rose but he couldn't help it.

"Unfortunately, he's not impotent, only infertile. She said that they tried everything to get her pregnant but it didn't work. And now I'm her last hope. She asked me—*me*, whether I couldn't brew a potion to make Gabe's sperm faster and stronger so that he could finally fuck her pregnant! And I surely wouldn't help her for free, she said. Compensation for my work would be negotiable. I don't want a charity fuck, I…"

His report ended in a grunt. His entire body trembled. He only didn't break because he feared Alissa's reaction. She said nothing. Hagen couldn't stand it anymore and looked at her. He saw terror on her face, horror. Hagen gasped.

"That is so cruel," Alissa whispered.

Her words made the barrel overflow and he sobbed. He wanted to lean towards her to cry at her bosom but she took his face into her hands and forced him to look at her.

"Hagen, what did you do after she asked you that?"

Fear swung in her voice. God, she feared that he had killed Juliana right away. "I threw her out. I shouted at her to get out; I couldn't think of anything else."

"Good," she said, relieved. "Good." Then she pulled him to her and let him cry, caressing his hair and his neck.

He cried the pain out, so relieved. Alissa also found Juliana's request outrageous. Cruel, she had called it. Yes, Juliana had been cruel. How could angels be cruel?

After a while, he finally calmed down and raised himself into a sitting position. Alissa was still caressing his neck. He stared at the spot where he had hit the wall.

"What will you do now?" Alissa asked.

Yes, it all boiled down to that question. "I don't know yet. This is too big to decide in a day."

"Yes, it is," she said.

"Did you get any sleep last night?" she asked after an endless moment of silence.

He shook his head.

"Try to get some rest. I'll clean up the mess."

"You don't have to do that, Alissa."

"But I want to."

She smiled at him and kissed his tear-smeared cheek. Then she got up and pulled at his arm. He struggled to his feet and shuffled next to her towards his bedroom.

"The bedroom is a mess too," he whispered.

"Then I'll clean that mess up as well."

"You really don't have to do that, you—"

"I know." Her firm tone allowed no further protest.

They stopped dead at the bedroom door. The central Juliana picture, number seven, the one that he hadn't smashed, lay right in the middle of the rumpled sheets.

Hagen started shivering again the moment he saw that picture. Alissa released his arm and made a step towards the bed.

"Please, don't..." Hagen said and Alissa paused, watching him. He took his gaze from the picture, fighting tears again.

"I'll take it and put it onto the cabinet over there, okay?" she said, ever so gently, and pointed at the cabinet that had been the base of his shrine, not knowing any better. She had never been in his bedroom before tonight.

Hagen managed to nod.

She Should Have Called Him Siegfried

Slowly, as if to verify that he wouldn't change his mind about the picture, Alissa took it and carefully placed it, face down, onto the cabinet. Hagen fought for his composure while she quickly scanned the room. Her eyes came to rest on the mess of smashed picture frames between the clothes rack and the window.

She returned to him and took his arm again. She pulled him towards the bed, made him lie down, and opened the upper buttons of his shirt and the button and zipper of his pants. Then she put the blankets over him and caressed his face.

"Try to sleep." She kissed his forehead. "Close your eyes." She kissed his eyelids.

He didn't know how, but he drifted off to sleep. Half-conscious, he heard the phone ring twice and that Alissa answered it both times. Since she did, he decided not to wake up. Later, she rummaged in the bedroom. She swept glass splinters onto a dustpan. Then she quietly snored beside him. He didn't know why, but her sleeping next to him in his bed touched him so deeply that he wanted to cry again, except that he was too tired and drunk from sleep to do so.

chapter 11

When Hagen woke up, he found Alissa lying next to him in his bed, dressed in his pajamas. She was still asleep with the make-up removed from her face and her well-styled hair in disarray. Now her forty-something years showed but that didn't make her any less beautiful. Hagen sneaked out of bed, trying to be quiet to let her sleep. He took a shower and was just rebandaging his hands, when Alissa appeared in his bathroom, still wearing his pajamas.

"Oh, let me help you with that," she said and fumbled at his dismal attempts to patch himself up. The swollen little finger and the entire side of his left hand had turned green and blue, and it hurt badly.

"Are you sure that nothing is broken?" she asked.

"No, I'm not sure. Guess I better see a doctor."

"You should."

He stood naked before her with only a towel wrapped around his middle. After she had bandaged his hands, she put hers onto his bare chest.

"Actually, I came here last night to get laid," she said and smiled provocatively at him. Strange how sexy she looked wearing his pajamas, without make-up, and her hair still in disorder. He pulled her to him and kissed her greedily as she unknotted the towel from his hips.

They shoved and pushed each other into his bedroom and a strange desire assaulted him out of nowhere.

"Can I bind your hands above your head to the bed?" he asked, looking at her, and was astonished to see a flash of fear in her eyes.

"Don't beat me."

"Oh no, no, no, never. I'd never beat you. I won't hurt you, I swear, only bind your hands; that's all."

She relaxed and gave in, although a hint of fear remained in her eyes and body.

He bound her wrists to the bed's frame with towels and then kissed and caressed her entire body. After a while, she truly relaxed, not fearing being beaten anymore and enjoyed his attention. She did him the favor and did what he had wanted to see, her head bent backwards between her arms as she came, her lovely throat stretched and arched between those arms and he himself came so hard that he shouted. Exhausted, he unbound her and kissed and licked every square inch of her throat.

She chuckled. "You sure love my throat, don't you?"

"It's so elegant, the way you bend it backwards when you come. It's doubly elegant when you have your arms over your head," he whispered and kissed her some more.

"That's what the bondage was for?"

"Yes."

"You have exquisite taste, Hagen."

"I'll take that as a compliment."

She chuckled and huddled closer to him.

"Am I a good lover?" he asked.

"Yes, you are," she said, naturally, and without a moment of hesitation.

───

Around noon on Saturday, they sat in Hagen's kitchen dressed in the two black bathrobes that he possessed and were eating toast with butter and jam for breakfast. Hagen knew that the time for decisions had come and she knew that as well.

She looked at him over the rim of her coffee cup. "What will you do now, Hagen?"

He felt sobered, in control again, and, to a certain degree, able to face the possibilities. "There are a couple of options."

She nodded.

No, he wasn't in control again and far from having his cool back. His voice quivered as he finally continued.

"I could…move on. Forget about her; never see her again in my life. Quit my job, leave town, and start elsewhere from scratch…" he lapsed into silence.

"I don't think you're that kind of man, Hagen."

"What kind of man am I?"

"You're possessed, obsessed. You'll always be obsessed with something; that's in your nature."

"Yeah, I guess you're right."

They stared at each other for a while and the fire in her eyes burned bright with that same obsession.

"Your ex-husband, did he beat you?" Hagen asked and she jumped.

"He did. I didn't kill him, but now I'd kill any man who'd dare to raise his hand against me. I'll have no man beating me and humiliating me ever again."

"I thought so." He sipped his coffee before he continued. "Then there's this other option…up until now, I've only done petty stuff with my potions. They all do something, but nothing really dangerous. None of the formulas that I possess can cause serious damage.

"My teacher told me this day would come. When I'd have to decide whether to stay with the petty stuff that is inconspicuous, that doesn't really harm or hurt, but that also has meager effects. Or whether to venture into the land of the real magic, the really powerful potions that mean life or death, sanity or madness. The day to decide has finally come."

He watched Alissa closely while he spoke and he saw the fire burning behind her calm façade, the greed for it all.

"Risk it all, get all or nothing," she said.

"Yes, it's tempting, isn't it? Juliana is offering me an opportunity to mess with Gabe. I have no idea about male fertility, but I do have an idea about love potions. I could make the milk sour. I could make him turn away from her. But of course she'd suspect me of doing things like that. It would have to be so subtle, so inconceivably subtle. It would have to be a work of art. Or I could brew a potion for her and give Gabe only vitamins. My price for his potion could be that she drinks hers."

"And the potion for her, what kind of potion would that be?" Her voice was a mere whisper.

"I've heard of a potion that would make her crazy about me, once and for all. It would have consequences, like a raging Gabe, maybe the police in my house threatening to check the cellar, having to move away from here with Juliana, having her lying at my feet begging for my attention…and my sperm…all of the time. Alienating everything and everyone, the neighbors, the family, my friends, my mother…but it's tempting, isn't it? It's so tempting."

Alissa was glowing now. "I, for my part, have had nothing long enough; I'm ready for everything. I always knew that there is stronger stuff than what you're giving Benjamin now. I want it; I volunteer. Let me administer the hard stuff to Benjamin. Nobody knows that I know you. No trace would lead back to you, I promise. Nobody believes in potions these days. Ben's wife would just think he's gone nuts. And if it works, you can prepare your departure with Juliana and then give her the potion."

Hagen lowered his eyes. "I'll think about it."

"What's there to think about? Do it! What do you have to lose? You won't get her without the hard stuff; that much should've become obvious. You must take what you want. Nobody's going to give it to you."

"It's not that easy. She said that…" Pain shot through his chest again at the mere thought of it. "She said that if I really loved her, I'd want her to be happy, that she's sorry it couldn't be with me, and that I'd help her if I really loved her. I—"

"Hagen, that's bullshit. She's using you. She tramples over your feelings. She only says that to get what she wants. She's self-centered. We all are. She wants to have a baby from her Gabe and she will do anything to get it, including torturing you. You have to turn it around. Get what *you* want for a change. It's as if she were asking you to die! If you really loved me, lower yourself under my feet and lick them!"

"They hurt you bad, didn't they," Hagen whispered.

"Yes, they did. And I'll have nobody doing that to me again, ever." Her whole body trembled.

"Why him? Why Benjamin Morrow?"

"I don't know. I started to fancy him when I was still stuck in that dreadful marriage. I came to that hotel five years ago and Ben seemed so honest, so nice, so knightly. He's fair and just and…I don't know, I fell for him. But he ignored me, not as an employee, but as a woman. I don't get it, his wife is chubby and ordinary, how can he not even look at me, how…I want him to leave her for me. I want to have a little piece of happiness for my own, I…" She lapsed into silence, fighting tears.

"Yeah, I know what you mean. You stand there, alone, with all these happy little people around you."

She nodded and drank more coffee as if to swallow her tears.

"Seriously, Alissa, the one thing I'm asking myself is whether it would make us any happier to cross the line. Would you be satisfied having Benjamin lying at your feet if you knew that it was only because he's been bewitched?"

She stared at him rationally with all greed gone for the moment. "We'll never find that out if we don't try, Hagen."

He took a deep breath. She was right. He envied Ivan for his courage to try out new things. Courage, he, Hagen, so far had never really possessed.

"True…" he said.

For a while neither of them spoke.

"I'll have to see my teacher. I'll have to convince her that I'm done with the petty stuff and that I want to move on to the real and powerful potions. She might ask things of me to prove that I mean it and that I'm willing and able to bear all consequences, including taking the secrets she'll teach me with me into my grave."

"You never mentioned this teacher before. Who is she?"

"An alchemist…a real one. It took me years to find her. She gave me a collection of harmless potions after I convinced her that I was serious about this. She made me her apprentice when she gave me those formulas and ever since then I've been reporting to her about my progress by writing letters. I haven't asked her for the hard stuff yet; it wouldn't have been appropriate. But now…I think I could ask her. The time is ripe. But she won't give me what we want for free; she'll ask for favors."

"What kind of favors?"

"Potions, of course, potions of consequence that she'll want me to brew and administer."

Alissa furrowed her brows. "To whom?"

"Certain people in positions of power."

"Are you telling me that there's a conspiracy going on?"

"Yes."

"Hagen, are you seriously telling me that there's a circle of old witches and sorcerers who have their hands in high politics and stuff?"

"Yes, and if I ask for the real potions, I'll become a member of their group," he paused. "And if you tell this to anybody, be assured, they'll find you and silence you, and they will do so before you can do any real damage."

She drew in her breath sharply; then she straightened herself and nodded. "Understood."

"So, I don't know how long it'll be until I get our potion formula from my teacher, maybe weeks, maybe months, maybe even longer."

"Also understood."

"Are you willing to wait?"

"Yes, I am."

"Good. And you may never, ever, ask me what it is that I'm brewing or how it works."

"I won't."

"And once we start with this, there'll be no way back."

"I don't want to go back anymore." She smiled at him glowing with excitement. He smiled back at her and nodded. "Are we done with the serious talk?" she asked after a moment.

"Yes."

"Then I want to go into your bedroom again and make love to you until I faint."

He chuckled and held his hand out for her. She rounded the table, took his hand, and led him back to his bedroom. She didn't faint, but he did.

chapter 12

When Hagen woke up again, Alissa was already showered, dressed, made-up, and styled. She was sitting by his bed watching him when he opened his eyes.

"I have a shift tonight. I usually have off on Saturday and Tuesday. We're a hotel; we have no weekend and we also have night shifts."

"Oh…yes, sure."

"Last night, while you were sleeping, two people called. One was an elderly man named George who said that he urgently needed to talk to you about something Helena had said."

Hagen sat up and stared incredulously at her. "Wait, wait, something that Helena had said?"

"Yes."

"Wow…I don't remember if I told you about her. Helena is a lady with a brain tumor that I've been brewing potions for. Usually she doesn't say much at all; she's hardly ever conscious."

"Well, then you better call George. Another guy named Ivan called and I had quite a bit of trouble getting rid of him. He insisted on coming over. He knew about Juliana's visit and was worried about you. I told him to come tonight at nine p.m. and that's in a few minutes."

Hagen smiled at her. "You're quite an organizer."

"Of course, I am. I'm the head receptionist in a huge five star hotel."

He crawled towards her. "Can I smudge your lipstick?"

"You can; that's a quick fix, but please don't touch my hair."

"Got it," he said and they kissed endlessly.

Finally, she pushed him away. "I should go so that this Ivan guy doesn't find me here. Who is he?"

"My best friend. We're old schoolmates. He knows all about Juliana and he was here when she came by the other day. And why don't you want to run into him?"

"I thought we were part of a conspiracy now and had to be careful."

"Well, yes, you're right…I'll go see my teacher tomorrow. It's quite a drive; I won't be home before midnight I suppose."

"Then I'll come by Monday night," she said.

"I'll be waiting for you."

She nodded and rose from the bed. At the door, she turned around to him once more and smiled at him, happily, conspiratorially, expectantly. He smiled back and watched her leave.

He got up a few moments later. He reeked of sex and his skin felt sticky. He went to the bathroom but didn't get far—the doorbell rang. He quickly threw on a bathrobe. It was the one Alissa had worn. It still smelled of her and he drank in her scent as he went to answer the door.

Ivan inspected him from head to toe. "Man! You all right?"

"More or less."

Ivan shoved him aside, closed the door, and looked around the entrance hall, as if he expected to find someone else in the house.

"What the hell happened and who's that woman?"

"Oh, she's my lover."

"You have a new lover? How come I don't know anything about her? And, man, is that smell what I think it is?"

"Yes, sorry."

"Where is she?"

"Gone, you just missed her."

"Who is she?"

"A potion customer."

"What the hell happened with Juliana? That Miriam woman said you were very bad off."

"Miriam?"

"The woman you reek of!"

"Oh…Miriam, yes…sure…"

What a girl, she had even thought to give Ivan a false name.

"Juliana…" Hagen said and lowered his eyes. They were still standing in the hallway. "Can we go into the living room? You're a doctor; maybe you could take a look at my hands."

"Your hands? What the fuck's going on?"

Hagen led the way into the living room and sat down on the sofa. Unwrapping his bandages, Hagen told Ivan the outlines of the Juliana disaster. Strange, now that he had made the decision to make her his once and for all, he could talk about her without crumbling.

Ivan stared at him with his lower jaw hanging. "Let me get this straight. She wants you…*You*…to brew a potion for her Gabe dude to make him fertile so that she gets pregnant when he fucks her?"

"Yes…"

"What a fucking bitch!"

Hagen chose to ignore that comment. "I threw her out and I hit the wall…hurt my hand. Could you take a look?"

Ivan still stared at him with his mouth open. "Hagen, that is gross!"

"Yes, it is."

"You're still in shock, aren't you? Otherwise you wouldn't be so calm."

"Oh, I wasn't calm yesterday. Cried my guts out in Miriam's arms."

Finally, Ivan's stare fell onto Hagen's hands.

"Jeez, I gotta X-ray that. Take a shower, get dressed, and I'll drive you to the hospital."

Half an hour later, Ivan drove Hagen in his Porsche towards the hospital while still fussing at him. "Hagen, I'm seriously worried. You're much too calm for what happened," Ivan said.

"Oh shit, I gotta call George." Hagen fumbled for his cell phone. "Sorry, just a second." He dialed George's number with his bruised fingers.

George picked up almost instantly. "Hagen, I'm so glad you called back. I was about to call again, but your friend Miriam said that it would be better if I didn't disturb you. How are you?"

"I'm okay, George. What happened? Miriam told me that Helena had said something."

"Yes, it was so amazing and I'm still disturbed. She had the longest and most lucid moment since I brought her back home. She spoke about you. She said that you're in trouble and that she has a message for you. It's a message she can only give you personally and that means she wants to see you. Now we have to find a moment when she's conscious and you are in the same room with her, which I find to be a rather daunting task."

Hagen's blood flow seemed to screech to a halt by the big issues that loomed behind what George said so airily. "When did she have that lucid moment?" he asked.

"On Thursday night...I didn't call you right away; I was too stunned and it was late. I called last night and your friend Miriam said you weren't well...Helena was right, wasn't she? She said she can see things...I find that all quite overwhelming. Are you okay?"

"I'm better now, George, but yes, this is remarkable. Maybe that's a side effect of the potion, or her cancer, or a combination of the two."

"Second sight?" George asked.

"Apparently. Look, George, I won't be in town tomorrow. However, as soon as I can make it, I'll visit you and Helena. Probably Tuesday, Wednesday at the latest, and, of course, I'll bring more potion."

"All right, Hagen, thank you. Do take care of yourself."

"Thanks, George, and don't worry, I'm fine, bye."

Hagen hung up and looked at Ivan.

"What was that all about and where are you going?" Ivan asked.

"I'm going to visit my teacher."

Ivan flinched. "Hell, man, you're thinking of something major, aren't you? That's why you're so calm."

"We'll see, I—"

"Man, seriously, don't do anything stupid. I know you don't wanna hear this, but damn it, Juliana's not worth it. She ain't nothing special. She's a monstrous bitch if she's asking something like that of you. Forget her finally and move on. You're always telling me that I'm nuts; yeah, maybe I am, but you're nuts too. You're gonna get some monster potion from your teacher, right? Either for her or for Gabe or for yourself, right? Stop it, man, right here and now."

"In contrast to you, I know what I'm doing, Ivan."

"Oh, man, this is crazy."

Their arrival at the hospital cut the discussion short. Ivan took an X-ray of Hagen's hand. A bone in the little finger had cracked. Hagen watched with wonder how professionally and calmly Ivan anesthetized his hand, set the bone, took care of every single cut, bandaged his hands, and gave him a bunch of medicine against inflammation and pain. After not even an hour, they were sitting in Ivan's Porsche again.

"Hagen, you got me stone cold worried. I don't want you to get into some shit because of Juliana. She already got you into a hell of a lot of shit with that rape stunt that she tried to pull off. It's enough, Hagen; she's really not worth it. Seems you have something going on with this Miriam woman. That's good. Focus on her.

"I do believe in your potions but I don't believe in miracles. There's a scientific explanation for all this. Even that vision I had with that teenager who had gotten impaled is explainable, somehow, I suppose. I'm on mind-enhancing drugs and you see all kinds of weird shit with them. But believe me, no potion in the world can make Juliana love you."

And that, Ivan, is where you're wrong, Hagen thought but did not say.

"Man, I know you're hurt, but it'll pass. It'll get better. Take some of the stuff you brew for me; that'll make you feel better. Don't do anything stupid. Don't drive to that mysterious teacher of yours. Don't do this."

It had to be his calm that was driving Ivan nuts and Hagen decided to cry. He had no problem crying. Ivan had a point in a way. Juliana wasn't worth it. She had never been. However, Hagen was beyond that now and ready for the big potions. Nevertheless, he cried for Juliana, the angel that he had forever lost.

Ivan sighed in relief. "Man, I'm so sorry. I really feel for you. I do. She's been super vile but it'll get better. You'll get over her now, finally. It'll get better from now on."

Ivan unloaded Hagen at home, put him onto the sofa, and drove to a nearby convenience store for a six-pack of beer. After Hagen had drunk one beer and Ivan five, Ivan seemed convinced that Hagen would heal and ushered him into bed. Then Ivan left to practice some drunken driving. Hagen only hoped that Ivan would get home safely without incident.

Hagen got up at six the next morning and left town to see his teacher.

⋈

Report No. 10 from Agent 9836B12
Subject: Hagen Patterson (HP)
Status: Results remain inconclusive.
Next action: Further investigation.
Details of current status:

1)   HP left town at 06:00 on Sunday morning. Destination unknown. Quit pursuit after one hour due to possibility of being discovered.

2)   HP seems to have had a minor accident. Hands are bandaged. Ivan Fuller took care of HP's injuries at the hospital where he works. Accident must have happened in HP's apartment. Reason etc. remain unknown. Awaiting HP's return at stakeout position.

chapter 13

SUNDAY, 12TH OF September

At noon on Sunday, Emma rang Hagen's doorbell holding a plate of homemade cookies. He still hadn't returned her set of keys to his apartment. She hadn't seen him since he had locked himself out.

After that awful phone call on Friday, she hadn't dared to disturb him on Saturday, also because she had seen Alissa's car parked in front of his house the entire time.

Almost twenty-four hours. Wonder how many times my boy got it up, Alberich said.

Now Alissa's car was gone and no one opened the door. Emma checked Hagen's garage and found it empty.

Now you'll speculate the whole day about where he's gone. Alberich sighed deeply.

Emma returned to her second floor and put the cookies into a container. Her son was thirty-one and had his own life. She had to get used to that. She had tried for a couple of years.

Quite unsuccessfully if I might add.

Emma sat in her empty kitchen. She stared at her refrigerator and then at the 1983 poster of *The Ring.* She didn't know what to do with her Sunday afternoon. She had taken care of the household and done the laundry.

Oh, I could entertain you in various ways.

I know all of them, no thanks, she thought back dryly and Alberich snickered.

She had an idea.

Now, I'm thrilled.

She reached for her phone, checked her personal phone book, and dialed.

"Yes?"

"Hello, George, it's Emma Patterson."

Alberich moaned in her head.

"Oh, Emma, it's so nice of you to call. How are you?"

"You know what, George? I haven't visited you and Helena in ages. Would you mind if I came over this afternoon?"

"Not at all. That's so kind of you, thank you."

"Great, I'll be there in an hour."

She hung up and Alberich grunted in her head.

Visiting death and her devoted husband? What a great pastime.

"Better than having to listen to you all day long," Emma hissed aloud under her breath and prepared to leave.

꧁꧂

Emma parked her car in front of George's house, which looked so much like her own: a suburban, neither rich nor poor, one-family house. And yet, dramas happened behind every door.

Uh, Emma gets poetic.

In George's house, Helena had fought cancer and death for two years already. Sudden terror gripped Emma and she shuddered.

Yes, exactly. No need to come here.

Emma tried to remember when she had been here last. She couldn't and, therefore, decided to say that it had been about half a year if George asked.

I don't remember either. What's there to remember anyway?

Emma took a Tupperware box filled with the cookies for Hagen from the passenger's seat and steeled her nerves for the sight of Helena. Emma didn't know her exact age, but Helena had to be around sixty-five, only a few years older than she was herself. If Emma suffered from cancer, she surely would die quickly. No one would be taking her home to nurse her, no loving husband and no loving son either.

Yes, unfortunately, my hands and body are not around to help you, my dear.

Emma rang the doorbell and George answered moments later.

"Emma, so nice of you to come by."

George smiled broadly at her. Helena had been blessed with such a husband.

Nice husband or not, she'd be better off dead.

"Hello, George, you look great."

"Oh, you look greater. Please come in."

"Thank you."

He ushered her into the house and Emma squirmed. It smelled of illness and death like in a hospital. Also, old people's odor mixed with detergent, disinfectant, and diapers.

Tell him to open the windows more often, Alberich said.

"I made some cookies yesterday." Emma offered the box to George.

"Oh thanks, homemade cookies, great. I haven't had any in a while. Ah, let me take your jacket." He helped her out of her jacket and put it onto a hanger before he took the cookies and led her into the living room.

Emma stared nervously at Helena in her wheelchair, and raised an astonished brow. She had expected Helena to look far worse than she did.

Oh, if you ask me, she looks horrible.

I didn't ask you, Emma thought back.

Helena looked rail thin but not as famished and near death as Emma remembered her. While her hair was gray and short, it was still full and neatly washed and styled. Her pale, nearly white face was smooth and peaceful. Fewer wrinkles seemed to surround her eyes than last time she had seen her. Helena's watery blue eyes looked expressionlessly into nowhere, with her head slightly tilted to the side. Her lips were thin and colorless but not pinched, and her white hands, thick blue veins shimmering below her fragile skin, lay motionless in her lap.

"George, Helena is looking better, much better than the last time I saw her."

"Oh really?" he asked, joy in his voice.

"Yes. I expected her to look worse, but she's looking better, definitely."

"I'm very glad to hear that. It's so hard for me to tell. I see her every day."

Emma approached Helena and knelt down beside her.

"When's the last time you saw her?" George asked.

"I'm embarrassed that it's been so long; about half a year, I think."

"Oh, never mind that...better than half a year ago. That's very encouraging." George beamed.

Emma put her head into Helena's line of sight, but her eyes didn't show the slightest reaction.

So quiet, Al? No biting comments? I'm surprised, Emma thought.

Nah...too much death, too close. His voice quivered. Emma held her breath; his voice never quivered.

"I strongly believe that she's getting better, too. She has lucid moments every few days now, two, three times a week," George said.

"Really? She recognizes you?"

"Oh yes, and she speaks to me."

"That's great, George. That's amazing. I mean, the doctors gave up on her over a year ago. What do they say? Have you sued them?"

George chuckled. "No, I haven't. They say it's a miracle; they're almost embarrassed."

"Sure they are."

"But I know why she's still alive and even better, and you know that too, Emma."

Emma got up and waved her hand at George, rejecting what he was going to say.

"You know my opinion about Hagen's potions, George."

George smiled nonchalantly. "Please sit down." He pointed at the sofa.

The furniture in his living room was twenty years old but far more modern than what Hagen had in his apartment. Despite that, the whole house conveyed wear, old from use, not antique by choice.

Emma sat down with George and opened the box of cookies. She eyed Helena uncomfortably. Alberich was far too quiet.

"I don't understand why you don't believe in your son, Emma."

"Of course, I believe in my son, but not his potions."

"They're an essential part of him. If you deny his potions, you're denying him too."

"I think what he does is quackery and irresponsible. I've never supported it and I never will."

"But how do you explain that?" George pointed at his wife.

"Her will to live and your loving care."

George shook his head. "I've seen the tumor on X-rays, MRIs, and whatever other pictures. No love and no will to live could keep anything like that at bay. What keeps this monster in check is Hagen's potion."

"We could argue about that for hours and neither of us would change our opinion, George."

"Well, I guess you're right. I'm only worried that Hagen doesn't get the credit he deserves."

134

"Hagen and I have a very complicated relationship. I love my son, very much, but certain issues between us remain unsolved and I'm afraid it'll stay that way. But tell me, what does Helena speak about when she's awake?"

George looked at her for a while, inspecting her, as if he was making decisions about what to tell her and what not. Emma shifted uncomfortably on the soft sofa. Well, George sided with Hagen, not with her. She'd forgive him for that. Alberich's silence unsettled her much more than George's inspecting glances anyway. She hated Al with all of her heart but, nevertheless, his presence and constant comments had become a part of her and it scared the hell out of her not to hear him babbling acidly.

"Oh, mostly she's thanking me for being there and taking care of her."

"There you are, never underestimate the power of love."

"I most certainly don't."

The old man grinned and his grin had something mischievous and adorable about it. For a moment, he looked like a young man again.

He took a cookie and munched on it. "Oh, they're great. Thank you. They're really good."

"I'm glad you like them. What and how do you feed Helena?" Emma asked.

"She can eat only mashed food. I'll soak some of the cookies in milk and mash them for her. But that's only a snack; she gets mostly special hospital food in pulp or liquid form."

Regina Glei

I am not alone. George is here, I know that, but there is also someone else. I cannot say that I like that other presence. I see darkness about and around that person, an air of loneliness, but also something deeper, more profound.

I know what it is—a person touched by evil. No, touch is a moment; this is permanent. It's a woman. Evil lives with her, in her, around her. She's a woman with a long past. She feels around my age, maybe a bit younger, and evil engulfs her life. I don't know that evil. I've never seen it, felt it, or encountered it yet and I'm very grateful for that.

How astonishing...the evil can sense me. It can feel my presence too, and I make it uncomfortable. The air around the woman quivers. Threads of darkness seek, but don't reach me. A shield, which I didn't know I possessed, protects me. The threads recoil when they try to close in.

Who is the woman? I know her from the time when I was healthy but now I know her in a different way. I didn't see the evil around her before, the darkness that dwells with her. I don't want her to be here; I want her to leave. I don't want her to be in my presence or in George's.

It has gotten cold in the room.

The evil around her knows that I can sense it. It doesn't like to be sensed. It lingers there in the dark and whispers. It is whispering to her! She knows. She talks to this evil, every day. It doesn't like that I can see these things, that it cannot hide from me. It's angry, because it knows that it cannot touch me. I'm out of its reach because I can see it and I know what it is. I can laugh in its face. I do laugh in its face. You have power over her, yes, but not over me.

I smile, because I'm safe and strong. So strange that I, weak as I am, close to death as I am, that I can be strong, that I am strong. I revel in that; I haven't felt strong in a long time. But I'll only relax and sleep again when the evil has left my house, when it has gone away from George. I'm worried about him; he doesn't see or sense this evil. I must protect him. I must stay strong.

***

Her Sunday afternoon well spent, Emma left George and Helena and drove back home.

Al? she thought.

Yes, my dear? The quiver in his voice had disappeared.

Why have you been so quiet? I don't think you were ever so quiet before, not in all those cursed thirty-two years that I've been housing you.

Must be a coincidence.

Liar. I know you too well, Al. It was Helena, right? She somehow disturbed you.

Rubbish, how could a half-dead, unconscious woman disturb me?

However, Emma did know him too well and he was disturbed.

Dream on, he said contemptuously.

Back home, Emma checked whether Hagen had returned yet. He hadn't. She sighed, ate dinner, and took care of her Richard Wagner homepage with a still astonishingly quiet Alberich in her head.

chapter 14

HAGEN HAD NEVER been a morning person. He spent his nights in his cellar. His study next to the lab had a small window that looked onto the lawn of his garden, but the lab itself had no window at all. Sometimes he spent entire nights in that room, mixing and stirring, and went to bed with the rising sun. Therefore he never hit the road at six in the morning; he usually drove to work at half past eight, and marveled at the unfamiliar atmosphere.

Traffic was thin, the weather clear, and it promised to become a fine day, ideal for a road trip to the countryside. Hagen almost forgot the serious reason for this excursion when he looked at the soft wooded hills around him.

If traffic remained light, the drive to Sandra's house would take four hours one way. He played no music in his car. He preferred listening to the vehicle's engine and the tires on the road. He opened the window a bit and enjoyed the cool morning air that smelled of wood and dust. It had been a dry summer.

Regina Glei

The endless woods reminded him of a movie he had once seen: *The Blair Witch Project.* It had been quite a blockbuster in its time. He smiled at the irony, since he was driving to visit what some people might consider a real witch, though he, Sandra, and their kind called their trade alchemy, not sorcery, for the lack of spells and wands.

Suddenly, he swerved to avoid bumping into the road kill that lay in the middle of his lane. It had been a fawn. An impulse made him slam his foot onto the brake. He parked the car close to the ditch and, hands in the pockets of his jacket, walked back to the fawn.

He stared down at it. Its guts spilled onto the road from its torn body. The blood was still fresh; the young animal had found its death during the past twenty-four hours. Flies buzzed around the carcass. Its small head was unharmed and its dead and empty eyes stared across the road into the woods.

Hagen looked up from the body of the fawn. The road lay empty and quiet. Wind whispered in the trees, birds chirped, the flies at his feet buzzed, and the leaves danced in the sun.

Why had this planet brought forth human beings? They had no place here. The asphalt road, his boots, the clothes he wore, his car, all of that was artificial. Humans were a mistake. Human machines had killed the fawn at his feet. Humans had stopped being a part of nature the moment they had converted from hunters and gatherers to cultivating and using the land. They had become alien to this planet. The earth had lost control over humans and constantly tried to correct that.

Hagen looked at the death at his feet until the sound of an approaching vehicle destroyed the glimpse of truth. Hagen jumped, becoming aware of the stench that rose from the corpse of the fawn and started nudging it with his boots towards the ditch next to the road. Flies flew up and he waved about with his bandaged hands to get them out of his face. He hid his hands in his pockets when the car slowed down.

A big SUV approached him, a man behind the wheel with a woman sitting next to him, a couple, no doubt, around Hagen's age. The man let down his window.

"Hey, you all right?" he asked.

"Yes, thanks. Wasn't my road kill. It must've happened last night. I just wanted to get it off the street."

The woman leaned over her husband or boyfriend to get a look. "Oh, a fawn…that's so sad."

"Happens all the time, Ma'am, unfortunately," Hagen said.

"Well, thanks for getting it off the road. Take care," the man said and hit the gas.

Hagen looked after them as they swerved past his Toyota. He continued nudging the fawn's carcass with his boot.

Humans…what a nuisance. Destroying it all, even this moment of clarity. The fawn slithered into the ditch. Hagen wiped his boots in the grass next to the road and walked back to his car.

Sandra lived in an old farmhouse with her next neighbor a hundred yards away—far enough for privacy but close enough for a good neighborhood. It was a few minutes past ten in the morning, when Hagen arrived. He parked his car next to Sandra's old pickup truck and took the bottle of wine that he had brought as a present from his backseat.

He rang the doorbell, which, like his, had a penetrating ring so that Sandra could hear it in the cellar.

It took a while before someone shuffled towards the door. Hagen felt an eye on him through the peephole before the locks snapped open.

Sandra smiled, not in the least surprised. He adored her for that.

"Hagen Patterson, it's been a while."

"It has. Hello, Sandra, it's been four years, I think."

"If you say so, it must be true," she said.

He remembered her as a remarkable lady and found his memory confirmed. She was a head shorter than he was, slender, and had snow white, hip length hair bound into a ponytail. She was a bit older than Helena, close to seventy, but was in brilliant shape and her face and whole countenance radiated a serenity and sovereignty that he had never seen in anyone else. Nothing could disturb this woman's calm. Her green eyes shone clear and at peace with herself and the world. Her sharp nose made her look alert and smart and she always had a soft smile on her lips. Hagen met her that day only for the third time but every time he saw her, he wished more and more that she were his mother.

"You look great," Hagen said and meant it.

She nodded at him. "Thanks. Please come in."

"Thank you. I brought a bottle of wine."

"Oh, how nice. Let's go into the living room."

"I hope I'm not disturbing?"

"Not at all, my husband is at church so we're alone."

"I didn't know you had a husband."

"Again. He's my third. One divorce, second husband died of some awful virus, and Norm is number three. He's of the trade."

"I see. Do you have children?"

"Yes, three, all adults and moved out."

"Wow, I didn't know that either."

She indicated a huge plush sofa. Her choices in clothing and furniture made Hagen squirm. Everything around Sandra was kitschy and over the top. She wore a wide, long skirt in all colors of the rainbow and a black blouse with frills that day.

"Why are you not surprised to see me, Sandra?" Hagen asked as he sat down.

"My students come in two categories: those who will come to visit me out of the blue one day and those who won't. I always had the feeling that you belonged to the first category. I'm more surprised that you didn't come sooner."

"And what do you say to those first category students?"

"I have one important question for them and it is: have you come here hoping to change *the* world or *your* world?"

The plush sofa made Hagen shudder. He had sunken into it to a frightening degree and feared the thing would swallow him alive. It smelled moldy and he thought he could see the gazillions of dust mites that crawled over it.

"What if I give the wrong answer to that?"

"No cheating, you must answer the question, Hagen, and be honest."

"My world," he said after a while.

"I see. Did you have breakfast?"

"Actually, no."

"Good. I was just about to eat some. Why don't you join me?"

"Thanks, I appreciate it," he said, glad to be getting out of that sofa.

He followed Sandra into the kitchen and stared at the tacky landscape pictures that hung everywhere. He couldn't remember them from his last visit.

"Those pictures…who—"

"Oh, they're my husband's. He's a painter, not a very good one as you can see, but I'm not complaining."

"He's of the trade and yet he goes to church?"

"Yes, some of us are able to harmonize our trade with God."

"That's amazing."

"He's an amazing man; that's why I married him."

She made Hagen sit down at her huge wooden kitchen table and laid out another place setting for him. Homemade bread, boiled eggs, jam, honey, bacon, and cheese waited on the table. The sight of food made Hagen realize how hungry he was.

"Please, help yourself," Sandra said.

"Thank you."

She Should Have Called Him Siegfried

"What happened to your hands?" she asked as she spread butter onto a slice of bread with a big knife.

"Oh, I…I beat up a wall in anger."

"And that anger makes you want to change your world?"

"No, there's more…humiliation, disregard for my person and my feelings."

"And now it's payback time? Brewing a potion that will convert the disregard into admiration?"

Hagen chewed harder on the piece of bread in his mouth, unable to swallow it, despite being hungry. "Sort of."

"Hurt feelings and now we're out for a little revenge?"

"Not revenge, punishment, corrective measures. Teaching someone that it'll have consequences, bad consequences, when she treats people like dirt."

"So, the woman in question has been mean and vicious, and now she needs to be corrected?"

"You weren't there; you don't know what she said and did. I'm not the bad guy…she is," Hagen said, trying not to get loud.

"But you'll become the bad guy by turning the tables. If you administer a powerful potion to her to turn her around against her will, you become a criminal."

"I know that."

"Are you sure that you truly understand what that means? Are you sure you're able to bear the consequences?"

"Yes, I am."

"With what exactly do you want to correct her?"

"With a love potion."

Sandra nodded. "You'll have to prove to me that you're able to bear the consequences."

"I'll do whatever you tell me."

"We'll see." She smiled a strawberry jam smeared smile at him.

They chatted about more harmless issues for the rest of the breakfast, mainly Helena's and Ivan's potions. Sandra knew all about them from the letters he wrote.

"I'm impressed that Helena's potion causes second sight," Sandra said. "That's rare for such a mild potion. I think you should change to more potent stuff to enhance the effect and also to prolong her lucid moments."

"I don't want to worsen her condition; I'm a bit afraid to change the potion."

"Discuss it with George. If he wants to risk it, why not try?"

Hagen nodded. "Okay, but I'm not familiar with a more potent brew for her."

"I have a formula I can give you."

"I see…I'm thrilled," he said, gratefully.

"I think you can risk it. She's now quite stable, isn't she?"

"Well, yes."

Sandra sipped her tea. Hagen watched her in awe. She had never met Ivan, George, or Helena and yet it seemed as if she had known them for years as she talked about them. In a way, she did. Apart from Hagen, she was the one most familiar with their conditions.

"And how is that potion for Alissa coming along?" Sandra asked.

"Showing small effects; Morrow talks to her and smiles at her."

"You could use him as a test subject for the potion that you're aiming at yourself."

Hagen drew in air. "That's exactly what I had in mind. So, you'll give me the formula?"

"In time, after you've proven yourself worthy."

"Thank you."

She nodded at him as if she had just promised to give him a nice Christmas present and not terrible power.

"Have you once done the same thing? Sat with your teacher and asked him or her to allow you into the next circle? Did he or she ask you that, *the* world or *your* world, and if so, what made you want to reach for more?" he asked.

"Yes, same thing, and I had wanted to change the world. I asked him to initiate me after they had shot Kennedy. I was twenty-five at the time and disturbed and upset. I felt helpless and didn't want to feel helpless any longer. My teacher laughed at me, sent me away, and told me to come back when I had learned my lesson.

"Five years later, I returned to him and told him that now I believed that there's no difference between *my* world and *the* world. It's the butterfly effect. When we intervene with our potions, we change the world a tiny little bit. Because of what we do today with our potions, the world will look different in a million years.

"Nature had decided that Helena should have died a year ago. She hasn't and now she has the second sight and who knows what she'll tell you. Your motives are selfish and arrogant, Hagen Patterson, but at least you have no delusions of grandeur."

"Why then do you support my low motives?"

"Most people who change something in this world are selfish, arrogant, and power-hungry, except Mahatma Gandhi perhaps. You are young Hagen. You are thirty-one now, right?" He nodded. "And you're good. You could make it far in the trade."

"Thanks."

"Let's go to the cellar," she said and got up, leaving the dirty plates of their breakfast behind.

Hagen tried not to show her his excitement. She had not allowed him into her cellar during their two previous encounters. As he walked behind her towards her sanctuary, much of his misery fell from him. It had been a good idea to come here and yes, he was ready for the serious stuff, for some true meddling with the world.

Sandra opened the door to the catacombs of her house and walked down old, rickety, wooden stairs that creaked with every step. There were several doors to the left and right of the dark cellar corridor and nothing but a naked bulb lit it. Hagen grinned at the pompous ass that he was with his chandelier hanging at the entrance to his cellar.

Sandra fished a big key chain from the layers of her skirt and opened one of the heavy wooden doors. Hagen held his breath as he entered. The room was huge, bigger than he had expected it to be, and a large ceramic-tiled workbench dominated it. Much like in his own cellar, myriads of vials and tubes with powders, grains, and liquids in all colors of the rainbow stood on it, resembling her skirt.

Sandra also had a huge cabinet standing against one wall and a large refrigerator, but she needed no pomp, like Hagen did, and had no formaldehyde collection. She walked straight for one door of the multi-door cabinet and opened it. Folders, not vials, stood inside and she took one of them.

Hagen tried to watch her, but his gaze was magically drawn to her table. He studied her current mixing and stirring and had no clue what she might be brewing. He sniffed at some of the vials but couldn't conclude what mix it was.

He looked at Sandra and her folders, five thick folders. He flinched, as he understood.

"Are all of those formulas?"

"Yes." She grinned broadly at him.

"Holy cow! Five folders with formulas?"

"If you get to be seventy years old, you'll have five folders with formulas too, Hagen."

He had to chuckle. "Got you."

"I'll make a few copies; I have a small copy machine in my study. In the meantime, don't you dare approach this cabinet. Instead, I want you to tell me what the red potion is in that vial to your left."

Hagen checked the table in front of him and pointed at a vial with a dark red liquid inside it. "This one?"

"Yes, I'll be back in a moment," she said and left the room with one of the five big folders under her arm.

Hagen stared for a moment at the open cabinet with the four other folders and shivered. Oh temptation—four folders filled with potion formulas. And he was just tinkering around with about sixty formulas and a few variations that he had created himself.

He forced his eyes away from the cabinet and took the vial with the red liquid. He sniffed at it—inconclusive, a sweet and sour aroma. He took another nose full: acidy. It had something fruity in it. He looked around the table and found a strip to test the pH value of the liquid. After dipping it in the vial, the pH strip read 3.8. He had an idea so he took a Bunsen burner and lit it. He waved the rim of the glass around the flame and found his assumption confirmed: the mark of lips graced the rim. He killed the flame of the burner and put it back in place just in time for Sandra to return.

"And?" she asked.

"You're pulling my leg. This is some sort of fruit juice."

"Have you tasted it yet?"

"No, was just about to."

He put the vial to his lips and sipped.

"I'm not sure what it is. It's not cranberry…but it's good."

"Pomegranate juice. It's good against high blood pressure."

"You have high blood pressure?"

"No, my husband does."

"Next time, give me a little more of a challenge," Hagen said with a grin.

"Well, I needed something that you could solve in two minutes."

She put the heavy folder back in its place and closed the cabinet door. She approached Hagen with several sheets of paper.

"Here, try those. When you have all the ingredients for them and can produce each of them within twenty-four hours, send me an e-mail. I'll give you my e-mail address in a moment. I have rules for e-mails. Never send a formula. Don't mention formulas. Never use the words alchemy, magic, formula, or anything like that, stick to good old letters for the important stuff.

"I now want a letter every two weeks. Once you have these potions ready, and once they're administered and working, you'll get more. You only have to come here when I tell you. Most formulas I send by registered mail. Only some very potent ones will you have to pick up in person.

"Needless to say, you do not, not for any reason, hand any formula to a third party unless I give you permission. Find a secure place where you can store the formulas. Get a safe. In e-mails, you only write messages, such as: the product is finished, awaiting instructions. We have couriers. They will pick up some of the potions you brew while others you'll have to send somewhere; instructions will follow. Understood?"

"Perfectly," he paused. "Those five folders over there, they're in a cabinet, not in a safe. You have even more?"

"Yes, Hagen, I have even more."

"Understood."

"Those in the safe are the ones that I'm not sending by registered mail. The one you want is among them. If you fulfill the upcoming tasks to my satisfaction, you'll get the formula that you're looking for in about three months. I hope that timeframe is acceptable for you."

"It is," he said quickly. Three months would pass like nothing; he had expected his apprenticeship to last longer.

Sandra wrote her e-mail address onto a piece of paper and gave it to him.

"Thank you, Sandra."

"The following three months will be your final trial period, Hagen. I'll decide after that whether you're ready, whether you need more time, or whether you'll never be ready. Those three months are also your last chance to withdraw from the trade. Once I decide that you're ready and you say yes, you'll be allowed access to crucial information. After that, you'll be of the trade until the day you die."

"I'm aware of that."

"Good. And now please excuse me, I have plans this afternoon and must prepare."

"Of course, thank you very much. I'll get to work on these right away." He waved the copies he had received.

Sandra smiled up at him. "I have high hopes for you, Hagen Patterson."

"Thank you."

"Let me show you out."

She brought him to his car, and Hagen started his Toyota's engine and drove off with Sandra waving after him. He felt better than he had in a damned long time. A tiny part of him was even grateful that Juliana had treated him so badly. Without her, he wouldn't have come here.

The importance of the moment weighed on him with a pleasant heaviness. He had entered a new stage of his life. He'd become a real and true alchemist and get into the possession of secrets.

He stared at the copies on his passenger's seat and couldn't stand it anymore. He had left Sandra's house behind him and parked at the edge of the road.

He picked up the copies and counted them first; Sandra had given him seven formulas. He quickly glanced over them. The first was clearly for Helena. He gasped, as he understood which ingredients would enhance her lucidity and also the hallucinogen part that appeared to result in second sight.

"Damn, why didn't I think of that myself?" he whispered.

He studied the six other potions. One looked like a stronger version of the anti-love potion that he already knew and he wondered how to get around the depressions his weaker version caused. One potion looked like an extreme happy maker. He had to chuckle. Whom did Sandra want to make so happy? The next potion caused him to whistle through his teeth; this looked like a potion evoking fear, strong fear. He didn't envy the receiver of this potion.

The fourth potion let a "Wow" slip through his lips. It looked like—he didn't know what to call it—a hypnotizing potion perhaps or a suggestion potion. Oh, shit. He could make Emma drink it and order her to tell him the identity of his father!

Sudden dizziness spun the world around him and he lowered his bandaged hand that held the copies into his lap. He leaned his head against the headrest of his seat. He still held mild stuff in his hand. They weren't locked in a safe and they didn't have the power to kill someone. And yet, happy makers, fear invokers, hypnotizing stuff, something that encouraged second sight….

The dizzy feeling lasted only a few seconds until a rush of excitement and thrill replaced it. He'd become an alchemist, a real alchemist, a meddler with the world.

Eagerly, he read potions five and six but had no idea for what they might be. He read the ingredients and brewing instructions again and again but couldn't figure out what they'd do. Well, he'd have to be patient. Patience, after all, was one of the main virtues of his trade. He had already learned that much.

He folded the precious copies neatly, hid them in the glove compartment, and restarted his car. He wondered whether he should make a detour of some sort. It had just turned one p.m. and he only needed four hours for the drive home. After a moment, he decided to look for a restaurant somewhere along the way that served venison.

chapter 15

EMMA HAD JUST eaten dinner and was going to settle down behind her computer to take care of her homepage when her doorbell rang. Delighted, she rushed to meet Hagen.

Ah, the faithful son, Alberich mocked. *Oh…not quite.* He snickered.

Emma tried not to frown. "Hello, Juliana."

"Hi, Aunt Emma, can I come in?"

"Sure."

Juliana looked extraordinarily serious and grim.

Some guests Emma led into the kitchen, some into the living room. George would have been a living room candidate, as was her brother, her cousin, and her friend Polly. Her friend Denise, Hagen, and Juliana were kitchen candidates she realized, and she found that quite odd.

Oh, you're right, interesting. I'll give that some thought, too, Alberich said.

"Cup of tea?" Emma asked.

"Oh, no, no, thank you."

"What's up?" Emma asked as she sat down and made an inviting gesture towards the chair opposite her.

Juliana paced the room instead of sitting down. "Have you seen Hagen since Thursday?"

"No. He's gone; must've taken his car early in the morning. I don't know where he is."

"Oh…" Juliana said.

She told him! The bitch asked him for a Gabe fertility potion.

Emma's feet grew cold. "Juliana, you didn't—"

"I'm afraid I did. I asked him for a potion for Gabe on Thursday night and Hagen freaked out."

"Oh no. How could you?"

Now Emma knew what that shouting and hammering had been about.

What did he hammer at? It can't have been her; she looks all right, Alberich said.

"I told you, Aunt Emma, I'm desperate."

"Oh, the poor boy," Emma muttered to herself.

"The poor boy? Ha! What about me?"

"What did he say to you?" Emma asked, her voice quivering.

"Nothing much…just how I could do this to him and then he threw me out."

"Good."

"Good? Aunt Emma!"

Emma, let her have it. That bitch is crazy.

"Damn it, Juliana…Why are you telling me this? Do you honestly expect me to help you? He's my son and I love him; I don't love you. I don't give a damn about you. You've caused him and me enough trouble. You're a selfish bitch." Emma stopped herself, terribly aware of her shrieking voice.

No, no, go on. Don't stop.

Juliana stared at her with her mouth open. "You're sick," she whispered. Then she shouted, "And Hagen's sick, too! You're a bunch of sick assholes! Curse you!" Juliana whirled around and left Emma's apartment running, smashing the door shut behind her.

Emma sat in her seat, hyperventilating, with her pulse running wild. Fear for her only son tore at her guts. She heard Juliana driving off with screeching tires.

What if he did something to himself? she thought.

No. He wouldn't have waited for that until Sunday. He took a ride; that's all.

Emma got up, left her apartment, and ran down the stairs. She checked Hagen's garage; he still hadn't returned. She ran back into her kitchen and grabbed her phone.

No, don't call him. Give him some time. Let him…ah… Alberich gave up when she dialed Hagen's mobile number.

"Hi, Mom," he said with not much love in his voice, bothered that she disturbed him, but he answered, alive and well.

Emma groaned with relief. "Hagen, where are you?"

"I'm driving, Mom; I'll be home in an hour, something wrong?"

"No, no, everything's fine."

"You sound upset."

"It's okay, but could you come up when you're back?"

He hesitated, clearly not enthused. "Sure, see you then." He hung up the phone.

Emma moaned with relief again and buried her face in her hands.

Calm down, Emma. If he didn't do something to himself between Thursday night and now, he's fine. He's not the suicidal type anyway.

"Al, do me a favor and shut up for a few fucking minutes," Emma hissed aloud and Alberich chuckled.

She couldn't work on her homepage, not now. Instead, she switched on her stereo and walked up and down through her apartment to the thundering of the *Twilight of the Gods.*

An hour later, Hagen returned as promised. Emma switched off the music to talk to him in the kitchen. She had prepared tea and had put the rest of the cookies she had baked the day before onto a plate.

He took her set of keys to his apartment out of his pants pocket and put them onto the table. She gasped at his bandaged hands.

Oops, what happened? Alberich asked in her head, his voice dripping with sarcasm.

"Ah, the keys, thanks...are you all right?"

Hagen looked critically at her. "What's wrong, Mom?"

"Juliana told me that she...what happened to your hands?" Emma couldn't keep her voice from trembling.

"Oh." Hagen avoided her eyes. He finally sat down and took a cookie. "I beat up the wall after she had left," he said, munching. "Ivan took care of my hands. He was astonishingly professional about that. First time I realized that he actually is a doctor."

"How do you feel?" His casual and calm demeanor only increased her horror.

Yes, I agree...he's too calm for Juliana treating him like this.

"Don't look at me like that, Mom. I won't run amok or something. I don't like what happened but I can deal with it."

"Can you?"

"I'm a big boy, Mom. Yes, I can deal with it."

I don't believe him one word, Alberich said.

Me neither, she thought back.

"Where have you been today?" she asked aloud.

"Took a drive and got some fresh air. It's all right, Mom; I'm fine. Those are good cookies." He took another one.

Emma shook her head. This was bad.

Yes...talking about cookies at the edge of doom is a bad sign.

"I'm glad you like them...what will you do now about Juliana?" Emma didn't even try to suppress the tremble in her voice anymore.

"Nothing. I told her to leave me alone."

"Does that mean you're giving up on her?" she asked, hopefully, though not quite believing that herself.

Oh, come on, Emma, never, not him, not my son.

Hagen finished his cookie and took a sip of tea before he finally looked at her again. "A part of me will never give her up, but another part of me has, yes."

"I'm glad to hear that."

Alberich made a sound of disbelief in her head and she shared his feeling.

Hagen nodded and took a third cookie.

"I noticed that Alissa has stayed at your place a couple of times, including yesterday."

"Mom, you're spying on me again. But yes, she helped me a great deal to get over Thursday's shock."

"That's good. Won't you introduce me to her?"

"I don't think Alissa would like that, but I'll ask her."

"Why wouldn't she like that?"

Emma, stop that. He'll never introduce her to you.

"She's a very private person. She's not keen on parental involvement, especially since she's older than I am and convinced that you'll hold that against her."

"I wouldn't do such a thing," Emma said. He was making that up; he had never talked to Alissa about his mother yet.

Sure, he hasn't. Why should he?

"Well, it's up to you and her, of course, but I'd be glad to make her acquaintance," Emma said.

"I'll let her know."

She was convinced that none of what he said would happen. She stared at him, trying to find the truth in his face, his eyes, his body language.

Yes, I agree; he's planning something. I wonder where he's been.

160

Emma tried to remember when she had lost access to him, when he had started to be distant and had stopped involving her in his life.

Emma, don't overdramatize this.

She realized that it had been a very long time ago, after he had returned from that summer camp when he had been fifteen.

"Hagen, I know I made mistakes and that I've not been the perfect mother but—"

"Stop it, Mom, please."

Yes, Emma, stop it.

"But I'll always be there for you and—"

"Mom, this is embarrassing."

"Why is it embarrassing? You block me off; you exclude me from your life. You—"

"Who's my father?" he asked and stared at her.

Oh, how much she feared his eyes and that burning question. Alberich chuckled in her head, wickedly, so wickedly. Oh, how much she hated him.

Yes, I know, Alberich said, deep enjoyment in every syllable.

"Damn it." Emma looked at her tea.

"As long as you cannot tell me that, don't give me crap about me excluding you from my life."

Speechless, Emma kept on staring at her tea, feeling her son's eyes boring into her.

Come on, tell him, Emma, tell him about the night of orgy, when you had sex with six men, five of them masked. How you smeared semen onto your entire body and -

Shut up! she shouted in her thoughts.

"As I thought," Hagen said when she didn't break the silence, and then he stood. "Thanks for the cookies."

The sarcasm in his voice bit into her like the fangs of a dog. After he left, she started to cry.

Why are you crying, Emma? Alberich asked. *You weren't embarrassed when it happened. Why have you been embarrassed ever since the following morning?*

I got carried away.

What's so bad about that? It was a great night.

"It was unholy! Evil! You are evil!" she shouted, aloud. "Leave me alone!"

Alberich chuckled maliciously in her head.

⚜

A bitter and foul taste in his mouth, Hagen entered his apartment. He went straight into his cellar and took the copies of the potion formulas from the inner pocket of his jacket as if they were a diamond necklace. He immediately checked which ingredients he had.

He had most of them, to his relief, except for five. Three of them would be relatively easy to obtain since he could steal them from his workplace. The remaining two represented a greater challenge. One he could come by via Ivan, but the last one—wow, he had no idea yet how to get his hands on opium. He smiled; that was part of the thrill and the challenge.

He stored the formula copies carefully in his study after having scanned and saved them on three different memory sticks and his computer's hard-drive. After putting them away, his gaze fell upon his desk. There still stood, from two nights before, the formaldehyde jar with Colleen Hardwood's hand next to the computer screen.

The play of generations. Had they survived, what would her children have asked her when she neared sixty? Had Colleen hidden any dark secrets like his mother? Hagen had felt shame in her today when he had asked about his father. He hadn't asked that directly in a long time.

He had often wondered whether he was a product of rape, but after today, he didn't believe so. Nevertheless, something shameful surrounded his conception. An orgy perhaps? He found it impossible to imagine Emma as part of an orgy.

He sat down at his desk and stared at Colleen's hand, a piece of beauty preserved. From a certain angle, the hand looked undamaged. He turned the glass slightly and the burns became visible. Fire eating away at flesh, the pain must have been unimaginable.

The perversity of Hagen being the owner of that hand sank in on him mightily. Ivan had had no right to saw that hand off its body. Hagen had no right to possess Colleen's hand now. He also had no right to the gout hand out on the rack in his lab. And yet, the gout hand was different. Someone had taken it as a sample for a terrible disease. Some relative or husband had approved the hand to be used for medical study; at least, Hagen presumed so. Colleen's hand, though, was different. Ivan had sawed it off without permission, without any practical or higher purpose.

Hagen couldn't let anyone see that hand. He'd lock it away in the safe that he was planning to buy. Colleen…he wished he had known her. Hagen's fingertips caressed the smooth glass.

How could he get out of Emma what had happened? He knew that she would never answer direct questioning and she'd never forgive him if he used the hypnotizing potion. Hagen stared and stared at Colleen's hand and drew in his breath sharply as he had an idea. Cindy….

Hagen sighed in satisfaction and decided to call it a day. It had been a long drive and the venison he had eaten lay a bit heavily in his stomach.

chapter 16

Monday morning, Hagen worked with an odd feeling in his guts. He should still be shattered and depressed, but felt better than ever and looked with excitement and expectation into the future, although Juliana had rammed in the dagger to its hilt. How could there be hope in death? He was rising like a phoenix from the ashes. He chuckled to himself at the thought.

Hagen went to the cafeteria for lunch and sat down facing the room, not the window, so that he'd spot Cindy immediately. She entered and caught his glance. Her brows rose as he smiled at her. She approached his table holding her tray.

"Hi," he said with a smile.

"May I?" she asked.

"Sure."

She sat down.

"I must apologize for Friday. I don't even remember what I said anymore, only that I've been in a very bad mood," he said.

"Yes, you were; I was worried. You look much better today."

"I also feel much better, thanks."

She shook her head and a smile curled her lips that made her look cute. "You're quite a rollercoaster."

"Rollercoaster?"

"Yes, one day friendly, one day mean, one day sad. I don't know what to think of you."

He chuckled and ate some bean sprouts. "Have you already e-mailed my mom about her Wagner page?"

She looked astonished at him. "Um, no, you didn't give the impression that you really wanted me to."

"Sure, why not? My mom is on a mission to make young people interested in opera. She's afraid that opera will die out because so few young people care."

"Really? I thought music finds you and not the other way round. That should be independent of age."

Hagen grinned at her. "That's my theory; Mom has another."

"Well, she doesn't have to convert me; opera already found me."

"She likes chatting with young people. Do her a favor and e-mail her. I told her about you so she's sort of waiting for your mail."

"Oh, well, sure," Cindy said.

Hagen flinched. He hadn't expected her to agree so easily. Now, he'd have to inform Emma quickly, before she gave Cindy a strange answer that revealed he hadn't told her about Cindy at all.

She Should Have Called Him Siegfried

After lunch, he called Emma at home and left a message on her answering machine, not in the mood to talk to her directly after yesterday's cookie conversation.

"Mom, it's me. You'll probably receive an e-mail from a new colleague of mine; her name is Cindy. She's a big opera fan and she knew about your website.

"I encouraged her to e-mail you. She's super shy, you know, and I told her that I already told you about her and that you're waiting for her e-mail. I had the feeling she wouldn't write if I didn't say something like that. When you answer her, please write something, like 'oh, yes, Hagen told me about you a few days ago.' Okay? Thanks."

Satisfied, he hung up and started his afternoon shift.

⌁

The moment Hagen left his workplace and got into his car, Ivan called him.

"Hey, man, you all right?" he asked.

"Hi, Ivan, yeah, I'm fine."

"How's the hand?"

"Hurts a bit, but I guess that's to be expected."

"Yeah, it's broken after all. How was your trip yesterday?"

"Very good. I have to prove myself, but if I don't screw up, Sandra will take me to the next level."

"Whew, what does that mean?"

"She has five big fat folders with potion formulas in a cabinet in her cellar and even more in a safe. All that I've done until now has just been tinkering at the outskirts of town. Now she'll let me into the city walls and when I don't screw up, I'll get to the castle one day. I'm so happy that I went to see her. Ah, I need you by the way; there's an ingredient that I need. But not tonight, I'm expecting Alissa. I'll call you tomorrow, okay?"

"Hold it, Hagen, you need to slow down."

"No, man, this is where I pick up speed and where I leave my petty meddling behind me," Hagen said, one hand on the steering wheel, one hand on the phone. Thrilled, Hagen waited for an answer and Ivan didn't disappoint him.

"I wanna have a sip from the good stuff."

Hagen chuckled. "You'll get it, man."

"What do you need?"

"Zoloft and...you don't happen to know where I can get some good old opium, do you?"

"Opium, whew-hew...Let me think about it. The Zoloft is no problem. Come by my place tomorrow after you're done at work and I wish you a hot night with your lady. You just blundered. So, it's Alissa and not Miriam?"

"Oh shit, yeah." Hagen laughed.

"See you tomorrow, man," Ivan said.

"Thanks."

Grinning, Hagen flipped his phone onto the passenger's seat and rode home, genuinely astonished at his good mood.

⚜

Alissa arrived at ten p.m. He pulled her into his house without a word and drowned her in kisses. He ruffled her elaborately styled hair and they made love right then and there at the entrance with her sitting on the shoe cabinet.

"Wow, that was urgent," she said with a smile after he had finished.

"Sorry," he said, quite overwhelmed himself.

"No, no, I enjoyed it." She held his face in her hands. "It seems your trip yesterday was successful."

"It was. Let's talk." He released her and pulled his pants back up, which made her chuckle.

He told her about the question Sandra had asked him, her cellar, about the folders, the three-month trial period, and the prospect to get the formula for the potion they were aiming at if he graduated. Alissa's cheeks were glowing by the time he finished.

"That's great," she said and unzipped his pants again.

Exhausted, they slept in each other's arms after another round of sex. He had bound her hands above her head to his bed again and this time, she had fully enjoyed it, no longer afraid of violence from him. He gave her a dosage for Benjamin the next morning while he got ready for work. Before Alissa left, she promised to come back Friday night at the latest.

Tuesday, 14th of September

At work, Hagen stole the three missing ingredients he could get from that source. He also learned during lunchtime that Cindy had written Emma an e-mail and that she had promptly answered.

"Your mom was so kind and so happy that I mailed her. I'm surprised that you told your mom about me."

"Sure, why not, young opera fans are rare."

Cindy beamed at him.

Oh dear, she adored him for having wasted a thought on her outside the office.

Hagen squirmed, but at the same time, his anger towards Emma waned a little. Sometimes she did do the right thing.

After work, Hagen rode to Ivan's place, as he had promised. Ivan was a surgeon and well paid. Nevertheless, he lived in an apartment, not a house, because it was serviced. A maid changed his bed linen, washed his clothes, vacuumed, and cleaned everything. Therefore, Ivan couldn't store detectable amounts of unlawful substances in his apartment and used the forgotten supply closet behind the archive in the hospital instead.

Ivan didn't give a damn about furniture or other aspects of the interior. He had rented the place furnished and owned nothing but his clothes, books, and some other personal items. Hagen felt like he was visiting the show room of a furniture shop whenever he went to Ivan's place.

"Ah, there you are; come in. Let me check your hands and change the bandages before we do anything else," Ivan greeted him and ushered him into his sterile living room. Hagen told him in more detail about Sandra's folders with potion formulas, unable to hide his excitement.

"What kind of potions does she want you to brew?" Ivan asked.

"Sorry, but I don't think it's wise to tell you."

"Hey, I'm providing the ingredients for them."

"And I appreciate it, but this is where the secret stuff truly kicks in. The less you know, the better, and you already know way too much, Ivan."

Ivan grumbled and put a last piece of tape on the new bandages for Hagen's hands.

"I don't know what two of the potions that I'm supposed to brew will do, at least not yet. The others I could figure out, but those two are a mystery. If there's any good stuff, I'll test it on you, I promise," Hagen said with a grin.

Ivan remained astonishingly serious. "What about Juliana?"

"What about her?"

"Thought you wanted to ask Sandra for a very special potion for Juliana."

Hagen lowered his eyes.

"You'll get it after you've proven yourself with the stuff she has asked you to brew now, right?"

Hagen looked firmly at his friend. "Yes."

"What kind of potion is that, Hagen?"

"What do you think?"

"Something that makes her…well, love you."

"What would you think about that?"

"I think that it'd go too far."

"You say that…*you*…who asked me for an anti-love potion for Amanda just a few days ago."

"That's different."

"You will have to explain that one to me."

"First of all, the stuff that you currently have is rather mild. Second, it's the number of years, Hagen. You've been after Juliana your whole life. She doesn't want you. That should be clear to you by now. Forget her and move on.

"If you give her a strong potion, that'll be like rape. You say that you didn't rape her ten years ago and I believe you. However, if you give her the strong stuff now, then you'll commit that crime and I don't want you to do that. Give her up, man; she ain't worth it."

"And I'm supposed to let her get away with that outrage of asking me for a fertility potion for Gabe?" Hagen said, trying to remain calm.

"If you wanna punish her, fine, but find something less severe."

Hagen grunted.

"I'll help you think about it. We have some time anyway, right? You don't have that super potion yet."

"No, not yet."

"It could destroy your life, Hagen. Too many people know that she doesn't want you. If they all see her suddenly lying at your feet, they'll ask questions. And there's Gabe. He won't stand idly by while you poison his wife, unless you wanna take care of him with another potion."

"I'll think about it," Hagen said reluctantly.

"That's all I ask. Don't get me wrong, man. She's a bitch and she ought to be punished for what she did to you, but you have to be smart about that punishment."

"Yeah, yeah, I know," Hagen grumbled.

"Good."

"Just one more thing. You and I, we believe in potions, because we've both tested them and we know what they can do, even though we've had only mild stuff so far. However, the majority of the people out there," Hagen waved at the window and the city beyond it, "they don't believe in that stuff anymore. This is the twenty-first century, nobody believes in potions."

"Wrong, man, very wrong. Don't underestimate the people, never do that. People believe in drugs. They all know that substances exist that influence the mind and body. They'll simply think that you cooked up your own psychedelic illegal drugs to make her willing, like one of them date rape drugs, and that's what you do and what your potions are. It doesn't matter what you call them. You call them potions. They call them illegal drugs. There ain't no difference."

Hagen sighed deeply. "Yes, yes, you're right."

"Hey, cheer up. You are going to get to brew some really cool shit and you'll get to know some really hot secrets. That rocks, man." Ivan grinned wickedly at him and Hagen had to chuckle, as he looked into his friend's beautiful and, in its beauty, treacherous face.

"By the way, I have good news. I can get opium, but it's gonna cost you."

"Wow, where from?"

"There's a drug dealer I know. I removed a bullet from him last year. He thought he wouldn't make it, but he did and he thinks I saved his life. I've never told him that his gunshot wound wasn't that bad after all. He can get me stuff. But I have to pay him and good old opium isn't on his everyday drug order list. It'll take a few days and it'll be expensive. How much do you want?"

"That's great, Ivan, thanks. Not much, five grams should do."

"He might not want to take the trouble of getting hold of the stuff if it's only five grams."

"Well, I'll take more, but I don't know if I can afford it. How much are we talking about?"

"Haven't negotiated a price yet. I wanted to know how much you needed first. Now I do. I'll haggle with him."

"Thanks, Ivan, that's awesome."

"No problem. By the way, got something for me?"

"Sure." Hagen got Ivan's potion out of his bag.

Ivan took the bottle with a wistful sigh that made Hagen chuckle.

"Got some good clean pot; wanna get high?" Ivan asked.

"Yeah, why not." Hagen grinned at his friend.

Fifteen minutes later, they lay stoned on Ivan's sofa and passed the smoke back and forth. Hagen felt heavy and light at the same time. He wasn't lying on the sofa anymore but floated a foot or so above it in the air.

Then he was driving his car through the woods and a whole herd of fawns approached him, thousands, millions of them. They trampled over his car, their tiny hooves clacked onto the metal and the windshield, and suddenly their faces changed into that of Juliana. All of the Julianas trampled over his car. Their hooves were breaking through the glass, kicking him, hurting him. He howled. He wanted them to stop and he tried to will them away, but he failed.

Instead, his body started to grow and grow and grow. His head broke through the roof of the Toyota. His body bulged out of it and smashed the car beneath him. He grew to tree height and the Juliana fawns at his feet shrieked and backed away from him in terror.

He grew ever more. Soon the trees below him looked like miniatures. He didn't care about the fawns anymore, which had shrunk to the size of ants, and looked over the rolling wooded hills. The view was fantastic.

Emma, equally tall and massive, waited under the setting sun and waved at him, calling him. He walked towards her, smashing trees and entire hills under his monstrous feet and some of the fleeing Juliana fawns too.

It sounded as if he was stepping on cockroaches when he crushed them beneath his enormous boots. Every death sounded different. The fawns made popping sounds and they shrieked in tiny, thin voices.

Although Emma didn't move, the distance to her remained the same no matter how far he walked. He reached a town and crunched houses beneath his shoes. He still didn't get closer to Emma and it was starting to anger him. However, at the same time, the vision faded and he drifted into a blissful state of happy suspension and a little while later, he fell asleep.

chapter 17

WEDNESDAY, 15TH OF September

His head heavy after Ivan's pot, Hagen enjoyed giving Cindy the rollercoaster again the next day.

"So, did you e-mail my mom about the fantasies you have of me?"

"What?" She looked puzzled at him.

"Did you ask her for advice how to turn me on?"

She moaned. "You know what? Sometimes you're really disgusting."

He grinned at her, and licked his upper lip with his tongue provokingly.

"Fuck you, asshole," she said, took her tray and sat down at another table.

He chuckled, but soon stopped, since watching how she ate alone with her back towards him made him dislike himself for how he treated her.

In the evening, he went home and ate a quick dinner. He had promised George to contact him on Tuesday or on Wednesday and it was already Wednesday evening. He brewed Helena's potion and drove to George's house.

George opened the door for him. "Hagen, I'm so glad you're here. Come in, please."

George scanned him from head to toe, as if to verify whether Hagen was all right. Hagen felt bad for having caused the old man worry. He should have stopped by earlier.

It had been three months since he had last seen Helena. What condition would she be in? George ushered him into the living room where Helena sat in her wheelchair.

"What can I get you to drink?" George asked.

"Oh, a soda would be great, thanks."

"On its way, how do you think she looks?"

"She looks better, George, definitely."

George patted Hagen's shoulder, beaming like a boy on Christmas Eve, before he left to get Hagen his soda.

Hagen stared in fascination at Helena and knelt down in front of her. Her hands lay in her lap; her bottomless blue eyes stared emptily into nowhere. Her white face under the gray hair looked calm and smooth. Hagen could have sworn she was less wrinkled than the last time he had seen her.

Hagen gently touched her hand. For the first time ever, he noticed her hands. White as snow with thick blue lines underneath her transparent skin, she had thin but noble and beautiful vampire-like hands. She didn't react to the touch in any way.

George returned with two glasses of soda. "Please sit down, Hagen."

"Thanks." Hagen sat down on an armchair next to Helena. "Before I forget, here's the potion for the next week." Hagen got the bottle out of his bag.

"Thank you. What has happened to your hands?"

"Oh, had a little mixing accident; it's not bad, almost healed."

"My God, is that what happened last Thursday?"

"Yes…what exactly did Helena say?"

George told him what she had said and ended with: "It was amazing. She was suddenly bright and clear, the old Helena." The old man let out a wistful sigh.

Hagen stared sideways at George's wife. "I'm here now, Helena…"

"I think that long moment of lucidity exhausted her; she hasn't woken up since last Thursday," George said, sadness in his voice.

Hagen stared at her; he studied the sharp line of her nose, her white cheeks.

"Hagen, you didn't make a mixing mistake, did you?"

Hagen looked into his soda glass. "Am I such a bad liar?"

"No, but the way Helena spoke about you made me think of troubles of the heart, not the body."

George's worried expression, the care in his face touched Hagen deeply. Oh yes, he would've liked George for a father.

"You're right, George, but I'm fine."

George opened his mouth but Hagen interrupted him.

"Really, I am. I wanted to discuss something important with you, and I beg you not to tell anyone about this."

"Of course, what is it?"

"I have come by a potion formula that is stronger than what we're giving Helena now. If things go well, it could...let me call it 'awaken' her. I don't know how the tumor will react, nobody knows that, and I don't know if the stronger potion would work at all. It could also be harmful. It could kill her in the worst case. It could wake her up in the best case. Or it could enhance her moments of lucidity, as well as that hint of second sight that she apparently had last week. Or it could simply not change anything."

George drew in his breath and leaned back into his sofa.

"You don't have to decide tonight, George. I don't have the new potion yet, I have to brew it first, but I could have it in a week or two. It's entirely up to you. We can go on with this." Hagen pointed at the bottle on the living room table. "I have no problem with that. But we could also try the new potion."

George nodded heavily and drank his soda. "How did you come across this new potion?"

"I'm afraid I cannot tell you that; the less that you know, the better for both of us."

"I see...Though I've been pushing for making her current potion stronger, I...that's a tough decision."

"It is, George. I know that."

"But it's also tempting…very tempting."

"Yes."

"Let me think about it."

"Sure, take your time. I now have the formula; all I need is your decision. You can think about it as long as you want."

George nodded.

⌖

I sense an unfamiliar presence in the room. A man. A young man. Something is with him, surrounds him, wraps itself around him. It's attached to him, like a shadow. Even if he wanted to get rid of it, he couldn't. Your shadow doesn't leave you, does it? He was born with that shadow. It's like a second skin, or let me call it an aura. Some people claim that they can see a person's aura. I've never believed them…until now. Auras do exist. I can see them now.

George is here too and, oh, my God, for the first time ever, I realize that I'm seeing his aura. It's green. He's like a tree, calm, deeply rooted in the earth, his self. The branches are reaching towards the sky. The leaves are stretching and stretching to catch a glimpse of the sun. He thinks that I am his sun. Oh, how sweet you are, George.

If George is a tree, then the young man is huddled inside a thundercloud. I almost cannot see him, so thick is the cloud. It wobbles and quivers and doesn't let him be free. There's not much I can get from the young man beneath the cloud, only the strongest emotions: sadness and desire, burning desire, for knowledge and love. There are two women whom he wants. And he knows that neither of them really loves him. That hurts. Much pain lingers under that cloud. I felt that pain before…it…it's Hagen Patterson. Ah, he is here, but…I am not ready, I don't know what to tell him.

The cloud around him is weird. It has a life of its own. George's tree does not; he is the tree. However, Hagen's cloud is different, as if another spirit, another soul, dwelled in that cloud.

And I know it. I felt it before. Different and yet similar, there's a connection between the spirit I felt before somewhere, sometime, and that cloud. I wish I could remember. I wish I could understand. Evil dwells in that cloud, that spirit.

Smoke…I see smoke. All around me. Fire. The fire is not here, not real. It's an evil fire. It has killed. Fire has burnt Colleen Hardwood. But who is she? I'm oddly sure that I've never known a person by that name. I try to push her away, to concentrate on the dark cloud around Hagen, but…oh…pain…the cloud awakened the alien beast in my head…in my head….

⌖

"Emma visited Helena and me last Sunday," George said.

"Really?" Hagen tried not to frown. "What did she want?"

"Oh, nothing, just a kaffeeklatsch. It was nice. I hadn't seen her in a while."

Yes, sure, she hadn't found anything better to do. She had just wanted to kill time in her worry about Hagen's whereabouts. Like the charity sex that Juliana had offered, it had been a charity visit—not really interested, not caring at all, only doing it because Emma had found nothing better with which to spend her time.

George and Hagen chatted some more about potions and homemade cookies before Hagen left George and Helena and drove home. He was eager to start brewing, finally, the new potions from Sandra's copies, at least those for which he had the ingredients. He locked himself away in his cellar and brewed until three in the morning.

Report No. 11 from Agent 9836B12
Subject: Hagen Patterson (HP)
Status: One source of illegal substances confirmed.
Next action: Further investigation.
Details of current status:

1)   Ivan Fuller has contact with a known drug dealer.
Name: Daven Harlow. Street name: The Punk. Investigation has shown that Fuller once operated on Harlow after a shooting and has since used Harlow as a source for marijuana and the occasional cocaine. In the interest of the overall investigation, it is highly recommended not to act now against Fuller or Harlow.

2)   HP has personally visited possible illegal substances recipient George Sears and his wife Helena for the first time since the start of the investigation.

3)   HP is now seeing potential illegal substances recipient Alissa Caradine on a regular basis. She stayed the night from Monday to Tuesday. The night from Tuesday to Wednesday, HP spent in Ivan Fuller's apartment.

4)   Will concentrate on the Fuller-Harlow connection and HP's other potential source for illegal substances = his company.

chapter 18

TUESDAY, 28TH OF September

At exactly nine in the evening, Hagen's doorbell rang. He looked through the peephole, raised a brow, opened the door and nodded at the man in front of him.

"Good evening, I have come to pick up a delivery for Mr. Johnson at St. James Street."

"No, St. Jacobs Street."

The man nodded and Hagen, finding Sandra's code words quite amusing, stepped aside to let him in.

"You want to sit down for a minute and have a cup of coffee?" Hagen asked the courier and the man bowed to him.

"That would be much appreciated, thank you."

The guy was a bit older than George and wore an old-fashioned black derby hat, and an expensive long black coat, cashmere, Hagen supposed, although it wasn't that cold yet. He also carried an elegant black walking stick with a silver duck's head stud, which made him fit perfectly into Hagen's antiques cluttered apartment.

The man took off his coat. He wore a black and impeccable five hundred dollar suit beneath it. Hagen hung the man's coat on a hanger in his corridor.

"This way, please." Hagen ushered him into his living room and he sat down on Hagen's sofa, still holding on to his walking stick.

"Milk and sugar?" Hagen asked.

"No, black, thank you."

"I'll be back in a moment."

Hagen grinned to himself while he prepared coffee for the courier in his kitchen. He liked people of principle. Returning to the living room, he served the courier his black coffee.

"How long have you worked for Sandra?"

"I'm not working for her, Mr. Patterson. I'm serving her, and I have done so for thirty odd years."

"I'm impressed."

"I'm honored to be serving you as well from now on, Mr. Patterson. I understand that you are one of Sandra's most promising students."

"Oh, thank you, I'm glad to hear that."

Hagen took a plastic bag from under his living room table and placed the bag on it. "Here's the product."

"Ah, thank you." The courier glanced inside the plastic bag. He nodded in satisfaction at the four bottles with thick brown liquid and put the bag next to him on the sofa.

She Should Have Called Him Siegfried

The courier would deliver potion number four from Sandra's copies and that potion unsettled Hagen the most. Rather a poison than a potion, it slowly and unnoticeably killed the person who received it. The man or woman who was taking that potion presumably didn't know he or she was being poisoned and would die of a seemingly natural death in the not too distant future. Hagen gave the man or woman another year at the most. Those who wanted that person dead were patient. Patience, again and again, proved to be one of the most important virtues of an alchemist.

So, here he was, turning into a criminal, a murderer who didn't even know the person he murdered. Hagen reached for his white coffee, and the three cubes of sugar he had put inside still couldn't mask the bitterness of the brew.

"Where do you live?" Hagen asked.

"I live everywhere, Mr. Patterson. I have residences in twenty-eight cities and meander between them."

"Oh wow, really?"

"Yes. I am fortunate. I came by a comfortable amount of money during my days."

"Not bad," Hagen said and grinned at the courier. "A comfortable amount of money is an interesting choice of words."

The courier bowed his head.

"Don't you ever get tired of traveling?"

"Never, it is my lifestyle. I get easily bored when I am not in motion."

Holy cow, this guy was nuts. Strange, but his craziness eased Hagen's pain of actively participating in an assassination.

"How many deliveries are you making for Sandra?"

"Quite a few, Mr. Patterson."

"Oh, please call me Hagen."

The courier bowed slightly. "As you wish, Hagen."

Hagen struggled to hide his bemusement. "To where will you deliver this potion?" Hagen pointed at the plastic bag next to the courier.

"That should be none of your concern, Hagen. Trust me; it's better for you not to know."

"Understood, sorry for asking. I'm still new to this."

"Never mind, Hagen."

"Why don't you brew yourself? Why are you a courier?"

"Oh, what you and Sandra do is a gift. A talent that I cannot claim to possess. I stand in awe before your creations and it would be inappropriate if I tried to be your equal."

"Oh, I see, well…thank you."

"No, thank you, Hagen, for joining the trade. You're doing the right thing. Someone has to give a damn and there are far too few who do. You're helping to make the world a better place."

"Well, I hope so."

"Oh, be assured, you do."

From whose perspective, I wonder, Hagen thought.

"I don't wish to be rude, but I just cannot help but ask. Has your first name anything to do with brewing potions, Hagen?"

188

"Well…I suppose it has."

The courier looked expectantly at him. "I'd be very grateful if you could enlighten me."

"Um…you know…until I was fifteen I never concerned myself with the supernatural, but then I went away from home for summer camp for the first time. Are you married?"

"I have been, twice."

"I see, well, before that summer, I had been immune to the charm of women and thought the girls in my class were stupid, loud, and giggling monsters. However, during that trip, I developed a fancy for Ms. Rosenbloom, my music teacher. She had been around thirty, terribly old from my perspective at the time, but I had found her hands most beautiful, especially when they played the violin that she had brought. I still have a weakness for beautiful hands, you know."

"Oh, I understand that." The courier nodded quite vehemently.

"I gave a damn for the violin's sounds. I actually hated its high screeching and scratching, but to watch those elegant hands playing the instrument and to imagine those hands doing interesting things to and with me….

"Ms. Rosenbloom of course thought I liked the music and one evening she spoke to me at the campfire after everyone else had gone to bed or was fooling around elsewhere. I knew that my mother has named me after a character in an opera and that Hagen had been the bad guy. But I had never cared much for my name or the story of that fictitious Hagen. What finally opened my eyes to my name and its meaning was how Ms. Rosenbloom told me the story that night.

"She said that in the world of the *Nibelung* magic is common and normal. It's a matter of course. It simply exists and is as real as trees and rocks. That'll end after the *Twilight of the Gods* and after the new world order has begun. That's what the opera is about, the end of an old world and the birth of a new one."

The courier nodded again vehemently, hanging at Hagen's lips with unconcealed interest. Hagen wondered what fascinated the courier so.

"She said that in the old world, magic is natural," Hagen continued. "As if it was nothing, we're being told that Hagen has brewed a potion for Siegfried to initiate his intrigue. Thinking of nothing evil, Siegfried drinks it and the potion makes him forget that he's in love with Brünhilde.

"Hagen's potion is the trigger for all that follows. Well, it starts with Hagen's father, Alberich, of course, and Siegfried's father, Wotan. But anyway, Ms. Rosenbloom said that I surely had an interesting namesake."

"Why have your parents chosen the name Hagen over Siegfried?"

"Ms. Rosenbloom asked me the same thing. My mother said Siegfried sounded too German. I told that Ms. Rosenbloom and she said that that reason would be kind of disappointing."

"Indeed."

"I have to admit that her comment bit in deep, even more so than magic being a natural phenomenon. I started to wonder whether my mother had given me my name more intentionally. I haven't found out to the present day by the way. But back then, at fifteen, I found it awesome that the Hagen of *The Ring* had contributed to his whole world's demise with one single potion. What incredible power, what endless possibilities for greatness and despair, slumber in a single potion."

"Oh yes…you really are a worthy apprentice of Sandra, you are." The courier beamed at him.

"I hope I am. So I began to mix and to stir. And the more I mixed and stirred, the more I saw how little man understands about the world and his own body and all the more the greed for knowledge was awakened."

The courier smiled gratefully at him. "Thank you for sharing this with me, Hagen. I find it most fascinating. I believe in fate and it is no coincidence that you are Sandra's most promising apprentice. You'll make it far in the trade, Hagen, and I can only repeat that I am honored to be able to serve you."

"Thank you."

The courier nodded, downed the rest of his black coffee and slapped his palms onto his upper thighs so loud and so hard that Hagen jumped. "Well then, I shall be on my way. I will come to pick up the product once a month."

"Yes, thank you, I'll be expecting you."

They both got up from their seats. The gentleman picked up his walking stick and his plastic bag, and they headed for the door. Hagen helped him into his coat and then he was gone. He drove a Bentley, stylish to the last.

"Holy crap," Hagen said to himself. Then he shook his head, chuckled, and returned to his cellar.

⋈

Wednesday, 29th of September

Home from work, Hagen checked his mailbox and fished out his phone bill and a letter. His stomach flipped. A woman's hand had scribbled his address onto a pinkish envelope. He turned the letter around to look at the sender: Juliana Daniels.

His fingers turned numb. He dropped his key twice before he was able to open his front door with it. He let his bag fall onto the floor, flung his jacket onto the shoe rack, and walked into the living room. He sat down on the sofa, where he had sat when she had recently pushed the knife deeper into his heart.

With a grunt, he ripped the letter open and took out a single pink sheet of stationary that carried Juliana's elegant and squiggly handwriting.

Hello Hagen,

He scoffed. Not even "Dear Hagen." He took a deep breath and read again.

Hello Hagen,

I'm very sorry to have caused you anguish the other day. I know that the situation isn't easy for either of us, but please try to understand my motivation. I didn't turn to you with my problem to hurt you but out of sheer desperation. You are a man; you don't know what it means to crave for a child. I need to have a baby; nothing else is on my mind. I have become obsessed with the need for a child. You might not understand the content of this obsession, but the nature of obsession is quite fa-

miliar to you, I believe. Therefore, I beg you to help me, Hagen. I'd be eternally grateful if you did.

Awaiting your reply anxiously.

Sincerely,

Juliana

With a moan, Hagen threw the letter onto the table and leaned back in his sofa. He stared at the ceiling. Damn, he'd have to wait another two and a half months at least to get the love potion. How was he supposed to deal with Juliana until then? How should he answer Juliana and when? He got out his cell phone and texted Alissa, asking her to come by as soon as possible.

Thursday, 30th of September

Alissa stood on Hagen's doorstep the next night.

He drank in her heavy perfume as he embraced her and pulled her inside.

"Do we make love before or after your problem?" she asked and smiled at him.

"Both," he said and she chuckled as he maneuvered her into the bedroom.

After their first time for this evening, they lay naked in his bed and he gave her Juliana's letter to read. She scoffed and shook her head as she read it, then handed it back to him. He folded it and put it back into its envelope.

"You have to take that chance, Hagen."

He sighed deeply and fingered Juliana's letter.

"This is a great opportunity to see her on a regular basis. How do you plan on administering the love potion if you never meet her?"

193

He frowned.

"Here's what you'll do. You brew a fertility potion for her husband…what was his name?"

"Gabriel."

"That consists of vitamins. You wait for a few days before you reply and ask her to come by in two weeks. That's how long you need to research and brew his potion. You start to administer the vitamins to Gabriel mid-October. You ask her to pick up a new dosage every two weeks or so. Mid-December, you'll hopefully get the formula for the love potion.

"That's two months. If you order her to pick up new potion every two weeks, the timing would be perfect. Then you have to see her four times or so and at the fifth or sixth time, around Christmas, you can hopefully administer the love potion." Alissa looked expectantly at him.

He still held Juliana's letter and turned it around and around in his hands. "I don't know if I can pull that off, Alissa. Lie to her face…I—"

"Of course, you can pull that off," she interrupted, "You have to."

She leaned over him, gently took the letter from his fingers, and put it onto the nightstand. She took his face into her hands next and looked him in the eye.

"You can do it, Hagen; it'll work. You'll gain her trust, at least a little bit. You don't have to ask her in, just give her the potion. When you have the love potion ready, you'll find some excuse to ask her into the house, it being Christmas or New Year's and all. You'll offer her a drink and there'll be the love potion in it." She caressed his cheek.

He took a deep breath. "All right," he said and pulled her to him to kiss her.

Alissa left around midnight. Hagen remained lying in his bed and looked at the wall that had once held his Juliana shrine. He had hung the central picture back in its place but the six surrounding it and the wedding picture remained stowed away in a cabinet.

He still felt Alissa all over him as he stared at Juliana's photograph. He groaned and put his pillow over his face. Maybe he should drink an anti-love potion and be done with women for the rest of his life. He got up, took a shower, and went back to bed.

chapter 19

Friday, 1st of October

Hello Juliana,

Hagen wrote in answer to her letter.

I need to do some research for what you have in mind. Give me about two weeks and let me know when would be a convenient time for you to pick up the product.

Sincerely

Hagen

⟞⟝

Tuesday, 5th of October

Dear Hagen,

She wrote back, "dear," not just "hello."

I hoped with all my heart that you would help me and now you are. I promise that you won't regret this. I can come by your place Thursday nights, around eight p.m., before I go to my gymnastics class. I will give you my cell phone number in case of emergency. I trust that you won't abuse having that number now. Let me know the appropriate Thursday.

All the best,

Juliana.

⟞⟝

Below her name, she had scribbled her phone number.

Hagen hit the armrest of his favorite armchair five times after reading her letter because of that awful comment about him abusing her cell phone number. His just healed little finger hurt badly after that for two days.

⌖

Thursday, 7th of October

Not so punctually, at a quarter past eight, Hagen's doorbell rang and he peeked through the peephole at another of Sandra's wondrous couriers. Hagen opened the door and looked down at a barely five feet tall woman, who was nearly as wide as she was tall. She smiled up at him from behind half an inch of make-up.

"Hello, Mr. Patterson, so nice to meet you. I didn't know you'd be so young. And so handsome! Ah, I forgot the password stuff...I'm supposed to pick up a delivery for a Mr. Johnson at St. James Street."

"Um, hi, no, it's St. Jacobs Street."

"Yes, sure. How could I forget that," she said and giggled.

Hagen stepped aside and had to squeeze himself against the wall of his corridor in order to let the lady pass. She was about fifty and was dressed in a square dress with square patterns on it. She had a white handbag over her shoulder, thick glasses on her nose, and a wig on her head, a bad one. One could see from a mile away that she wore a wig.

"How about a cup of coffee?"

"Oh, yes, please, thanks. Ah, that's so nice to have you on my route now, a lovely young man. Sandra, that wicked witch, didn't tell me that you're so young."

She waddled into his living room, and let herself sink into his sofa. The sofa complained with a puffing sound and for a moment, Hagen feared it would break in the middle.

"Milk and sugar?"

"Both, and plenty of them, please."

"Coming."

In his kitchen, Hagen grinned broadly while he placed four cubes of sugar into the lady's coffee. He then balanced two coffee cups back into the living room. There he found that the lady had already dug up the plastic bag with the potions from under the living room table and examined them.

"That's my delivery, I guess."

"It is indeed."

Hagen put the coffee in front of her.

"Ah, thank you." She reached for her cup before he had even sat down and emptied it with one big gulp.

"Um, you want another?"

"No, no, one's enough. My doctor told me not to drink too much coffee anyway."

Hagen nodded and took a sip from his own cup.

"So, you're the new animal potion guy."

Hagen almost swallowed his coffee the wrong way. He had brewed the potion, number five from Sandra's copies, without having a clue for what it would actually be used. He had hoped somehow to find out from the courier what this thing did, and apparently he would.

"Um, animals?"

"Oh, Mrs. Henderson is so amazing. Lately she has managed to establish communication with her cat. That's a first. Dogs and horses are no problem, but cats… now that's a different story. They are such individualists, such wild and free minds."

Holy cow—literally. Mrs. Henderson, whoever she was, imagined she could talk to animals thanks to that potion? Hagen stifled a grin. He believed in potions, yes, but talking to and understanding animals? To influence the human psyche was one thing, to establish communication with animals was quite a different pair of shoes. Blessed be Mrs. Henderson that she was mad enough to believe a potion could do a thing like that.

"Is that so? That's amazing indeed."

"Yes. I'm so happy that I got involved with the trade, you know. It has opened my mind to all the infinite possibilities between heaven and earth. It's such an enormous world out there. I'm selling Tupperware, you know; that's how I get around. I was getting tired of it, frankly, but the trade has made my day. I've come to love traveling again."

"Why don't you brew yourself?"

She giggled and waved a fat hand. Hagen stared at her thick, sausage-like fingers, so big and fleshy that she could hardly make a fist. What a difference they were from the fingers of Colleen, Juliana, or Alissa. He'd even prefer to be touched by the gout hand of death than by those stumps of meat.

"Oh no, I'm not smart enough for that. I'm happy to meddle with the world by delivering. To brew is for charming men like you, and that's even a rhyme."

She beamed broadly at him and Hagen wrung a smile from his lips. He definitely preferred the twenty-eight cities gentleman.

The lady clapped her fat hands together and the movement made her arms wobble. "Well then, I shall be on my way. I'll see you in a few weeks, Mr. Patterson."

"Please call me Hagen."

"Oh, thank you. You're so sweet." She heaved herself from the sofa with an agility he had not expected, took the plastic bag, and waddled towards the front door.

"Oh, my God," Hagen said, grinned, and shook his head as he had closed the door behind her.

⚔

Thursday, 14ᵗʰ of October

Hagen had ordered Juliana to come to see him on October fourteen. At a quarter to eight that evening, he paced from the front door, through his living room, into the kitchen, and back. He carried a bottle of Gabriel's fertility potion under his arm, a slightly yellow colored vitamin juice.

Damn, how much he'd have loved to pour the poison that the twenty-eight cities gentleman now delivered into that drink. No, it wouldn't rid him of Gabe fast enough. And he wouldn't suffer. He wanted Gabe to suffer, the guy whose sperm was no good, the guy who had Juliana whenever he wanted despite that.

Hagen grunted and wiped his face; his skin felt oily and sticky. He wiped his palms on his jeans. He wished Alissa were here to cheer for him.

Who was classier, Alissa or Juliana? Alissa, definitely. He stopped pacing. Was she really classier? Well, they were entirely different types. They both played with people, yes, but in contrast to Juliana, Alissa admitted doing that.

His doorbell rang and Hagen jumped so hard that he almost let Gabe's bottle drop. He had stopped in the middle of his living room and now rushed towards the door. He checked through the peephole. Yes, it was her.

He opened the door and stared at her. Her long brown hair hung loosely around her shoulders. She wore a trendy white tracksuit with red stripes at the sides and red sneakers.

"Hello, Hagen."

"Hi…" Why did he lose his ability to speak in her presence?

"I really appreciate what you're doing. Really. I know that it's difficult for you. That makes it even the more—"

"Here." He interrupted her and held out the bottle with vitamins for Gabe. "Administer fifty milliliters each day in fruit juice or vitamin drinks or whatever soft drink. Don't mix it with alcohol and preferably not with a soda that contains carbonic acid either. Don't serve it in water; he'd taste that. That's a seven hundred milliliter bottle so this dosage is good for two weeks. Come back every two weeks to get a new bottle."

"Thank you. Understood. When do you think I can expect an effect?"

"No idea, I've haven't treated male infertility yet. You went to doctors for a year or something and they couldn't help either. Don't expect miracles. Maybe Gabe is beyond help. I cannot give you any guarantee whatsoever that it'll work."

She looked at the floor. Her downcast eyes ripped out his heart. How her hair fell into her face made him want to put his hand under her chin, raise it, and kiss her blood red lips.

"I understand. Thank you for trying, Hagen, really."

He was still holding out the bottle for her to take. When he didn't answer her last comment, she finally took the bottle, careful not to touch his hand.

"See you in two weeks then; I'll drop by again at eight. If anything's wrong, you can send me a message on my cell phone."

"See you then, Juliana."

She took a step backwards and he closed the door in her face. He leaned his forehead against the door and took three deep breaths to calm his hammering heart.

Part 2

chapter 20

With snow chains under his wheels, Hagen drove to Sandra's house. It had started to snow on Wednesday and he needed the extra traction to get there. He interpreted it as a good sign that she had invited him to stay the night from Saturday to Sunday. He still couldn't quite believe it yet that he would drive home with *the* formula in his pocket.

Sandra warmly welcomed him and Hagen met her third husband, Norm. After hearing from Sandra that he went to church and seeing his tacky landscape paintings, Norm was quite different from what Hagen had expected. The guy sent a chill into his very bones. Although they were of approximately the same age, Norm had nothing of George's harmless and cute appearance but looked like a cunning and ruthless man. He had brutal lines around his mouth and piercing gray-blue eyes. Surely at least one murder by potion went on this man's account. Well, on Hagen's too, he delivered poison now as well. Norm smelled strongly of "Old Spice."

The last time Hagen had smelled that, it had been on his uncle twenty-five years ago and the odor had given him a headache.

They talked shop enthusiastically, three alchemists under one roof, until Hagen couldn't stand it anymore.

"By the way, have I graduated?"

Sandra smiled broadly. "With honors, Hagen, with honors. You fulfilled all the requirements, you got all the ingredients, delivered on time, and the potions work. If you want, you can be a member of the inner circle from today onwards. Do you want that?"

Hagen straightened his hair and took a deep breath. "Jeez, I'm as excited as if you had just asked me to marry you. Yes, I want."

"Great. Welcome to the trade, Hagen," Sandra said and embraced him and Norm did too. He smelled as if he had poured half a liter of "Old Spice" over himself.

"Welcome, Hagen, this is a great moment." Norm patted Hagen's shoulder so hard that it hurt. Intentionally, Hagen was sure.

⚞⚟

Sandra had accommodated him in a simple but clean and cozy guestroom with a colorful day blanket, which she knitted herself, covering the bed. Hagen lay on his back, stared at the ceiling and felt astonishingly calm and sober after having gained access to the inner circle of alchemists.

Just how much would, should, and could he meddle with the world? The shadow of doubt threatened to descend upon him. The weight of responsibility wrapped itself around his chest. He grunted. He wouldn't think about big issues now. He had to stop being a spoiler. Ivan would be able to revel in success, just like he had enjoyed having been celebrated by his entire hospital for saving that impaled girl. Hagen wouldn't allow doubt to gnaw at his success now, he wouldn't. He turned onto his side, determined to fall asleep.

<hr />

Sunday, 12th of December

Down in her cellar, Sandra gave Hagen eight copies and one of them was *the* one, the love potion. He studied it eagerly and whistled through his teeth at the ingredients.

Awed, he looked up at Sandra and Norm. Sandra wore a unique indoor, comfortable piece of clothing: a huge, homemade knitted sack with sleeves in it, knit from thick wool. It was surely wonderfully warm, but bewildering to look at in its ring pattern, rainbows—five of them in sequence. Norm matched her style. He wore pants, luckily, but an equally homemade pullover with more rainbows on it although the blue band dominated.

"How old is this potion? Who was the first one to find this formula? I cannot imagine how anyone can find such a formula…" Hagen asked, marveling at the magic sheet of paper in front of him.

Sandra smiled broadly at him. "Nobody knows how old this potion really is, but it's old. Very old. You can trace simpler versions of it back to Roman times."

"You're kidding."

"No, I'm not. However, there's something very important that you must know. One ingredient is missing from the ingredient list."

"What? Why?"

"You have to find that last ingredient yourself, Hagen. If you have absolutely no clue, ask me, but first try to find the missing component. When you brew the potion according to this formula, the result will be a black, thick, unsavory soup. The missing ingredient is a liquid and when added, the potion turns for a moment into what looks like liquid gold before it loses its color and becomes an easy to administer transparent fluid, only slightly thicker than water and almost tasteless. It's best administered in fruit juice or wine."

"Wow…no heating or anything when adding the last ingredient?"

"No, room temperature, and it'll change from black to gold and transparent."

"I know of no liquid ingredient that does that."

Sandra, as well as Norm, smiled conspiratorially at him.

"You'll figure it out; I have no doubt," Norm said.

"All right." Hagen puffed up his chest. "I'm up to the challenge."

"I know you are." Sandra smiled broadly at him. "By the way, I don't want to discourage your own research, but I really need a particular potion urgently. You'll find an amnesia potion among the copies."

"Oh." Hagen looked eagerly through the rest of the eight copies he had received.

"You've been heading in the right direction with yours; don't be hurt in your pride. Look at it as a little coaching, for that's all it is."

Hagen read through the ingredients of the amnesia potion and gasped. "I'll be damned. Wow…now I get it. No worries, Sandra, I'm not offended. I still need a lot of coaching. This is great, how could I not get that? Ah…"

He looked up from the amnesia potion formula at Norm and Sandra and found them grinning broadly. He had to chuckle and they laughed with him.

"Continue experimenting with your amnesia potion. The formula that I've given you causes general amnesia. What you're aiming at is selective memory loss. As far as I know, no amnesia potion like that exists yet. It would be an immense breakthrough if you could add that angle to the potion and thus create a new one."

"Great, I'll try." Hagen nodded enthusiastically.

"One more thing. There are people out there," Sandra waved her arm at the ceiling, "who don't like what we are doing. There is quite an intense cat and mice game going on. They try to find us and take us out and get our potion formulas. Be careful with whatever you do and never underestimate the enemy. They are good at what they do, just as we are."

Goose bumps crawled over his arms. "Who exactly are they, Sandra?"

"Government. Not officially though, these agents are of the kind who'd never reveal whom they are working for."

"Wow…okay, I'll be careful."

"Adhere to the rules of communication that I explained to you earlier and you should be fine."

"Understood," he said, but the copies in his hands suddenly felt like lead.

⌖

After many compliments and goodbyes, Hagen finally got into his car and, deep in thought, steered carefully along the snow-covered country road that wound itself through the woods. The snow first sloshed and then crunched beneath his tires as he drove deeper and deeper into the hills. The sun had come out and sparkled in the powdered sugar that covered the trees. It looked beautiful and yet he felt like crying.

He now had his love potion. The one potion he had come here to get, that he had sold his soul and life for…in a way. But…he'd lose Alissa after he brewed that potion and, damn it, he didn't want her to lie happily in the arms of Benjamin Morrow.

What if he lied to Alissa and told her that he had failed Sandra's test? No, that wouldn't work. Alissa would see his lie, she'd look through him, and she'd know that he now had the formula.

Hagen continued driving, swallowing tears, but then he smiled bitterly. In contrast to other people, he had options. He could take the happy maker drug that he made for someone somewhere.

He stopped his car by the side of the road, half in a snowdrift. Like he had done after his visit to Sandra three months ago, he looked through the copies. He understood the amnesia potion and the one for Juliana, but the other six remained a mystery. He arched his brows. Wow, the closer he came to the castle, the

212

weirder the potions got. Well, he'd find out what they'd be good for whilst brewing them, hopefully.

He drove on through the dead landscape. "No, Hagen, it's sleeping, not dead. Don't be so morbid," he said aloud in his empty car.

chapter 21

THE CREATURE IN my head has turned from an alien monster to a Great Dane to a toy poodle. The magic potion has tamed and trained it though I fear that one day, the poodle will bite back and become a Great Dane or an alien monster again. For now though, the beast is cute and small. I'm so much closer to the surface of being than I was before the new potion. Alive and awake: two quite different states of existence. A plant is alive, animals are, microbes are—what have I been during the past year? Alive, yes, but not awake. It's not cynicism to call someone unconscious a vegetable, it's the truth. I've been a vegetable for a year, longer than that. My mind is still clouded and my moments of actual wakening are still short and rare and I treasure each of them.

However, even when I'm not awake, I still see things. I know things that I shouldn't be able to see or know. I now know that George was actually relieved when Carl died. He never told me. He never told anyone. He was too ashamed to admit that he was glad not to have to be the father of a crippled son. I cannot despise him for that. Quite the opposite, it gives me hope that George will forgive me when I tell him some time in the future, before the end, that I took the pill in secret to avoid another pregnancy.

I now know that the nurse who is sometimes here is a lesbian. She keeps that secret. Not in front of her friends and family, there she has come out. But she never did so at her workplace, afraid that she'd face bullying, prejudice, meanness, and so forth from her coworkers and her patients.

I like her much better since I know that she's a lesbian, because it is her natural state. I respect her decision to lead a double life. Bad experience has told her to keep quiet about her sexual orientation. I apologize for my fellow men and women.

And how do I know all these things? I see people's auras when they are close to me. One aura unsettles me greatly—the one of the healer, to whom I owe my moments of clarity and beyond. An evil shadow dwells around Hagen Patterson, and inside flickers the tiny light that is he.

I'm not afraid of the shadow. It's connected to him. It cannot suddenly leap across the room to possess another person; it's attached to his soul. However, I'm afraid for Hagen, for I know that I must tell him about that thundercloud around him and I must manage to be conscious when he comes to visit.

I hear movement in the room. I tell the poodle in my head to be quiet and open my eyes. "George?" I smile at him.

"Oh, bless you, honey, good morning."

George beams at me like a lit Christmas tree and kisses my forehead. "Is there anything I can get you?" he asks.

"Some tea would be nice."

"Lady Gray?"

"Oh, yes, thank you...George, I have had a name in my head for quite a while now. You and I, have we ever known someone named Colleen Hardwood?"

George furrows his white furry brows. They have whitened during my year of vegetating, now all the gray is gone.

"No, honey, that name doesn't ring a bell."

"I wonder who she was..."

"Was?"

"Yes, she's dead and I know how she died. She burned in a fire."

"Oh, my God, that's terrible."

George's shock is so genuine, honest and pure that I cannot but love him for it.

"I wonder who she was and why I remember her."

"You've come to see and know lots of weird things, Helena, my love. You're very special."

He kisses my cheek. He's proud and I have to smile at his naiveté, because it's not to my credit that I'm special now, but to Hagen and his potions.

I say nothing though and smile back at him.

"Let me get you your tea, honey, stay awake." George says and hurries out of the room.

I look around and my gaze falls onto the window and my heart leaps and bounces. Snow covers the world. I had never thought that I'd see snow again. I'm defying death. Every minute that I win against him is a victory. I have already lived much longer than Colleen Hardwood. She died at the age of thirty-eight. She had three children. I flinch and feel my breath rattling through my old lungs. Two of her children had died in that fire with her and her husband. Oh, what a tragedy, only one daughter is left. One daughter….

Colleen's DNA lives on while mine will not. It died with the death of Carl. Well, my kids would probably only have gotten cancer too. I'm not sad that I remain childless. I realize that I'm not sad about anything, really. A few regrets, yes, but only a few.

chapter 22

REPORT NO. 32 from Agent 9836B12
Subject: Hagen Patterson (HP)
Status: Courier movement.
Next action: Further investigation.
Details of current status:

1) Over the weekend, HP drove away, taking the same road into the woodlands as roughly three months ago. Again, pursuit was impossible due to too lonely of a road. HP would have noticed any shadowing attempt.

2) Investigations about his four couriers have been completed and have been sent separately. Interference not recommended for the time being. Couriers to be shadowed, if resources allow so, for possible identification of the end-customers of the potions and other alchemists for whom they are couriers.

3) Could still not verify the company HP is working at as a source for illegal substances

due to lack of access but it seems more than likely that his company and Ivan Fuller are HP's main sources for ingredients. His company doesn't seem to be aware of any abuse. Amounts HP is stealing must be miniscule.

4) Since I suspect that HP received new formulas during his absence, I will concentrate my stake out on potential new couriers.

5) Juliana Daniels, HP's high school love interest, is now confirmed as a recipient of allegedly illegal substances. See attached photos of a transaction in HP's doorway. She did not enter the house.

She Should Have Called Him Siegfried

Monday, 13th of December

With her eyes glowing, Alissa looked up at Hagen after their first urgent kisses on his doorstep Monday night. "You got it?" she asked.

"I did."

He disliked the greed in her eyes, the fire, the expectation, and anticipation. He wanted to yell and shout at her, "What can this Benjamin guy give you that I cannot? He's even another three years older than you. How can you love a guy who is forty-five when you could have a man who is thirty-one?" But he swallowed the words.

"Oh, that's exciting." She kissed his lips.

"Don't celebrate too soon. One ingredient is missing."

"What?"

He told her about the missing component issue.

"What's that crap? You did everything this teacher of yours asked for and you did more than that, what's this new test now?"

"I don't know…let me study the formula for a while and hopefully I can figure it out. We've been patient for months; we can just as well be patient for a few more days."

She sighed deeply and he kissed her neck, her throat, her lovely throat, and worked his way up to her lips. They made love in his bedroom and Hagen wanted to cry. Why was he condemned to love the wrong women?

Tuesday, 14th of December

On Tuesday, Hagen had lunch in the cafeteria at his workplace. He hadn't done so on Monday. He had been unwilling to face Cindy, his mom's new best friend.

After intensive e-mail contact, Cindy and Emma had met and now Cindy was hanging out with Emma ridiculously often. Emma mollycoddled Cindy to her heart's content. She was the daughter she had never had, finally someone who shared her passion for Wagner. Hagen strongly suspected that Cindy only hung out with Emma to be close to Hagen and he avoided her like the plague, sneaking in and out of his apartment like a criminal when Cindy visited Emma upstairs.

"Hi there, where've you been all weekend and yesterday?" she asked after she sat down at his table without invitation.

"That's none of your business, my dear."

Cindy scoffed. "You shouldn't worry your mom. She tried to reach you and you weren't there, no message, nothing. You could at least tell her that you'll be out of town for a while."

"Why should I? It's my life and my weekend. I can do with my time whatever I want. I don't owe my mother anything."

"Only your birth."

"Oh, don't give me this crap. I didn't ask to be born. That honor-your-parents shit gets on my nerves. At least half of the world's parents don't deserve gratitude from their children."

"Emma is a wonderful woman, and it was damned hard for her to raise you all on her own, without a husband or grandparents to help her."

"Yeah, don't you wonder why my grandparents cast her out?"

"Because she'd had the bad luck to get pregnant without being married and your super conservative grandparents couldn't live with that."

Good, very good! Emma had started talking to Cindy about her past, exactly as Hagen had wanted. One day, she'd tell Cindy about Hagen's father and he'd get it out of her, no doubt. He had to suppress a grin of victory.

"You sure? Did you talk to my grandparents? I'm convinced they have a different perspective on all of this."

"Have you talked to them?" she asked suspiciously.

"No, I've tried to once, when I was a teenager, but they didn't want to have anything to do with their bastard grandson."

"That's outrageous. How can they do things like that?"

"Maybe they know who my father is," Hagen said. Then he grinned and shrugged.

"No, they're just conservative assholes."

"Oh, and Emma isn't obliged to show them her gratitude for having thrown her into this world?" Hagen asked.

"Come on, that's different."

"Is it? Aha." He continued to shove food into his mouth.

"Seriously, Hagen, Emma loves you, and it saddens her that you're so distant and don't involve her in your life."

"She knows the price tag on that."

"You lived quite well without your father for thirty-one years. Why can't you let that go?"

Hagen laughed out loud. "You have no idea what it feels like if you don't know who your old man is and neither does she. You've seen that old Toyota that I'm driving? My mother gave it to me for my eighteenth birthday. Back then, I thought about selling it and buying a plane ticket to Germany with the money and looking for my father.

"I searched mom's rooms, while she was out, for any hint to the man whose DNA is in my body. I found nothing, except for the tickets to the Bayreuth Festival that hang framed above her stereo. She could've bought them anywhere so they're no real evidence either. I don't even know if she's actually ever been there.

"Since I had nothing to go on, I kept my car and didn't fly to Germany. It gnaws at me every day not to know who my father is and it pisses me off that she won't even talk about it. It's a non-negotiable price tag and now I've lost my appetite, want my dessert?"

Without waiting for an answer, he dumped a bowl of vanilla pudding onto her tray. Then he took his tray, got up, and stomped away from her.

That had gone very well. Cindy would now start bugging Emma for information on his father for sure. The cry to solve a mystery demanded it. And, once awakened, nothing could stand in the way of female curiosity.

She Should Have Called Him Siegfried

That evening, Hagen sat at home and studied the eight formulas he had received. He listed what kind of ingredients he needed and jotted down ideas on how to obtain them. He hadn't been able to concentrate on it Sunday night after his return, too frustrated by his fear of losing Alissa. He sighed when the doorbell interrupted him. It was Ivan.

Ivan had stopped bitching at Hagen about the potion he planned for Juliana when Hagen had given him a sample of the happy maker potion that he now brewed for one of Sandra's couriers. Well, Ivan had also paid for it. Ivan had bought the opium needed for this potion because Hagen had been unable to pay the ludicrous price the drug dealer had wanted for it.

"Hey, man, may I congratulate the mighty alchemist on his admission into the inner circle?" Ivan asked with a grin, as Hagen led him into his cellar.

"Yes, you may, Master Ivan."

"Uh-huh. Congratulations. Got any hot new formulas?"

"Yes, plenty, but I don't know yet what they're good for."

Ivan chuckled. "If there's hot stuff among them, you know whom to test them on."

"Sure."

"Any weird ingredients you'll need for them?"

"Actually, I'm just listing what I have and don't have."

"Ah, I see."

Ivan looked at the nearly one hundred tubes, vials, and vessels on Hagen's workbench before he went to study, for the hundredth time, Hagen's formaldehyde collection. With Ivan busy, Hagen resumed checking ingredients.

"Where's Colleen's hand?" Ivan asked.

"In the safe."

"Wow, why did you put it there?"

Hagen looked up from his lists. "You know, don't get me wrong, I really appreciate the gift and I adore that hand, but the way you got it is so gross and illegal that I felt weird about it and put the hand into my new safe," Hagen said and grinned to lessen any offense.

Ivan chuckled. "Yeah, that was a bold move."

Hagen looked back at his lists.

"The Juliana potion…you got that one too?" Ivan asked.

"Yes, but there's an ingredient missing that I have to find myself, another little test it seems."

"Wow, that's a harsh test. There are gazillions of options. How are you supposed to find the right one?"

"I don't know yet." Hagen studied his lists but felt Ivan's eyes on him.

"You all right?" Ivan asked, worry in his voice.

"No…I don't want to lose Alissa. I know that I will when she gives her Benjamin that potion."

"Then don't give her the right one. This ain't exact science. Let her think that she is giving him the right one and then, if it doesn't work, just bad luck."

"Yeah, you'd totally do that, wouldn't you?"

226

"Man, come on, what did you expect to hear from me?"

"I can't betray Alissa like that," Hagen said.

"Why not?"

"It just wouldn't be right."

"But giving that stuff to Juliana would be right?"

Hagen moaned and buried his face in his hands.

"Yeah, with the cool potions comes the responsibility, hm?" Ivan said so sober and thoughtful that Hagen had to look up at him.

"Seems so."

"I can't help you with that, man. That's your decision. I can only tell you what I'd do if I were in your place and that is to give Alissa the wrong potion, try to be happy with her, and give Juliana nothing and forget about her."

Hagen grunted.

"What's that sneer for?"

"That choice is so typically you, the way of least resistance."

"Sure, why not? What's the merit of what you're planning?"

"I don't know, Ivan...I don't know anything anymore..."

"Man, you're in a bad mood, hm? Go through your new potions and let me know if I can be of assistance concerning rare components. Give me my happy maker and I'll be out of here to let you brood by yourself, you're depressing me," Ivan said but grinned warmly at his friend.

Hagen went over to the refrigerator. He handed Ivan a bottle of his potion.

"Think about it, man, vitamins for Benjamin, Alissa for you, and Juliana for Gabe. You gotta introduce me to that Alissa girl."

"The hell I will, you'll only tease us about her being too old for me," Hagen said with a grin.

Ivan chuckled. "Thanks man, and see ya, I'll let myself out. Call me when you need me for ingredients."

"I will, thanks."

Hagen watched Ivan leave his cellar and, with a sigh, turned back to his new potion formulas.

⁂

I don't know why you like that girl, Alberich said in Emma's head. *She's awful.*

She's not. She's a wonderful, intelligent, and smart young lady, Emma thought back angrily.

Cindy sat in front of her at her kitchen table and they were playing cards. Cindy was a kitchen girl as well, definitely. They had made an apple pie together on Sunday and had just eaten its last remains for dessert.

Well, I do admit having Cindy around is better than going to see that dying witch Helena.

Stop being so nasty.

"I had lunch with Hagen again today," Cindy said.

"Did he tell you where he went over the weekend?"

"Of course not…but did you know that he apparently contacted your parents, I mean his grandparents, when he was a teenager?"

Baffled, Emma let her playing cards drop. "No, I didn't know that."

"Hagen said that they refused to talk to him, their bastard grandson…I think that's very harsh. Why would your parents not even talk to Hagen?"

Emma shuffled uncomfortably in her seat while Alberich chuckled in her head.

"I mean, that your parents were angry with you, I can still sort of understand," Cindy continued while Emma remained quiet. "Conservative, catholic, and all, but that they even don't talk to Hagen, I mean, it's not his fault, is it?"

Touched by evil. Haha, Alberich shouted."Well, my parents are special in their own way."

One day, my dear, your card house of secrecy and lies will crumble and I'm eagerly waiting for that day and I'll laugh and dance on your grave.

Shut up! Emma thought back, finding it increasingly difficult to keep the rage and hatred for him out of her face.

Yes, crumble, crumble!

With an utmost surge of will, Emma forced herself to smile at Cindy.

"He's really suffering from not knowing who his father is, I think," Cindy said.

Emma stared at the cards in her lap.

Saturday, 18th of December

With sweat on his forehead and pinched lips, Hagen brewed and brewed, he mixed and stirred, he added and heated, and then he let the grayish mix cool down. He turned to the next potion, and kept moving so not to have to think. He worked and worked, he hardly slept, pushing the decisions away, postponing them day after day.

He mixed and stirred some more, and then his eyes fell back on the love potion. He drew in his breath. He had gotten it right this time. The grayish mixture had turned as black as the night. In awe, he took the flask with the potion and shook it slightly. It had become a thick, slimy, deeply black liquid that oozed and wobbled inside the vial.

He dipped a finger into the brew and rubbed what stuck to his finger against his thumb. He sniffed the oily and viscous liquid. Almost no smell, only a slight coppery whiff. How the hell was this stuff ever supposed to turn from black over to gold and then transparent?

During his attempts to brew the love potion, he had occupied his mind with speculating what the missing ingredient could be rather than the consequences of this thing. He split what he had brewed into ten tiny dosages and applied the candidates one after the other, well aware that he didn't really want any of them to work. They did him the favor; none of the ten turned the black slime into gold.

For a moment, he stood still in front of his test tubes and listened to the silence in his cellar. He wiped at the sweat on his forehead. He looked at his wristwatch and sighed. It was four in the morning. He didn't even know what day it was. He looked again at his watch; it had a calendar as well. Oh. Saturday morning, he wouldn't have to go to the company today...dreadful thought. How could he avoid having to think about consequences when he had no work to distract him? He was dead tired. He lacked sleep; he had only slept three or four hours each night the entire week. He pushed all thoughts away and went to bed.

～⚔～

Hagen woke up twelve hours later at four in the afternoon. He sighed deeply and studied the ceiling. He had no more excuses or means to escape the decisions that he had to reach. Would he do that? Deny Alissa her happiness and try to keep her for himself? Could he do that? Give her vitamins for Benjamin with a straight face, claiming it was the love potion?

He got out of bed.

No…no lying. Not to her. She'd never forgive him if she found out the truth. And a tiny possibility still remained that the love potion wouldn't work. Then he could win her honestly. He wasn't Ivan. He couldn't betray her like that. It just wouldn't be right, and he didn't have the final ingredient yet anyway.

He took a shower, had something to eat, and returned to his cellar to think in earnest about the missing ingredient. He brewed a large amount of love potion. Luckily, the known ingredients were commonplace and he had plenty of them. Well, if the basic recipe had been known since Roman times, they would have to be common. He split the love potion into a bunch of vials and contemplated the possibilities. What could make this thing whole? What would be the room temperature liquid that would turn this potion into…what? What exactly did a love potion mean?

"You have power over the one who loves you. I have power over Ivan and my mother, Juliana and Alissa have power over me, and Benjamin has power over Alissa," he said aloud. This potion meant power, simple as that, the power over one person.

Hagen stood there and pondered and tried another few ingredients. None of them worked.

Half an hour later, Alissa marveled at three vials filled with black liquid that Hagen hadn't yet tried with a final possible ingredient. The unsuccessful ones, he had already thrown away.

"Can't you ask your teacher?" Alissa asked.

"I could, but I haven't exhausted all resources and ideas yet. I think it's important to understand this potion, to truly grasp what the final ingredient is, instead of simply being told what it is."

"You fear it won't work otherwise?"

"Yes, that's one aspect. I'm not sure, but another might be that if you but want it enough, you'll find the right ingredient. If you don't find it, then that means you don't really want to use this potion."

She looked up at him with worry in her eyes. "You have doubts?"

Hagen wiped his hands on his lab coat. "Well, a bit, yes."

"You want to accept Juliana's charity sex? I hadn't thought you'd be that kind of man, Hagen," she said, disappointment in her voice.

He winced.

"She treats you like a piece of dirt. She thinks that she's receiving a fertility potion for Gabe from you. She's using you most viciously; she—"

"I know," he interrupted. He looked away from her, unable to stand her gaze.

"Please, Hagen," she suddenly begged, "you must find the right ingredient. Please."

He looked into her eyes again and the despair, the need, the longing, that he saw in them tore at his guts. Her craving, wasn't for him, but for Benjamin.

"I'll find the right ingredient. I'll find it," he promised and she nodded and smiled painfully.

Why couldn't she feel his love for her when he slept with her? Hagen fought tears. He wanted her to be happy, he did. That it would be someone else who could make her happy...that hurt so bad. Pain clamped around his heart like a vise.

chapter 23

WEDNESDAY, 22ND OF December

Every Wednesday now, Hagen visited George and Helena. Partially because Hagen wanted to give Helena the chance to be awake during his presence, but mostly it was because her progress fascinated him. According to George, the new potion was working very well and Helena indeed looked better every time he visited her, even a hint of color had crept into her cheeks and she had gained some weight.

Hagen sat next to George on the sofa with Helena opposite them in her wheelchair. Hagen sipped the soda that George had served him.

"It's amazing; I think she really has the second sight though I don't know what it means or what it's good for. She has already talked three times about a woman called Colleen Hardwood. She—"

George interrupted himself when Hagen coughed and gasped, soda had gotten into his airway.

"You okay?" George asked and patted Hagen on the back.

Hagen coughed and struggled, nearly choking.

"I'm fine, only swallowed the wrong way," he said in a raspy voice. "Please go on, what about this Colleen Hardwood lady?"

"I don't know, never heard that name before. I'm sure that we never knew a woman named Colleen Hardwood. Helena says she's dead, she was thirty-eight years old, and she died in a fire with her husband and two children. Recently. Now how odd is that? Why would Helena know these things and down to so much detail?"

Hagen had thought that he had been ready for supernatural things, but now panic rumbled through his guts. How on earth could Helena know about Colleen Hardwood, right down to her age and how she had died? And why did Helena know about Colleen Hardwood?

"Hagen? Do you know this lady?" George asked with suspicion in his voice.

Shit, Hagen had lost control over his facial muscles.

"No, I don't," Hagen said quickly, still with a hoarse throat. He wasn't even lying. He had never met Colleen, only her sawed off hand in his safe.

"That's amazing, why would she know how a perfect stranger has died?" Hagen asked to restart the conversation.

"I don't know. It scares me. I mean, why this lady? There must be a connection to her around Helena somewhere." George still looked suspiciously at him.

"Well, maybe there'll be a connection in the future?"

"How? According to Helena, this lady is dead."

"Good point."

She Should Have Called Him Siegfried

Hagen stared at Helena. She sat apathetic, unmoving in her wheelchair. Her eyes were open but her gaze unfocused, apparently unaware of his or George's presence.

Hagen's feet and hands had turned to ice. Damn, magic *did* exist in this world. Only something supernatural could give Helena knowledge about Colleen. But why? Colleen was dead and Hagen had never met her. He couldn't think of one reason why his cancer potion with second sight side effects made Helena aware of Colleen.

However, if something like that were possible, then the love potion would work, too. Benjamin would love Alissa and maybe Juliana would finally love him.

Staring at Helena, he admitted to his greatest fear: the potion would work for Benjamin but not for Juliana, and Hagen would be left behind with nothing. Damn, he had to believe in this potion. It would succeed for Alissa and for him as well.

Thank you, Helena, thank you for giving me courage, he thought towards her.

Hagen soon left Helena and George and drove back home in a daze. Magic was real. The impossible was possible. And he, Hagen, made it possible.

Back home, he immediately wrote Sandra a letter to tell her about Helena's remarkable insight. He didn't mention Colleen's name to Sandra. He only wrote that he had found unmistakable proof for supernatural things going on—after all, he couldn't easily reveal his connection to Colleen.

With new vigor and hope, he brewed another batch of the love potion and tried some new ingredients on them.

Power. Yes, the power to change the world waited at his fingertips. Why had he been so depressed and listless since his return from Sandra? He had no reason to be. Sandra had admitted him into the inner circle. He had become a true alchemist.

What he mixed and brewed changed the world a tiny little bit. How many could say that of themselves? Some politicians and large company bosses maybe, but it wouldn't be many. And now, he, Hagen Patterson, was one of the few people who made a difference.

Juliana, she would be his and, oh damn, yes, of course, they would have a family. He could and would give her the babies that she wanted. They'd have a whole bunch of kids, at least six, three girls and three boys. He had always wanted to have brothers and sisters.

He'd stand at Juliana's side with a newborn baby in her arms. She would look up from the baby and smile at him with heavenly happiness in her eyes.

He mixed and stirred and wracked his brain for the final ingredient. What could it be? What would it be? He stayed up until the wee hours of the morning, this time out of enthusiasm.

<hr />

I am uneasy. The shadow has been here again. It now comes to visit me regularly. I know that underneath the thundercloud is Hagen, but I'm afraid to wake up and talk to him because of the thing around him. I want to warn him, to help him, but I don't know what the thing will do if I'm awake. I don't fear for myself but for Hagen. I fear that it'll turn against him if I tell him about it.

After his visit today, I'm sure that he doesn't know about the thing. I cannot fathom what would happen if he knew. Would that knowledge help him or would it destroy him? It is this thing that I need to talk to him about, I know that now. I'm surprised that I already knew it weeks, even months ago. Back then, I had nothing but a vague hunch, now I know so much more. It is evil.

That cloud wraps itself around Emma too. She has passed part of the cloud on to her son. She couldn't help that, I suppose. It probably happened at Hagen's birth.

Does Emma know that? I'd have to see her to find out the truth. But Emma doesn't come to visit me anymore. Her evil guest sees to that, I'm sure.

The poodle in my head is astonishingly quiet today. Will it allow me to open my eyes? Let me try. There was snow the last time I woke up. I wonder if it has melted.

"George?" I ask and realize that he's not in the room with me. Ah, I hear his footsteps on the stairs. "George?"

"Oh, yes, my love. Oh, you're awake. How are you?"

"Is there still snow, George?"

"Yes, there is."

His eyes are bright with delight, and he rolls my wheelchair to the window. I look out and smile at the world covered in powdered sugar. It looks clean and innocent.

"It's beautiful. I didn't think I'd see this again."

George hugs me from behind and kisses my cheek. "Yes, it's beautiful and it's even more beautiful that you're here with me."

"Thank you, George, for everything."

"Thank you for being here, my love. Don't leave me, stay with me for much much longer."

"I'll try," I say and he kisses my cheek a second time.

"Good. You missed Hagen, dear; he was here just two hours ago."

"Oh, too bad," I say, hoping that George doesn't notice I am glad to have missed him.

"Next time, honey, he now comes every Wednesday."

"Okay."

"You know, I told him about Colleen Hardwood and he didn't admit it, but I think he knew her."

I look up at George in astonishment. So I know about her because of Hagen? "Really?"

"I'm not sure, but the way he reacted…yes, I think he knows her."

"Oh…" I wince. The poodle in my head barks and I have to close my eyes. I'm suddenly tired, very tired.

"Let me take you to bed, honey," I hear George say before poodle's howling drowns out his voice.

⚜

Thursday, 23rd of December

On Wednesdays, Hagen drove to see Helena and George and he enjoyed the couple's company. However, every other Thursday, the day of Juliana's visit, had turned into a day of horror. Self-consciously, he descended into his cellar after work and a quick dinner of instant pizza and took a bottle of vitamin brew for Gabe from his fridge. He stared at his black attempts at love potions that dominated his workbench and hastily left the cellar to wait for Juliana. She always came at eight p.m. sharp; it was five minutes to eight now.

He stared at the small package of chocolate on his shoe rack. Should he really give it to her? Would she have a Christmas present for him? He would bet she hadn't even thought of it.

Gymnastics class…the mere thought of Juliana in tight leggings, stretching her adorable body in all possible and impossible ways, made Hagen shiver with desire. He quickly banned the picture of her in revealing clothing from his mind and waited behind the closed front door.

How small he was now. During lunch, he had been talking mean again to Cindy, putting her down. He had been offensive and rude and now Juliana reduced him to a slave that cowered before his mighty master. He hated himself.

The doorbell rang, as punctually as ever. He opened the door and Juliana stood in front of him. She had bound her long brown hair back into a ponytail with one lock hanging into her face. She wore no make-up, fresh and natural and yet lady-like, and had on a pink, girlish tracksuit (and below it she surely wore those tight leggings and a t-shirt), stylish sneakers, and a down coat thrown over the tracksuit to protect her from the cold. Very few women could look elegant in such an outfit, but Juliana was one of them.

"Hi, Hagen."

The way she said his name made him squirm. Huskily, apprehensively, and yet a hint of gratitude tinted her voice.

"Hello, Juliana, how are you?"

Her perfume reached him, heavy and flowery, he drank in her scent, shivering.

"Oh fine, thanks. How are you?"

"Can't complain," he said and offered her the bottle for Gabe.

"Thank you, I really appreciate it." She said that every time.

He nodded at her. Usually she left at that point, but that day she lingered. Cold wind blew into the house and made Hagen shiver even more. Should he give her the chocolate now? She apparently had no present for him, or did she?

"It's been two months since I started to administer the potion. When do you think we can expect an effect?"

Oh shit...she was getting impatient. What if she found out that he was only giving Gabe vitamins?

"I don't know, Juliana. As I said before, you went to doctors for a year and they couldn't help. Don't expect miracles from me."

"Well, you're obviously not poisoning him, he's fine, but what guarantee do I have that there's really a fertility potion inside this bottle and not something totally different?"

"You're crossing the line, Juliana, again," he hissed. "Do you think this is easy for me? And all I get as a reward is distrust? Damn you!"

With that, he shoved her out of the door. Trembling, and not only from cold, he leaned against the closed door, realizing that she still stood at its other side, only a few inches and wood and glass separating them.

"I'm sorry, Hagen." The door muffled her voice. The apology sounded thin and half-hearted.

He didn't know what to do, whether to answer.

"See you in two weeks, Merry Christmas and a Happy New Year," she said and then left.

Breathing hard, he remained leaning against the door. Sweat broke out on his forehead, a cold sweat. She'd soon find out that the bottle contained nothing but vitamins. If she did, she would never see him again.

He'd have to give her the love potion soon, very soon. He had to find the missing ingredient within the next two weeks, as soon as possible. In addition, he needed to test it via Alissa on Benjamin before he could give it to Juliana.

In two weeks, he'd be able to ask Juliana in after tonight's disaster. In two weeks would be his chance to administer the potion through a drink he could offer her, one that she would have to accept to atone for her behavior. He had to find the damned missing ingredient. Now!

Moaning, he pushed himself away from the door. His gaze fell on the chocolate package that he hadn't given her. He took it, smashed the box on the shoe rack a few times, and then threw it into a corner. He rushed down into his cellar. He mixed and stirred wildly that night, but without any positive results, unable to focus on his task.

※

Friday, 24th of December

After work Friday night, Christmas Eve, Hagen couldn't sit still anymore. He had tried every ingredient he could think of. Everything.

He wandered in circles around and around his workbench. He didn't want to ask Sandra, not yet. Not even two weeks had passed since he had received the formula, too soon to give up and crawl back to her for help. However, time was breathing down his neck. He had to find the missing ingredient this weekend so that Alissa would have enough time to test the potion on Benjamin.

What could it be, this last ingredient, and why wasn't it listed in the formula in the first place? How much of it would he need? Had he already found the right one and administered too much or not enough? How could he know? It had to be something special and yet…Roman times…he had to think simpler. Up until now, he had tried chemicals and medicines. He should try more ordinary stuff. So he tried with vinegar, oil, and water, all to no effect.

"Think in basics, Hagen," he whispered to himself. "This potion is about love and power. It gives you power over a human being. And you don't just give this potion to anyone, but someone special, the human you desire, whom you want to make yours. A human that has so far rejected you, that doesn't want your love…tears! Maybe it's tears!"

Damn, he was much too excited for tears. He didn't even have onions in the house to make him cry.

No, he'd bet it had to be heartfelt tears so onions would be cheating.

But…bodily fluids…what if it was blood? Hagen gasped. Yes! Blood…you bind yourself to the person you love with blood; you persuade that person to love you back by making him or her drink your blood. Blood was worth a try and easier to generate than tears.

He took one of the yet untested vials with black slimy fluid and put it down in front of him. He grabbed a knife from his tool set at the left hand side of the workbench that lay next to the sink. He held the knife's blade into the fire of a Bunsen burner to disinfect it. Then he poured pure alcohol over the blade and sliced his thumb. It hurt, it reminded him of the night that had started all this, when Juliana had pushed the dagger deeper into his heart and when he had cut and broken his fingers.

He watched a drop of blood emerging from his cut thumb and held it over the test vial. A thick, dark red drop plunged into the black liquid and then another drop and another. He stared expectantly at the vial.

Something started to happen. The black liquid swirled inside the vial, without any assistance. Lighter and darker streaks emerged while the black liquid absorbed his drops of blood. A shimmer started to appear from the vial. The blackness brightened. Rapidly, the color changed and Hagen held his breath. The liquid sparkled in a warmer and warmer gold. Hagen yelped in delight. That was it! He had found it! Blood.

The liquid shone from within for a moment. It twinkled like a tiny sun, a jewel that caught the light from the lamp under the ceiling and turned it into pure… power. Breathlessly, Hagen watched magic at work. How the molecules inside the vial changed and became more than they had been: An instrument, a tool to control, and to break someone's will.

Black was the heart that brewed the potion, filled with greed and desire. Gold was the color for which countless people killed and died, the color of power, the symbol of might. And transparent like water, clear and innocent was the victim that didn't know yet it would be charmed and manipulated, subjected to domination and suppression.

Hypnotized, Hagen stared at the display of colors before him and watched the gold fade. A minute later, something transparent and pure, something slightly thicker than water, sloshed gently inside the vial. Hagen took the vial and held it up to the light of his chandelier above the workbench, so aware of what he held in his hand.

Power.

"Merry Christmas, Hagen," he whispered to himself, put the vial down, and settled onto the stool that stood behind him. He let the moment sink in, while he stared at the vial with its magic potion. The instrument to make Juliana his—he had found it.

He had never before had this power. He had tried every tactic that he thought possible, had begged, ignored, and adored. Everything had failed.

He was tired of failing.

He fished his cell phone out of his lab coat pocket and wrote Alissa a text message. "Found a Christmas present," he wrote and nothing else.

His finger hovered over the send button. There would be no way back if he pressed the button.

He did it. A strange peace washed over him, when the message started its way through the ether. He reveled in it for a moment, enjoying the silence in his cellar. Then he got up, threw away all the failed attempts at the love potion, and started brewing a fresh batch for Benjamin Morrow.

Five minutes after he had finished brewing the potion, his doorbell rang. Hagen left his lab coat on and walked upstairs. It was close to midnight, he noticed. He didn't check who stood behind the door. He knew who had come to visit him.

Alissa's cheeks were flushed with excitement.

"Got your message." She slipped inside. "What's the missing ingredient?" she asked, breathless and shivering.

She looked fantastic; she had come straight from the hotel. She wore a business suit, as always, a white blouse with golden threads in it—how befitting—a long, expensive cashmere coat, leather gloves, which she just took off, and long, high-heeled boots.

"Come and see."

He smiled at her and helped her out of the coat. After a welcoming kiss, he led her downstairs and around his workbench. They stopped in front of the vial with Benjamin's potion.

"It's still black," she said in disappointment.

"Yes, because only you can provide the last ingredient. It's your blood, Alissa."

Her eyes widened and her jaw slackened, but only for a moment. She drew in air and nodded. "Makes sense."

"Yes, doesn't it?"

He took the knife again and held the blade to a flaming Bunsen burner. He waited until it had cooled down and poured alcohol over the blade before he handed the knife to her.

"Where?" she asked, fear in her voice.

He showed her his thumb.

"Okay."

She grimaced as she cut her thumb. She cut deep and blood shot out of the small wound. She held her thumb quickly over the vial with the black potion.

"For us, Benjamin, for us," she whispered.

Hagen and Alissa watched her blood dripping into the vial. They watched the black swirling, the little sun of gold rising, and Alissa gasped and giggled. She grabbed Hagen's arm in excitement with her unhurt hand.

"Oh, my God," she said when the gold faded and became transparent. "Oh, this is amazing. I don't know what to say…Thank you, Hagen, thank you."

"We don't know yet if it'll work."

"It will. I'm sure. I know it." Her eyes sparkled in the light of the chandelier.

Hagen smiled at her and took the vial with Benjamin's potion. He poured it into a small bottle with a screw cap and closed it. He offered the bottle to Alissa and she took it in awe.

"Best administered in fruit juice or wine," he said.

She nodded and put the bottle into her handbag. He solemnly put a Band-Aid around her hurt thumb. After he was finished, she flung her arms around Hagen's neck, and kissed him.

Her kiss hurt. Her passion and her fire burned him. He knew that if the potion worked, this would be their last night together. Desperately, he kissed her back and, ridding each other of their clothing, they stumbled upstairs into his bedroom. He made love to her as he had never made love to any woman before, so aware of the coming loss, and so aware that she wanted Benjamin to do what he did.

She left him the following afternoon with Benjamin's potion in her handbag and anxious anticipation in her eyes.

After she was gone, he drank the entire bottle of expensive wine that she had given him for Christmas before he went upstairs to have Christmas dinner with Emma.

chapter 24

MONDAY, 27TH OF December

Hagen found himself able to wait in relative patience for the result of the love potion being tested on Benjamin Morrow. If the potion worked, he'd be responsible for the broken heart of Morrow's wife, divorce, suffering children, and so forth, but he knew none of those people, had never met them. If you don't know someone, it's hard to feel sympathy. Morrow was no different from all the other people for whom he brewed potions and that Sandra's couriers delivered to their victims. He knew Alissa though, had not betrayed her and had done his best to make her happy.

He sat at his usual table in his company's cafeteria and smiled at Cindy who was approaching him with her tray. She sat down opposite him and smiled back.

"Merry Christmas, how was your weekend?"

"Good, and Merry Christmas to you as well," he said.

Should he be nice or awful to her that day?

"You did anything special?"

"Hardly got out of bed with my girlfriend." So, awful it was.

Cindy sighed and shook her head.

"What's that sigh supposed to mean?"

"That I'm bored with your nasty days."

He chuckled. "Hung out with my mom again all Sunday?"

"Yes, I did."

"Jeez, ain't got anything better to do? Some Christmas party? Trying to get laid?"

"Men have the tendency to attach too much importance to sex."

Hagen grinned at her. "You don't even realize that you're making progress, Cindy. Three months ago, you never would've said anything like that. Your self-confidence is growing. Congratulations."

"Oh, wow, I'm touched. A compliment. Out of Hagen's mouth. I will have to mention that in my diary."

"Good, good, you're really making progress."

"I always wonder where you got that malicious streak from, Emma is so nice."

"Well, must be my infamous father then."

Cindy sighed once more. "That topic again."

"Sure. Since I don't presume you want to hear details from my Christmas in bed."

Cindy took a sip from her soda and looked at him over the rim of her glass. "Gotta admit that Emma makes quite a secret out of your dad and I've started to wonder why. Can't imagine what's so terrible about it that she avoids that topic like the plague."

Ah, very good. Female curiosity had started to dig into the mystery. He only had to wait.

"I'm amazed that you have apparently grasped a tiny bit of an outline of what I've been feeling for some twenty-nine years or so."

"What's your first memory?" she asked.

"Playing doctor and nurse with Juliana."

She shook her head. "That's a lie."

"Interesting, why do you think so?"

"You were five when you first played doctor and nurse with Juliana, Emma told me. You've only known her since she was four, which was when her mom moved in with your uncle. You must have memories from before that. Usually people have their first memories from around age three."

Hagen grinned broadly. Hell, Cindy had gotten close to Emma. Excellent.

"That's not fair. You hear all sorts of stories about me from Emma but I don't have such leverage over you."

She grinned. "Yeah, it feels good to have the upper hand for a change. So, what's your real first memory?"

"How Emma spanked me because I had broken one of her precious *Nibelung* twelve-inch LPs."

"Oh, come on, that's a lie too."

"No, it's not. That's my first memory, honest to God, and I was around three years old, indeed." He answered her merciless glare fully.

"That's not true, that's not your first memory, is it?"

"It is, I swear. Guess that's another reason why I like neither her nor Wagner."

"That's such a sad first memory."

"Yeah, isn't it?" He scratched the last bits of food from his plate. "You can ask Emma about it. I'm sure she remembers that story."

"I will."

Hagen took his tray and got up although Cindy wasn't finished yet.

"Fine, see you later," Hagen said.

⌐╫╦

Hagen waited for the love potion result and brewed according to Sandra's schedule. The courier with residences in twenty-eight cities came by to pick up a bunch of potions from Hagen on Monday night. He went by the name of Sam Millard, surely a false name. They sat in Hagen's living room sipping coffee.

"I must tell you that I have an odd feeling recently, Hagen," Sam said after the small talk was finished. "As if someone followed me."

Hagen jumped and put down his coffee cup.

"Can you be more specific?"

"The classic routine: cars following me, people walking behind me, the feeling of eyes on me all the time...I've been a courier for many years. I had such a feeling only once, about ten years ago and now again, and it started since I have you on my route, I'm afraid."

Hagen's hands wanted to tremble; he put his palms onto his thighs.

"You think I am compromised?"

"Maybe. You should keep your eyes open. Wide open."

"Jeez..." Hagen fidgeted in his seat. "What happened ten years ago?"

"Unfortunately someone on my route was taken out."

"What does that mean?"

"An alchemist suddenly disappeared, he was found a few weeks later, dead, in a river close to his house. His lab had been raided and his work destroyed, much of it had been thrown into that river. Very irresponsible, don't you think? To dump all these chemicals into a river."

"Indeed." Hagen cleared his throat. "Who are these people who're after us?"

"Secret governmental organizations, professional spies…" Sam trailed off and shrugged.

"Why has only that one guy been taken out, why not the other people on your route?"

"I don't know. I am very careful, of course."

"Sorry, but driving a Bentley is not what I consider to be low-key."

Sam smiled thinly. "I have various cars in my cities of residence, only one of them is a Bentley."

"Oh, I see, sorry."

"Never mind. I'm just telling you that you need to be extremely careful, Hagen. This is a critical time for you. You have just emerged as a member of the inner circle. That is the most dangerous time, in fact. You need to control sharply who knows about your cellar and who doesn't."

Hagen nodded. "Understood, and thank you for your warning."

"You're more than welcome. I'd highly regret if something happened to Sandra's most promising successor."

Sam smiled at him, so hopeful and well meaning that it oddly touched Hagen. Before, Sam had called him and apprentice, now a successor.

"Thank you."

After Sam had left, Hagen slumped onto his sofa again and listened into the silence of his apartment. He checked his cell phone, still no message from Alissa. He sent her one, asking whether everything was all right. No answer.

He listed in his head who knew about his cellar and his secret line of work: Sandra, Norm, the couriers, his mother, Alissa, Ivan, George, Helena and Juliana. Only the couriers were new to that knowledge. Did a mole hide among them? Hagen grunted in anger. He thought about his neighborhood. Indeed, there was an empty house, across the street, three houses down. He'd check that house for illegal residents at the next best opportunity.

⚜

Tuesday, 28th of December

By Tuesday night, Hagen's calm gradually vanished. He sent Alissa another text message. "You okay?" he asked.

No answer.

He brewed potions to distract himself. Finally, at eleven p.m., his doorbell rang. He almost dropped the vial he was holding. He put it down hastily and stormed upstairs. He tore open the door and Alissa stood in front of him.

She looked different. Her face looked softer, younger, and her eyes had a glow to them that he hadn't seen before, a girlish glow, a happy glow. She slipped inside and pushed the door shut behind her.

"Hagen, it's a miracle." Her voice quivered. "It works!"

"Really? Come on, tell me everything."

He pulled her into the living room and they sat down side by side on his sofa while it poured out of her.

"It works even better than I had ever expected. It's natural. It all seems so natural. It's as if he hasn't even drunk the potion.

"We had our after Christmas party yesterday. We always have a party the first Monday after Christmas when things have wound down at the hotel. During the party, I poured the potion into Ben's wine and he drank all of it. Half an hour later, he looked at me and he looked at me with different eyes.

"Another half an hour later, he sat next to me and we talked and talked. One party member after the other went home until only the two of us were left and he kept on talking about work, his kids, anything, and then he suddenly kissed me. I took him to my apartment and we made love the whole night!" Her eyes filled with tears and her hands trembled while she spoke.

"It was all so natural and easy. In the morning, he said stuff like how we should've done that ages ago and that he had wanted me for such a long time. And he told me that he was having trouble with his wife and he was thinking about divorce and whether I'd stay with him because he doesn't want to be alone.

"It's magic, Hagen, it is magic! It's fantastic. He loves me, Hagen. He really loves me! It's as if he has always loved me, all he needed was a nudge in the right direction, and the potion gave him that nudge." She laughed and tears poured over her cheeks.

Hagen stared at her with his mouth hanging open, fighting the pain of loss that crept into his stomach.

"Oh, Hagen, I don't know what to say or to do. This is so big. There's nothing in the whole world that I could do to properly thank you. You made this possible. You did an incredible thing for me and I can never pay you back, never. I love you too, Hagen, I do, really, but...I must be with Benjamin now, I..." She choked on her tears and couldn't speak anymore.

"I know, Alissa, that was part of the deal, remember? I'm glad to hear that it works and your happiness is reward enough for me."

Each word hurt. He was happy for her, yes, but pain surged through him like the fire that had killed Colleen Hardwood.

"It'll work for you too, I'm sure. Juliana will be yours. She'll love you, Hagen, and don't worry, there'll be nothing forced about it. It'll all come naturally. She'll love you back. It works, Hagen, it works!"

She laughed and tears shone on her cheeks and in her eyes. Alissa had never been so wonderful and the pain of losing her felt like someone opening up his chest with hammer and chisel.

"Yes, it works," he said and nodded.

"I…I have to go now. I…if there's anything I can do for you, no matter what it is, I'll do it. I owe you so much, more than any human has ever owed anyone. I don't know how to thank you, I…" She cried again.

Hagen caressed her hair. "It's all right, Alissa, go and be happy."

He couldn't help it that tears shot to his eyes. He got up from the sofa, trying to hide his tears from her. To swallow them was the most difficult thing he had ever done.

"Yes, I will be. I promise," she said and laughed.

He walked her to the door. She flung her arms around his neck and pressed a kiss onto his cheek.

"Go and be happy yourself with Juliana. And thank you."

She turned and left. The door swung shut behind her, leaving a breeze of ice-cold winter night air in the doorway. For a moment, Hagen stood like a statue before he sank to his knees and sobbed.

He had never met Benjamin Morrow, but what Alissa had said…natural, as if he had only needed a nudge in the right direction. Surely, Morrow had secretly desired Alissa but had never dared to show her his feelings. Being married and being her boss, he had probably dreaded the consequences, the problems, but at least in principle, he had wanted Alissa.

Juliana didn't want Hagen; she never had. It wouldn't be natural. The potion wouldn't nudge her in the right direction; it'd have to turn her around completely. He knew that unerringly, with biting certainty.

Hagen and Juliana would never be like Alissa and Benjamin.

Why was there no piece of happiness for him in this world? Why? He'd take it for himself, that piece, he'd take it. Juliana would be his. The potion would work on Juliana too, differently, sure, but it would work.

He swallowed his tears and rose to his feet. In eight days, he'd administer his love potion.

chapter 25

Sobered and calm, Hagen sat on George's sofa the next evening and watched the apathetic Helena.

"Helena was conscious for a few moments only two hours after you left last week, Hagen. She's conscious every two, three days now. Tomorrow I'll take her to the hospital for her regular checkup. I'm very excited. Maybe the tumor has shrunk." George shuffled in his seat like a child.

His happiness resembled Alissa's, the happiness of fulfilled love. Hagen frowned.

"I wouldn't count too much on that, George, but, of course, I'm happy to hear that she now has so many clear moments. Any new second sight stuff?"

"No, not since last week…what's the matter, Hagen? You seem…grim, are you all right?"

For a moment, he wondered what to tell George. He should tell him something so that Juliana moving into his place or anything similar wouldn't come as a total surprise to everyone.

"My girlfriend and I, we separated."

"Oh no, I'm so sorry. May I ask what happened?"

"Sorry, George, I…"

"Never mind. It's okay. Everything I say now will sound like a platitude, but believe me, the pain will ease."

"I suppose so," Hagen said.

⌦⌫

He is here. I can feel his presence. I could wake up now and tell him about the evil thing that engulfs him, but something holds me back. The tiny light inside the thundercloud that is Hagen is so dim today. Depressed. Something happened. He's unhappy. He lost something, someone…not to death though. What is it? Oh, it's love. He lost one of the two women he loves… again to another man.

I don't envy him. I remember how he feels. As a teenager, before I met George, I'd been madly in love with that boy, Abner Mills. He rejected me. It devastated me, and I cried for days and weeks. If I tell Hagen now about the darkness around him, it'll surely do more bad than good.

Strange. I fear telling him. I'm looking for excuses not to have to tell him. I must analyze that fear. Is it the fear of being the bearer of bad news or is it more? Am I personally afraid of the thing around him after all? I don't know. I'll tell him next week. I will. I promise you, Hagen.

Oh, I remember something. George told me that he thinks Hagen knows Colleen Hardwood. So if he does…then there must be another message hidden in the fact that I know her name. What is that message? What?

Thursday, 30th of December

Stoically, Hagen went to work. He had no desire to meet Cindy for lunch. He ate lunch outside in a restaurant off the company ground for the third day in a row. He did not have the nerve to deal with her and, through her, with his mother.

In the evening, he brewed potions from Sandra's list, wanting to be alone, but Ivan didn't do him the favor. He stood on Hagen's doorstep at nine p.m. and Hagen led him down to the cellar.

"You okay, man?" Ivan asked. "You haven't called me, you don't answer your phone, and you don't answer e-mails. What the hell is going on? Merry Christmas by the way and here are some supplies." Ivan put a vinyl bag onto an empty spot on the workbench.

Hagen checked the bag and its ingredients. "Oh, thanks."

He looked up at Ivan. He doubted that it would do any good to talk to him about what had happened. However, he knew quite well that Ivan wouldn't leave without answers.

"I found the missing ingredient, brewed the potion for Alissa or more correctly her Benjamin, she administered, it worked. And now I lost her."

He started emptying Ivan's bag.

"Holy shit. Why did you do that?"

"I couldn't betray Alissa, I just couldn't."

Ivan sighed deeply. "Hagen, you're hopeless. It's as if you want to be unhappy."

"Likewise."

Ivan groaned. "And now? Now what? And what's the missing ingredient?"

"Blood."

"Oh…"

"And now what…good question, dunno," Hagen said.

"Give up on Juliana, man, give up on her. Listen to me, I mean it."

Hagen shrugged. "Change of topic, I've been wondering why you haven't come to see me much earlier. You must've run out of potion a while ago."

Ivan smirked. "Oh, I'm currently on withdrawal."

Baffled, Hagen raised his brows. "Seriously?"

"Yeah. I admit that it's hard, but so far I'm being pretty damn brave I think."

He beamed with pride. The usual dark shadows below his eyes had disappeared. Ivan looked great, better than ever.

"Wow…why? And why now? I've been preaching for half an eternity that you should stop taking all this stuff and now when I'm not preaching you do so? What's going on?"

Hagen could hardly believe his eyes. His pretty friend was blushing. Realization struck Hagen like a sledgehammer.

"You're in love…"

Ivan blushed even more. "Hell, I'm discovered. I'm sorry, man. I didn't want to tell you because you're having so much trouble with that subject yourself at the moment. Don't be mad at me, okay?"

"Who?" Hagen asked blankly.

"You'll laugh at me." He squirmed. He looked like a schoolboy caught in the act with a cheerleader.

"Do I know her?" Hagen asked, not yet knowing what he should feel.

"Yeah…it's Amanda." Ivan's cheeks glowed crimson.

"Who?" Hagen asked, not understanding.

"Oh, come on, the nurse. The one we fled from, that I fled from, you let her into your house after that and told her that I was a useless and unfaithful piece of shit."

Hagen gasped. "How…what…"

"I don't know. She gave up on me, she followed your advice, and somehow…I don't know…it opened my eyes. Not immediately, I…it's hard to explain.

"I didn't talk to Amanda for a month, but then we had a night shift together and nothing much was going on so we started talking. Nothing else happened then, but we arranged a date for two days later and that night the chemistry worked and it's still working, somehow. Nobody is more amazed about that than I am, take my word for it."

"How long?" Hagen asked, dazed.

"About two months now, she moved into my apartment two weeks ago."

"She moved in with you? Already?"

"Yeah…and currently she's helping me to come off all the drugs. I don't know…she's marvelous. You brought us together, sort of. I wanted to thank you for that."

They stared at each other for a few moments. Ivan smiled sheepishly, happily, in love, and a little guiltily. Alissa was happy and in love, and now even Ivan? In hot shame, Hagen looked at the floor.

"Well," Hagen cleared his throat, his spit tasted of bile. "That's good for you. I'm happy to hear that. Don't let that moment and her slip away."

"I won't, thanks," Ivan said, relieved. "And listen to me, give up on Juliana. Make a fresh start. Tell me that you're at least thinking about it."

"I'll think about it," Hagen said. "Look, thanks for the ingredients. One of the couriers will come tomorrow and I have to brew some stuff, let's talk later, okay?"

"Well, sure…take care, man. Don't take it so hard, okay? Alissa was too old for you anyway." Ivan continued muttering banalities until Hagen had shoved him out of the front door.

He closed the door behind Ivan and took a deep breath. Ivan, who had dared anything, who had done everything, would get away with it and would live happily ever after together with Amanda the nurse? He didn't begrudge Alissa her luck and her love, she deserved it, but Ivan?

"Fuck you!" Hagen shouted.

He stormed into his living room and looked for something to smash. He took a pillow from the sofa and smashed it a good ten times with all of his might, grunting and shouting, onto the backrest of the sofa.

He found the package with chocolate for Juliana in a corner, tore it apart, and smashed it against the wall.

His doorbell rang. With a growl, he ran for the door and threw it open. He looked at a worried Emma.

"Hagen, what's going on?"

"Leave me the fuck alone!"

"Hagen, what—"

"I don't want to talk to you now!" he shouted and slammed the door shut so hard that the glass in the frames rattled, then he collapsed crying.

"Hagen—" Emma said, muffled by the door.

"Go away!" Hagen shouted and sobbed even harder.

⚔

In terror, Emma stood in front of the door behind which her son sobbed.

Emma, do what he says and leave him alone, Alberich said in her head, astonishingly earnest and concerned.

Close to tears, Emma turned around and walked upstairs to her own apartment. "If I only knew how to help him," she whispered to herself as she slipped inside and hung her coat back onto the clothes rack.

He's thirty-one years old. So far, he has been quite capable of coping with life. Everyone has ups and downs. He's down at the moment but it won't last forever. Let him be for Christ's sake.

Emma moaned when she sat down at her kitchen table and stared into nowhere. *It's never been this bad before.*

Oh, it has, forgot the rape incident and the abortion? It was far worse back then.

Grudgingly, she had to admit that Alberich had a point.

Of course. He'll get over it, Emma, whatever it is.

Emma shook her head. *I have a bad feeling about this, Al. He now has means to defend himself or to attack. He didn't have that ten years ago.*

Yes, finally…

Emma looked up at the 1983 poster of *The Ring*. Alberich's tone made her shudder.

You won't get him, Al. I won't let you.

What do you mean, Emma?

Emma steadied herself.

You know damn well what I mean.

Do I?

No, she wouldn't let his threatening intimidate her.

Once he's the potion master that you want him to be, you'll try to take him over. But I won't let you.

Alberich laughed out loud in her head.

And how am I supposed to accomplish that, Emma?

I don't know, but I won't let you near him. You won't get him.

We'll see, Emma, we'll see, Al said and his voice dripped with mockery.

You want him to come close to failing with his potions, right? You want him to get into real deep shit…and then you'll pop up, and get him out of the mess to make him willing to accept you. You want to get to him with that 'together we can rule the galaxy' kind of shit, right?

Alberich snickered. *Thanks for your ideas and I've always admired your wild imagination, Emma.*

268

"Fucking bastard! I won't let you have him, I won't," Emma hissed under her breath.

And how do you plan on stopping me, Emma?

We'll see, Al, we'll see, she said, trying to mock him back.

Emma stared grimly at *The Ring* poster. She needed an ally. Cindy...maybe Cindy could help.

Alberich laughed in her head. *That kid? I shiver in fear at the mere thought of her coming to your rescue, Emma.*

Emma ignored him, got up, and reached for her phone while Alberich continued to chuckle in her head.

☙❧

Friday, 31st of December

Despite it being New Year's Eve, Hagen went to work and brewed and mixed at the company, grateful for his job, which allowed him to concentrate on mundane and normal stuff for a few hours. He was alone in his lab. All his colleagues had taken off and were preparing for their New Year's Eve parties with their families and friends.

Hagen frowned in irritation when the door to his lab opened and Cindy entered. She checked around and he hated how her face lit up when she realized that he was alone and that she had him cornered.

"Hi, Hagen."

"What do you want?"

"You're constantly avoiding me at lunch. You're not even coming to the cafeteria anymore."

"So? Can't remember it saying in my contract that I must have lunch with Cindy."

She chose to ignore that. "You okay?"

Hagen finally stopped mixing and stirring and looked her in the eye. "Let me guess, my mom asked you to check on me."

"Yeah, because she's very worried about you. You were raving mad yesterday, she said, shouting, crying, and smashing things."

Hagen grunted at her. "Cindy, my dear, try to imagine for a moment that you were in my shoes. Let's say that you had a bad day yesterday and your mom comes running. You send her away and ask her to leave you alone. What does mom do? She phones a friend of hers who happens to be working at the same place as you do, gossips everything she heard down to the tiniest detail, and then asks your friend to go check on you the next day at work. Now, honestly, would you like that?"

"Well, no."

"Then leave me the hell alone before I get angry again."

"Hagen, your mom wants to help you and so do I."

He made a threatening step towards her and she backed away. "I don't want your fucking help and I want mom's fucking help even less! And now get the fuck out!"

"Happy New Year," Cindy said bitingly, turned on her heel, and left the lab.

Hagen grabbed a towel from a lab table and, grunting, threw it to the floor. What had he done to deserve this?

He turned back to his test tubes and vials. He would administer the potion to Juliana and leave with her. They would go away, far away. They needed chemists elsewhere too. He could send George the potion for Helena by registered mail or he could use one of Sandra's couriers to get the potion to her.

Yes, he'd leave. With Juliana. He'd give Gabe that hypnotic suggestion potion. Gabe would leave them alone. He'd see to that; he'd make the suggestion potion a real strong one.

Satisfied with his plans, he got back to work.

⚜

That evening, the street he lived in was deserted and dark, everyone at New Year's Eve parties. With a baseball bat hidded under his winter coat, a syringe filled with a strong sedative in one coat pocket and a kitchen towel, plus flashlight, in the other, Hagen sneaked to the deserted house down the road. The former owners had been victims of the economic crisis and had abandoned the place. No new buyer had emerged since. He made sure nobody watched him and sneaked to the back entrance of the house.

He had been on the watch for tails ever since Sam, the twenty-eight cities man, had told him about his hunch of being followed, but had noticed nothing out of the ordinary.

He tried the back entrance door and found it locked. He took his baseball bat, wrapped its end in the kitchen towel and with a swift stab, he smashed the glass around the doorknob. Easy enough and not even very loud. He had considered etching the doorknob with acid, but that would have been much too obviously pointing at his secret cellar.

He sneaked his arm through the broken glass and opened the door from the inside. He wore leather gloves. He took out his flashlight and entered the house, bat in one hand, flashlight in the other. He checked out the second floor first and found every room empty. It was a nice house, bigger than Emma's and more modern too. From two rooms in the second floor he could see his house through a window, through one of them even his entrance door, but nothing indicated that anybody had recently been inside this room. Hagen checked the attic, empty as well. He checked the ground floor and the cellar, but the place was completely deserted except for corpses of flies on the kitchen floor. If anybody was watching Hagen, it wasn't from this building. Hopefully, Sam worried for no reason.

Hagen returned to his cellar and ignored all New Year celebrations. Instead, he brewed to change the world.

⌖

Sunday, 2ⁿᵈ of January

A new year, a new life. Hagen didn't brew on January first or second. He had research to do. He sat behind his computer for hours and searched for a good place to work and to live with Juliana. He couldn't move too far away because the place would have to be within driving distance from his current home. He couldn't give people from a moving company access to his cellar. He'd have to rent a truck and move all the ingredients and equipment himself.

He measured his garage to determine how big a truck could fit in there. Luckily, he could access the garage from a door from his kitchen, otherwise he'd have trouble putting all the vials, tubes, and formaldehyde jars into the truck. He could hardly carry them over the lawn for all the neighbors to see, could he?

Hagen decided on a town with a reasonably big chemical company where he could apply for a job about an eight-hour drive from his hometown. To have Sandra in driving distance seemed important as well and from the new place, it'd be an hour quicker to get to her house.

He surfed the net for suitable houses. The new place would also need a door into the house through the garage and an appropriate cellar.

Planning and searching felt good. He'd start anew with Juliana by his side. He'd start a family with her, six kids. That was no joke; he wanted to have a bunch of children with her. And he'd become a mighty alchemist and once he was seventy, he'd also have five or six binders full of potions and a couple more in a safe, and then would look for apprentices to continue the trade and pass on the knowledge.

His doorbell rang. He groaned and walked upstairs. It was Sunday afternoon.

He peeked through the peephole and groaned again. Incredible. Emma *and* Cindy stood on the doorstep. He opened and looked critically at them, blocking the doorway.

"Hi, Hagen, Happy New Year," Emma said. "We felt that we owe you an apology. I shouldn't have asked Cindy to check on you at work. It's just that I was so worried."

Cindy nodded and continued. "You don't have to go out to eat lunch. I can sit at another table in the cafeteria if you don't want to talk."

"Happy New Year, and wow, I'm impressed by this display of remorse," Hagen said.

"We made some cake this afternoon." Emma offered Hagen a Tupperware box.

"Thanks." He took the box. Cindy and Emma smiled broadly at him. "I appreciate the change of tactics. Thanks and good day."

They stepped from his porch, retreating.

"See you soon, Hagen," Emma said.

"Bye-bye," Cindy added and waved her gloved hand like a child.

Hagen carried the cake to his kitchen. He checked inside the Tupperware box and the cake, plum cake, looked good. He had a piece. Yes, it had been a good idea to bring Emma and Cindy together. Cindy would take care of Emma after he had left.

He smiled. He should thank Ivan. Ivan had put the nail into the coffin of the old Hagen. On Thursday, he'd rise from the ashes with Juliana at his side and leave the old world behind him.

chapter 26

MONDAY, 3RD OF January

On Monday, Hagen ate lunch in the cafeteria again, alone. Cindy sat at the other end of the room with two guys from her lab. Hagen was able to persuade himself to smile and nod at her.

In the evening, while riding home, Hagen had, for the first time ever, the odd feeling that someone followed him. He studied the cars behind him and for a while, a Chrysler stuck to his taillights. Hagen made a detour that led him past Ivan's and his old, abandoned factory and the Chrysler was gone.

"You're getting paranoid, man," he whispered to himself and drove home. No Chrysler in sight anywhere.

Tuesday, 4th of January

On Tuesday evening, Ivan came by uninvited as usual. Luckily, Hagen had thrown away all his attempted love potions and no vials of black liquid graced his workbench anymore. He wanted to brew Juliana's potion on Wednesday night after he had returned from his visit to Helena.

Ivan scanned his workbench suspiciously, presumably looking for love potion. "What are you working on at the moment?" he asked.

"One of the potions I got from Sandra. I still don't know what it's for and even if it's the coolest potion ever, I won't tell you. Amanda probably wouldn't like that."

Ivan chuckled. "No, she wouldn't."

Hagen mixed and stirred.

"Have you heard anything from Alissa?"

"Yeah, a few text messages, she's in seventh heaven."

"Wow…that's amazing."

"Yep."

"Have you reached a decision about Juliana?"

"I think that this Benjamin guy secretly loved Alissa and that's why it went so well. I doubt it would go that well with Juliana…I'm inclined to follow your advice and give up on her. Maybe I'll go away for a while. If she finds out that I've just been giving Gabe vitamins, I'll have to leave anyway to escape her assassination attempts."

"Wow…I'd miss you badly, but yes, maybe that would be for the best. I'm proud of you, man. Looks like you've finally grown up."

"You too, although I have trouble imagining you raising kids and telling them to be careful about drugs."

Ivan laughed heartily.

"Bet your kids will all become actors or beauty queens, Amanda is a damned pretty girl, too."

Ivan laughed even harder. "Nah, the fine DNA got all spent with us, bet our kids will be ugly as hell."

"Maybe." Hagen grinned at his friend, convinced that they both felt it: the magic between them was gone.

"Well, I'll leave you to your brewing. Tell me when you need help with moving or anything else."

"I sure will."

"I'll let myself out. See ya," Ivan said and left the cellar.

Deep in thought, Hagen watched him go. Ivan had been a good friend. It would take a while before Hagen could find a friend like him again. Wistfully, he brewed the potion for Helena.

Wednesday, 5th of January

On Wednesday night, Hagen drove to George's house with a strange feeling in his stomach. Depending on what happened with Juliana the following day, this might be the last time that he met George and Helena.

Once there, he greeted George and they followed their weekly ritual. While George got the refreshments, Hagen watched Helena, unresponsive as always on his visits. He looked at Helena's frail body in her wheel-chair. How much longer would she live?

George returned from the kitchen and put a soda for Hagen onto the living room table. "I'm worried. She hasn't had a waking moment in about ten days."

"Really? So long?"

"Yes." George sighed deeply.

"How was her checkup?"

"Oh, fine, the doctors are so amazed by her stable condition. The tumor hasn't shrunk, but it hasn't grown either."

"Well, that's good news."

"It is."

Hagen and George looked at Helena, as suddenly one of her hands in her lap twitched. Hagen couldn't believe it, but the old lady's eyes were focusing. She was searching, finding, looking at him.

She smiled and George held his breath.

"Hagen..." Helena said faintly.

Hagen jumped to his feet and rushed to her side, kneeling down next to her wheelchair. George joined him and stood at her other side.

"Hello, Helena, so nice to see you."

"I heard your voice...I don't know how long I can stay awake. I saved my energy for your visit."

"I'm utterly overwhelmed, Helena. It's great to talk to you."

She was completely lucid, wide-awake, and life sparkled in her eyes, along with worry.

"Hagen, I have strange things to tell you."

"Whatever it is, it's okay, tell me."

"I can see things since I've been taking your potions. Strange things that I have no explanations for."

"I know. George told me."

"I can see people's auras...sort of. And you...you are not alone, Hagen. There's someone with you, an evil spirit. You must have gotten it from Emma. She was here a few weeks or months ago and I saw that evil thing around her too. Your shadow and hers are related. Something dwells with Emma and I think she knows about it, is aware of it, maybe she even communicates to it. And it's around you too, but you don't know of it, do you?"

"No," Hagen whispered, baffled.

"It dominates her, but it doesn't dominate you…at least not yet. I fear that it'll want to take you over some day or it'll want to influence you at the very least. You must not let it. You must fight it. Emma has lost the fight against the thing, but you still have a chance."

"Where did it come from? What is it? I don't understand…"

"I don't know. I only know that this thing has been with you since your birth. My head starts to hurt…but I have more to tell you."

He nodded.

"Colleen Hardwood, she died in a fire. You know her, don't you?"

"In a way…" Hagen said.

"Beware of fire, Hagen. I don't know what that means, but I have this weird sentence in my head since your last visit. Colleen fears that her hand will burn twice."

Hagen barely avoided falling backwards onto his butt.

"You seem to know what that means, that's good," Helena said and smiled but pain showed in her face.

"My head hurts," she said and lowered her eyes.

"Honey, you must rest," George whispered, worried.

"The spirit around me, does it have anything to do with my father, Helena?" Hagen asked and she looked once more at him, eyes widened in terror.

"Yes," she said, awed, afraid. "He *is* your father... that cloud around you is his spirit."

Hagen held his breath.

Helena shivered and closed her eyes. Her breath rattled in her lungs.

"Helena?" George said, so worried. "I must take her to bed. She's exhausted. Stay here for a moment, Hagen, will you? It won't take long."

"Yes, sure," Hagen muttered, got up, and returned to the sofa where he sat down while George lifted Helena's frail body from the wheelchair and carried her upstairs.

Hagen stared at her empty wheelchair. Colleen didn't want her hand to be burned twice and an evil spirit that was his father's dwelled around him and Emma? Ridiculous. But who was he to draw a line between the possible and the impossible? He made impossible things possible every day.

Paralyzed, he sat on George's sofa and waited for him to return. He did so twenty minutes later.

"Is she okay?" Hagen asked.

"Yes, I think so."

"I'm sorry that I exhausted her."

"No, no, that's all right. She wanted to talk to you for so long. I'm convinced that she noticed when you were here previously. As she said, she saved up her energy for tonight. Though, frankly, I didn't understand her. The spirit of your father surrounding you? And Emma too?" With a sigh, George sat down and shook his head before he continued. "If I remember correctly, you don't know who your father is, do you?"

"No, I don't. Emma has never told me, despite frequent begging. The only thing I know is that I must've been conceived during her infamous trip to Germany and that there's something shameful about it."

"Well, it seems that Emma is the key to some of these riddles."

Hagen scoffed. "Hell will freeze over before she tells me anything."

"Confront her with what Helena has said, maybe that'll make her talk."

"I doubt it."

"This Colleen Hardwood thing unsettles me even more though, what the hell does that mean? Her hand doesn't want to burn twice, why her hand?"

"I know an explanation for this, George, but it's too gross to tell you, sorry. No, I'm more unsettled by this spirit-of-my-father issue."

"So you *do* know Colleen Hardwood," George said, a bit of accusation in his voice.

"Yes and no, I've never met her, but I know about her."

"Amazing, so amazing…" George whispered; wonder replacing the suspicion in his voice.

"I think I should leave now, George. I have a lot to think about. And I have to decide whether to confront my mother with what Helena told me."

"Do it, every child should know who his father is. She owes you an explanation."

"I have thought so for some thirty years, George, no success so far...All the best for Helena, and thank her for me when she wakes up the next time."

"I'll do that and thank you too, Hagen."

⌇

Half an hour later, Hagen sat back in his cellar on one of his stools in front of his workbench. Fire. He'd have to be careful about fire from now on, especially after Juliana would have drunk the love potion. Gabe... maybe he'd want to set his house on fire when he didn't get Juliana back or something like that.

Hagen got up and started brewing the hypnotic suggestion potion for Gabe. He carefully read the list of instructions on Sandra's sheet. Below the ingredients and brewing instructions stood two final paragraphs:

> Scope of effect: During administration, the administrating party needs to suggest to the receiver what the receiver is supposed to do. Success is proportional to the number of times the receiver is being suggested the item and even more so to the simplicity of the sentence. The shorter and clearer the message, the higher the chance of success will be. Sentences with five words or less repeated about twenty times during administration show the highest success rates.
> Be careful in your choice of words. For example, if the administrator wants the subject to forget that he has an appointment the next day, the appropriate message would be "I have no appointment tomorrow." The subject will start repeating the sentence and will be led to believe that he has no appointment the next day.

⌇

While Hagen brewed, he feverishly thought of which sentence to put into Gabe's head. He favored "I've never loved Juliana." However, there was also "I don't care about Juliana," or simply "I hate Juliana."

Sighing, unable to decide, Hagen continued brewing. After he had finished the suggestion potion for Gabe, he brewed Juliana's love potion, concentrating on the naked task and trying to ignore the tension in his shoulders, stomach—everywhere.

Soon the black-as-night potion stood in front of him and he solemnly repeated what he had done two weeks ago. He took a knife from the workbench and flamed it over a Bunsen burner. He let the blade cool down, poured alcohol over it, and then cut into his barely healed thumb, deliberately. He wanted to feel the pain. He cut deeper than two weeks before and held his thumb over the vial.

"For us, Juliana, for us," he whispered, like Alissa had done, as his blood dropped into the potion.

In awe, he watched the dark liquid turn to gold and then to transparency. It was done.

He poured the potion into a bottle with a screw cap and brought it, along with the suggestion potion for Gabe, to his fridge in the kitchen. Gabe's potion was the color of apple juice, impossible to confuse them. The bottle filled with the dose of fake fertility potion was larger than the two real potions and already waited in the kitchen's fridge. Finally, he prepared chloroform and a handkerchief to knock Gabe out if he came complaining, just in case.

Hagen got ready for bed and stood in his pajamas in front of the central picture from his former shrine. Her picture hadn't done it in a long time, but that night it warped again into three dimensions. He admired Juliana's sharp nose, her full lips, her noble cheekbones, the hollows of her eyes, and her flat ears. He bowed towards the picture.

"Tomorrow, you'll be mine," he whispered and kissed the cold glass and her lips behind it.

He slept surprisingly well that night.

chapter 27

THURSDAY, 6TH OF January

Hagen waited at home for Juliana after a seemingly endless day at work, trying to keep his fingers from trembling. What if she didn't come? What if the last visit had made her believe that Gabe's potion contained something different than fertility potion? What if she'd had the potion analyzed somehow and had found out it indeed contained nothing but vitamins dissolved in water?

At five to eight, he waited behind his front door with his guts rumbling. He heard a car...it continued on down the street. He wiped his damp, cold hands on his jeans.

Another car. It stopped and its door slammed shut. He heard no steps approach, she had to be wearing sneakers again. Even though he was expecting it, he jerked as if ten thousand volts rattled through his body when his doorbell rang.

Juliana stood in front of him.

"Hi, Hagen, Happy New Year."

"Hello, Juliana, Happy New Year. Would you mind coming in for five minutes?"

She raised an astonished brow. "Not at all."

He let her inside the hall. She wore the same type of outfit as last time, except that this tracksuit was red, not pink. She took off her coat, hung it on a hook, and followed him into the living room.

"Please sit down. No alcohol due to driving and sports, I guess, how about a juice?" He prayed that she didn't notice how goddamned nervous he was.

"Don't bother, it's all right," she said.

"Well, I'll get myself something to drink."

He hurried into the kitchen, tore open his fridge and poured apple juice into two glasses that he had already prepared. He had chosen the smallest glasses he owned to increase the chance that she'd drink all of it. He took the love potion and poured it into her glass.

Calm down! he thought. *If it doesn't work today, it'll work another time.*

He took the vitamins for Gabe, tucked the bottle under his arm, and carried the two glasses with juice to the living room. There he found her sitting on his sofa, one leg elegantly folded over the other. He put down the glass filled with love potion in front of her and set Gabe's bottle next to her glass. Then he settled down and sipped from his own juice.

"Thank you. Hagen, what's in that fertility potion?" she asked and—Yes! Yes!—she did it. She took her glass of apple juice and drank it half down.

He feared that she'd be able to hear his heightened heartbeat from across the sofa so he quickly answered, "Potion recipes are secret, Juliana. The secrecy comes with the trade, but I can tell you that there's a lot of exotic stuff in there, and illegal stuff too, a bit of ivory, for example, or bull's testicles, Chinese herbal medicine, and so forth."

"Wow." Doubt drained her voice. "Sorry I snapped at you last time. Whatever is in there, Gabe's fine and I'm glad you're apparently not trying to poison him."

"It wouldn't help our relationship if I did that, would it? So, be assured, this stuff is real." Hagen pointed at the bottle for Gabe. "No guarantee though that it'll work."

"Understood. Would you like to talk compensation?" Juliana asked.

"No, I've got my pride. There might not be much left of it, but some still is and I don't want charity sex."

"I see...I thought you had asked me in to discuss compensation."

"No, it's okay. Same as you, I just felt awkward about last time, that's all."

"Well, let me know if you change your mind about compensation."

He wanted to shout with joy as she reached for her apple juice again and drank the rest of it. "I will," he said.

She put the empty glass down and placed the bottle for Gabe into her bag. She got up and Hagen stood with her.

"Well then, thank you and see you in two weeks," she said as she turned to leave.

He escorted her to the door and helped her into her coat, drinking in her scent, though careful not to touch and upset her. "See you," he said.

She smiled once more at him, forcedly, before she left. Trembling, he stood behind the closed door. His hands had turned to ice. No way back. She had drunk the potion...and now? What would happen now? With Benjamin, it had started to work after half an hour... Juliana would be at her gymnastics class by then.

"Calm down, damn it," he hissed aloud. "Calm down."

He walked in circles through his apartment. Should he go into his cellar and brew something? No, too nervous. His thoughts jumped from disaster to seventh heaven scenarios.

He also couldn't ignore what Helena had said the day before. Emma...he'd have to deal with his mother and that shadow around them. The hypnotic suggestion potion he had brewed for Gabe would work for his mother as well. He already knew the sentence for her—tell Hagen about his father. He'd brew a batch for Emma tomorrow. He'd do it, Emma owed him answers. Even if she couldn't forgive him for it, he would be leaving with Juliana anyway, at least he hoped so.

Oh, God...he couldn't stand the tension. He checked his assorted medical supplies and took a tranquilizer pill. How would Juliana react? What would happen now? What?

Even with the tranquilizer, his hands were shaking and he couldn't stop pacing around his apartment. Maybe nothing would happen tonight; maybe nothing would happen at all. How long did her gymnastics class last? Two hours at the most?

Oh, he was going mad. He'd have to take something much harder than that tranquilizer to be able to sleep tonight.

At half past ten, he almost suffered a heart attack when his doorbell rang. Could that be her? Would it be her? He ran to his door and looked through the peephole. His hammering heart missed a few beats. It was Juliana.

He opened the door. Her hair was down and her cheeks glowed rosy from the exercise. She looked at him with a disturbed look in her eyes.

"Hi, can we talk?" she asked.

"Sure."

He let her in, trying to keep his shaking under control. She closed the door behind her.

"What's up?" he asked, afraid of the answer.

"Hagen, I'm really having trouble with your 'charity sex' expression. I…it wouldn't be like that. I…" she looked up at him.

He held his breath as he stared into her eyes. What should he do? What could he do? What should he say?

"Sex with Gabe is only business…around ovulation period," she whispered. "I'm sorry, Hagen. I've treated you so badly, all this time, I—"

Yes! Yes! His heart leaped and bounced in his chest. He moved close and embraced her. He kissed her and she kissed him back, her breath hot on his cheek. He kissed and kissed her, forgetting everything, all of his worries. Juliana lay in his arms and he kissed her.

He shoved his tongue into her mouth and sucked the very life out of her and she let him. She let him. She didn't fight him. She lay in his arms and kissed him back willingly. He couldn't believe it. Blessed potion!

His hands wandered over her body, fumbled with her clothes, and slipped into her panties. She moaned. He couldn't believe his ears. She moaned…she wanted him. He wanted to shout when he felt her hands fumbling at the zipper of his bulging pants. They rid each other rapidly of their clothing and he half carried her to his bedroom.

It was divine. It didn't matter that she only lay in his arms because of the potion. He ignored that they skipped the topic of protection. She wouldn't be taking the pill if she was so desperately trying to get pregnant from Gabe, but Hagen didn't care.

He could bear that he had lost Alissa and Ivan. He could bear not knowing his father's identity. For ten years, since that first night with her, he hadn't really been happy, and now he was. All that wanting, all those desires, got purged when he finally found himself doing and not just standing idly by and watching. He loved her with everything he had and she loved him back. She was enjoying what he did, how could she not? He told her a hundred times that he loved her.

"I know, Hagen," she finally whispered.

"Tell me you love me too, at least a tiny little bit, please," he begged.

"Yes, a tiny little bit, Hagen, somehow."

She smiled such a beautiful smile that it physically hurt him. He groaned and drowned her in kisses and made love to her again. It worked! The potion had worked! Now everything would be all right. Everything.

At four in the morning, he finally slept, completely exhausted, but happy, happy for the first time in ten years.

⋈

Friday, 7th of January

Hagen's alarm clock rang and ripped him from a deep sleep. Disoriented, he sat upright in his bed. Juliana moaned next to him, unwilling to wake.

Juliana. He looked down at her. Incredible. Juliana lay in his bed, naked, like him. The bed reeked of sex. He stared at her small but well-formed breasts for a moment, caressed them, and bowed down to kiss her lips.

What would he do if what had happened ten years ago would now repeat itself? He wouldn't be able to bear it again if that look of horror crept into her eyes at the realization that she had slept with him. He didn't want to wake her and face the chance, but he knew he must.

"Hey, I'm afraid we have to get up," he said. "Lab and school."

Juliana jerked awake. "Oh shit! I have to go home and redress. I can't go to school in a tracksuit."

She sat upright next to him and stared at Hagen, disbelief in her eyes. Hagen gasped. Now she would freak out and accuse him of rape.

"What the hell do I tell Gabe?" she asked.

"A friend of yours at the gymnastics group had a nervous breakdown because her mother died and you stayed with her for the night?"

She raised a brow and then nodded. "Yes, that sounds good. Can I get in the bathroom first?"

"Sure," he said, relieved, so relieved that she didn't accuse him of anything.

Juliana hurried to leave and twenty minutes later, they stood in his doorway. Hagen was only dressed in a bathrobe and she wore her tracksuit. He kissed her passionately, enjoying that she kissed him back.

"When can I see you again?" he asked.

"I don't know, Hagen. I'm very confused by what is happening."

He held his breath. He'd have to say something meaningful now to disperse her doubts. "You haven't had fun having sex in ages. You know that I am and always will be there for you so you took the opportunity when it was available."

"Such a cold comment from you?" She eyed him suspiciously. "That's unexpected. Yes, but I guess you're right. I…I have to think about what happened last night, Hagen. I can't promise anything now."

"I know. It's okay. But I'm here for you, always, and you can do with me whatever you want, you know that."

"Yes, I know that."

She nodded and kissed him. He pressed her to him, feeling that she *wanted* to kiss him, that she *enjoyed* kissing him.

"See you," she said when she finally released him.

"Yes, see you." He reluctantly let her go.

He moaned in joy and relief. Then he smiled to himself. Damn, that had been the best possible outcome he could've imagined. Alissa was right, the potion had performed a miracle, and in a way that felt natural. Natural in terms of Juliana and Hagen, but natural nonetheless, and she'd come back to him, she would. She'd be his. She was his already. He squealed with joy, then went to get ready for work.

⌇

He had lunch alone in the cafeteria but Cindy must have seen him beaming. She dropped by his table on her way to the used tray conveyor belt.

"Hey, you're beaming like a nuclear power station. You get back together with your girlfriend?" Her voice dripped with jealousy.

"Hi, Cindy, yes, something like that."

"Congratulations," she said and he nodded. When he offered no further information, she nodded back and walked towards the conveyor belt.

He watched her leave. He had to be very careful with her. She'd relay everything he told her to Emma without doubt or delay.

⌇

Hagen drove straight home and brewed a batch of hypnotic suggestion potion for Emma. When would Juliana come to see him again? What about her job? What about Gabe?

At nine p.m., his doorbell rang and he sprinted upstairs. He quivered with joy, threw open the door, and pulled Juliana inside the hallway. He kissed her. He couldn't help it, he had to kiss her. He had dreamt of her all day long, every day of his life. She kissed him back but he felt her hesitation. He stopped and looked at her.

"Gabe was very upset. He left ten messages on my cell phone. For the moment, he bought the story about the gymnastics lady whose mother has died, but…Hagen, I don't understand what's going on. Have you given me some potion or something?" Her voice quivered.

"No, I haven't. What are you talking about?" How astonishing, he lied straight to her face without even a brow twitching.

"Did you put something in that apple juice you gave me?"

"No, Juliana, damn it, no. You know why you're here. You finally noticed that Gabe is a wimp. He can't and won't get you pregnant. He can't give you the babies you want, I can. You know that I'm crazy about you, always have been. You finally realized that I'm the man you want and who can make you happy, not Gabe."

"Have I realized that?" she mumbled.

"Yes, you have. And don't tell me that you didn't enjoy what happened last night. You didn't pretend. Can you look me in the eye and claim that you faked it?"

She looked him in the eye and shook her head. "No, I didn't pretend. It was good, yes."

"There you are. It's you and me, Juliana. That's the way it was always supposed to be. We made a few detours along the way but they are behind us now. You're mine and I'm yours. I'll make you happy and we'll raise a family," he said and kissed her.

She kissed him back, but he still felt hesitation.

"Let's get away from here; I want to make a fresh start with you and without my mother, Gabe, or gossiping neighbors. Let's leave, Juliana, just you and I."

"Hagen, wait, this is all going awfully fast."

Damn, he had to be patient. He had to be careful not to force things too much now.

"I'm sorry; it's just that I'm so madly in love with you. I always have been. Always." He pulled her to him and held on tight.

"Why? Why me? Why still, after all I've done to you?"

"I don't know. You're the one; you always have been and you always will be. You're the woman for whom I was made. I've loved you since I was five years old."

"You're crazy, Hagen," she said, not upset, just a little sad.

"Why so sad?"

"I don't know."

"Let me make you happy," he whispered and kissed her throat.

"No, Hagen, don't. I don't understand what's happening or why I want you suddenly. I—"

"Because you're sex starved and have a man in your arms who'll do everything you desire. Because you've been worrying about sex and babies for years, always trying and never getting what you wanted," he said between kisses.

"I'm not on the pill, Hagen. You could get me pregnant." Her defenses were crumbling.

"I thought you wanted to get pregnant more than anything else?"

"Yes, but…I'm so confused."

"Don't think and just do." He rubbed his fingers against the jeans between her legs and she moaned.

"I have to go back home. I—"

"Only once," he whispered and pulled her into the living room and onto his sofa. She gave in and opened his pants. She was hungry, not as hungry as he was, but hungry enough.

Half an hour later, she left him and he remained sitting exhausted on the sofa, not even walking her to the door. He stared at the ceiling and felt astonishingly sober.

The coming few days would be the most critical. Of course, she suspected him of not being innocent about her change of mind. Gabe would notice something too. Hagen steeled his nerves. Yes, the coming days would get tough, but he was ready to fight…and win.

Determined, he got up and continued preparing for their move to a new place.

chapter 28

SATURDAY, 8TH OF January

On Saturday afternoon, Juliana stood in his doorway again. He pulled her inside and kissed her greedily. She kissed him back, but after the first few urgent kisses, she pushed him away.

"You put something into that apple juice, Hagen, I'm sure of it. What was it?"

"Nothing. You're imagining things."

"Bullshit! I want you; I can't stop thinking about you. I've never wanted or couldn't stop thinking about you before that night."

"I can only repeat that your frustration in your marriage has opened your eyes to what I have to offer."

She scoffed. "This isn't natural."

"Why do you always have to hurt me? What have I done to you?" he said, so astonished that he could still lie into her face.

"Oh, Hagen, I…damn you." She flung her arms around him and kissed him; then she opened the zipper of his pants.

Later, he bound her hands above her head to the bedpost with a pair of recently acquired handcuffs. He didn't ask her permission and she didn't complain. She just enjoyed it and groaned with pleasure. When he was finished, he left her tied to the bed, naked.

He took a shower and studied his reflection in the mirror, not knowing what to do. She wanted him, yes, but she also knew. She had repeated, more than once, that this wasn't natural while they had made love.

He threw on a bathrobe, returned to the bedroom, and stared at her. Her face was calm but knowing.

"What did you put into that apple juice, Hagen?"

So amazing…she lay naked and handcuffed, defenseless on his bed, and yet she was in control. He didn't like that.

"Love potion. A strong one."

She simply nodded.

They remained quiet for a few moments.

"I've never really believed in your hocus-pocus, not even when I asked for a potion for Gabe, but, wow, that stuff's good."

"It is," he said, standing by the bed and looking down at her.

"I like what you're doing with me. This is great sex, it's better than with Gabe, because you're so goddamn mad and desperate and obsessed. But it just doesn't feel right. I've never loved you, and now a part of me does. That's amazing stuff you brewed there."

"Yes," he answered and sat down on the edge of the bed next to her.

"What's going to happen now?" she asked.

She Should Have Called Him Siegfried

"I'll go away with you. We'll have a family together. When things have settled down, you'll file for divorce from Gabe and then we can marry."

"Gabe will never go along with that, unless you have a potion for him, too. Do you?"

"Yes," he said.

"What kind of potion?"

"A suggestive one. I'll make him, let me call it, 'un-love' you."

"Don't hurt him."

"I won't. Well, maybe I'll have to a little to make him swallow it."

"You're mad, Hagen, and I'm frightened by how calm this conversation is."

"Yes, it's a bit weird."

"Are you not ashamed, even a little bit?" she asked.

"No. I'm not really hurting anyone, am I? I'm only giving slight pushes in the direction that I want things to go. I've learned one thing though, give someone power and he'll use it. It's impossible to resist when you have the means. We're all trying to make the world fit our needs. It's just that some people are more ruthless about it than others. Generally, the winners are the ones who are more ruthless. I've been losing for too long and I won't lose any longer."

"I'll fight you if I can," she said, still so calm.

"That's good. I wouldn't want you to be docile and nothing but an empty shell." He leaned over her and kissed her.

"Fuck me," she whispered.

"With pleasure," he said and kissed her throat.

It had long turned dark by the time Hagen sat in his kitchen eating instant pizza. Juliana had gone to take a shower after he had un-cuffed her. When she joined him in the kitchen, she was towel drying her hair and was wearing his second bathrobe.

"Want some?" He pointed at the pizza.

"Yes, sex makes hungry." She sat down and reached for the pizza with an elegant hand. She looked at him over the pizza slice she held, munching. "Is there an antidote to that love potion?"

"Not that I know of."

"Once you drink it, you're done for?"

"Yes."

"How does that work?"

"I don't know. It's magic. I only mixed the ingredients."

"A part of me still refuses to believe this shit."

Grease from the pizza smeared her long fingers.

"You came here to be with me and have sex with me for three days in a row. There must be something to that potion."

"Apparently...though Gabe won't believe me, not one word."

"It's your own fault. If you hadn't asked me for that damned fertility potion, I think I would've given up on you."

She sighed deeply and shoved the last bit of pizza into her mouth, chewing thoughtfully, then she licked her greasy fingers one after the other. "Did you really put fertility potion into those bottles?"

"No, vitamins. I have no formula for a fertility potion. I seriously considered poisoning Gabe. You gave me a very tempting opportunity to be rid of him and I thought long and hard about it. But, of course, you would've known that I had poisoned him and never would have forgiven me, so I refrained from that temptation." It felt good to tell her the naked truth, no need for lies anymore—at least so he thought.

She wiped her fingers with the bathrobe. "Who guarantees you that the next time I come to visit I won't have a gun in my purse and shoot you in the head?"

"Nobody. But I wouldn't mind, Juliana. I'm beyond that. I don't want to live without you anymore and ask yourself this, would Gabe die for you? I doubt it. I'll do anything for you, Juliana, anything. I'll care for you if you get sick, like George cares for Helena. You'll never have to be lonely. I'll be with you until the end. And I'll be a good father to our children."

"The worst thing about all of this is that I believe you."

He smiled at her, broadly.

"Let's see if I can resist you," she said and got up. "I'll go home now."

"Sure."

"You won't hinder me?"

"Of course not."

"Damn, you're sure of your fucking potion, aren't you?"

"I am."

"Farewell, Hagen."

"See you soon, Juliana."

He remained sitting at the kitchen table as she left the room. He heard her rummaging around, getting dressed, and then the front door shut. He took a deep breath after she had left. She would return. He wondered how he could be so sure and couldn't explain it to himself, he simply was. She'd be back the next day.

⌘

Sunday, 9th of January

Juliana stood on his doorstep Sunday afternoon at three p.m. He pulled her inside and kissed her and, as he had once done with Alissa, they had their first urgent time for this afternoon with her sitting on his shoe rack. Afterwards, they dressed again and sat down in the living room.

"I told Gabe that you gave me a love potion," she said.

"What did he say?"

"He laughed, called it nonsense. I asked him to make love to me and he did."

"How was it?" Hagen asked, unable to deny the sting of dread in his guts.

"Dull."

The sting eased.

"He's nice and normal and…boring. He doesn't have your despair. You're burning; he's simmering. He has developed a complex, thinks he's inferior. He has changed since he found out that his sperm are no good. Men are such fragile creatures. Scratch their pride but a little and they crumble.

302

"I think he'll show up here soon. I told him I was going to see you. He didn't believe me. You should get your suggestive potion for him ready."

"And while I give it to him, you'll shoot me in the head?" he asked.

"Maybe."

"Then I'd better tie you to the bed."

"Yeah, I can't guarantee what's going to happen if I see the two of you together."

He offered her his hand, she took it and he led her to his bedroom.

"You're truly amazing, Juliana. Although you drank the potion, I have the feeling you're still playing with me. I'm waiting to be backstabbed at any second."

"And I'm waiting for the moment when that potion of yours will stop working and I will scream in disgust when you touch me."

"It's been almost four days since you drank the potion. The change is done."

She sat down on his bed and he got the handcuffs from a drawer in his nightstand. He chained her left hand to the bed and started kissing her. She kissed him back passionately, hungrily.

He had once thought her to be a holy, suffering nun. The past few days had revised his view of her completely. She was a poisonous snake and he waited for her to bite and kill him. And yet, he wouldn't want things to be any different.

She fumbled with his shirt, but he wound himself out of her grip. "Gotta prepare for Gabe," he said and left her sitting on his bed.

He hurried into his cellar and got the chloroform, the handkerchief, and a piece of rope. He checked the suggestion potion inside his fridge in the kitchen. The bottle was still waiting.

His doorbell rang. He jumped and hastily threw the rope into the cold and as good as never used oven for lack of a better hiding place, poured chloroform into the handkerchief, then rushed for the door.

He checked through the peephole and steeled his nerves before he opened.

"Hi, Hagen, her car is parked outside so I suppose Juliana is here?"

"Hi, Gabe, yes, she is, please come in."

Gabe gasped, flashed angry eyes at Hagen, and entered.

Gabriel Daniels, Hagen's rival, the smart, slick, handsome business man, whose sperm was good for nothing, was an inch taller than Hagen. Gabe was well built and blond, though he didn't come close to Ivan's beauty. He was attractive but soft around the nose and had sad, brown eyes. Hagen wondered whether he even possessed enough testosterone to grow a beard. Hagen let Gabe walk past him.

"What is Julie doing here?" Gabe asked.

Hagen closed the door. With swift and rapid motions, he put his left arm from behind around Gabe's chest and with the right hand, he pressed the chloroform-soaked handkerchief over his mouth and nose. Completely surprised, Gabe moaned, tried to shake his attacker off, and to wrestle Hagen's hand from his face. Hagen didn't let up. Gabe thrashed about; hit Hagen in the side, who grunted but held on. Gabe whirled around, carrying Hagen with him, and smashed him against the shoe rack where he had made love to Juliana not even an hour ago. Hagen groaned when the blow knocked the wind out of him but still hung on tightly.

Next, Gabe smashed Hagen into the wall opposite the shoe rack but with waning force. His moaning and groaning became weaker as the chloroform started to work. Finally, Gabe's muscles slackened and he collapsed.

Breathing hard, Hagen stuffed the chloroform handkerchief into his pants pocket. He grabbed Gabe under the arms and hauled him into the kitchen where he put him onto a chair with a great deal of effort. He took the rope from the oven, quickly bound Gabe to the chair by his hands, feet, and chest, and then gagged him. He had to giggle. He had never done anything like this before; better than any movie and so addictive.

He put the biggest knife he owned on the table. It was sharp enough to slice Gabe's throat. He had no idea when Gabe would wake up. Oh, of course, Hagen had sal ammoniac among his ingredients, as every well-equipped alchemist did.

Hagen hurried into his cellar, soon found the smelling salts and ran back upstairs. He held the ammoniac under his rival's nose. Gabe shivered, his eyes flickered open, and after a moment, he realized that he was bound and gagged. He rattled at his bonds, struggling and moaning. Hagen put the smelling salts down onto his kitchen table and took the knife instead, holding it to Gabe's throat.

Gabe yelled but the gag muffled his voice to a harmless grunt.

"Gabe, my friend."

Hate and fear flashed in Gabe's eyes.

"Here is what's going to happen. I'll open your gag and you'll drink a potion. It's not poisonous. It won't harm you. I don't want to hurt you, but I will if you shout or do anything foolish.

"Here's the essence of what I'd like you to do or more correctly not to do. Juliana is mine now. She is well and healthy, don't worry. She now loves me. I gave her a potion to that effect. I'll go away with her and I'll make her as many babies as she wants, something that you cannot do, I've learned."

Gabe struggled and fought against his bonds, groaning pathetically, anger and shame in his eyes.

"I want you to give up on Juliana and I want you to not go to the police. That's all, just these two things. The potion I'll give you will help you to comply with those two requests. It won't hurt at all and you'll live happily ever after. So, no police and give up on Juliana, that's it. Got it?"

Gabe moaned and struggled some more.

"I mean it, Gabe. I'll slice your throat if you scream. I have no scruples anymore. I'll have Juliana for myself or I'll die, no options in between. And if you force me to kill you, I'll do so. Do you understand me?"

Gabe grunted.

"Nod with your eyelids if you understand me."

She Should Have Called Him Siegfried

Hagen increased the pressure on the knife to Gabe's throat, staring fiercely at Gabe, and finally the helpless man opened and closed his eyes in agreement.

"Very well."

Hagen placed the knife onto the kitchen table and got the suggestion potion out of the fridge. He took the gag from Gabe's mouth. Gabe gasped and coughed.

"You're fucking mad, Hagen. You'll never get away with this," Gabe said in conversational volume.

"We'll see."

"Where is Juliana?"

"In the bedroom."

"What have you done to her?"

"Nothing, don't shout her name or something…" Hagen warned.

Gabe grunted.

"Drink this." Hagen put the bottle to Gabe's lips.

"The hell I will."

Hagen shrugged and pinched Gabe's nose shut between thumb and index finger of his right hand. Gabe fought him but eventually had to open his mouth to breathe. Hagen poured the potion into Gabe's mouth, dropped the bottle, and pressed his hand under Gabe's chin to force it shut. He thrashed about, his face turned red, and he had to swallow. Hagen released his nose and mouth and Gabe gasped for breath.

"I've never loved Juliana," Hagen said and after a short pause, "I won't call the police. I've never loved Juliana. I won't call the police. I've never loved Juliana. I won't call the police."

He had already said the sentence five times before Gabe was finally able to speak again. He opened his mouth to say something but his eyes glazed over and he only drooled. Hagen took Gabe's face into his hands and stared at him, his nose hovering an inch above Gabe's.

"I've never loved Juliana. I won't call the police. I've never loved Juliana. I won't call the police."

Hagen chanted the two sentences. He poured his will and his strength into every word as he forced them upon Gabe. He repeated them and repeated them and Gabe's jaw started to move. Hagen hammered the two sentences into Gabe's head, his entire being, with all the will and power he could muster. He rejoiced when his victim started to repeat the sentences.

"I've never loved Juliana. I won't call the police," Gabe whispered.

Hagen kept on repeating the sentences and Gabe's voice became firmer and firmer, as he repeated after his attacker. Hagen fell into rhythm with Gabe and they said the sentences together.

He lowered his voice gradually and let Gabe repeat the sentences by himself. Hagen had lost count, but he had said these two sentences at least fifty times, not twenty. Surely, the message had reached home despite being longer than the potion instructions had recommended.

Gabe continued saying these two sentences long after Hagen had stopped. Hagen quickly untied Gabe, pulled him to his feet, and moved him forward. Still mumbling the two sentences, he followed Hagen's pushing and elbowing without much assistance but also without resistance.

Hagen shoved Gabe outside. He locked the entrance door and watched anxiously through the peephole to see what Gabe was doing. He swayed and seemed to be waking up. He looked around in irritation, and then staggered to his car. He looked at Hagen's house, as if he didn't know where he was or what had happened. After a moment, he shook his head as if to clear it, got into his vehicle, and drove off.

Hagen heaved a big sigh of relief.

Intoxicating, the things he could do with his potions. He had had no idea! And yes, before he left with Juliana, he'd make his mother drink that suggestion potion and have her tell him about his father.

He waited two more minutes but Gabe didn't return.

Hagen checked again whether he had locked the door, he had, and returned to the bedroom. He found Juliana leaning against the wall with her legs folded elegantly over each other on the bed, her left hand still tied to the bedpost.

"And?" she asked.

"It went well. Gabe is unharmed and quite likely cured of you now. I'm dying to know what he'll be like when you return home." Hagen started to unbutton his shirt.

"No cure for his potion either?" Juliana asked.

"Not that I know of."

"Don't you want to use your mighty potions for better purposes than making Gabe 'unlove' me? Hell, if you could make the President drink this thing, you could tell him to stop all wars."

"Secrecy is the alpha and omega of my trade. We alchemists cannot practice our art in the open. If we did, they'd hunt us down and kill us. The balance between secrecy and power is the key to success. In the future, you'll be able to play that game together with me and I have the distinct hunch that you'll highly enjoy that."

"Interesting prospects," she said, and then she couldn't say anything else because he drowned her in kisses and started to undress her.

Their lovemaking got more intense every time. He had a feeling that the love potion worked better every day. She gave herself to him. She asked him not to stop and she dug the fingers of her free right hand into his back. She belonged to him, finally.

Drained, he un-cuffed her. Soaked in sweat, they lay side by side.

"I'll go home now," she said.

"Yes, sure."

"If Gabe is hurt, feels bad, or if anything has happened to him, I'll kill you."

"Understood."

She sat up. "I'm going to take a shower."

She left the room and he remained lying in bed. He was exhausted but satisfied and fulfilled. Life was good.

She didn't return to the bedroom to say good-bye, she simply left. The front door unlocked and fell shut. He got up, relocked the door, and took a shower. Then he ate something and went back to bed. He was tired; his new life took its toll on him.

⚞⚟

Monday, 10th of January

Hagen had no desire to meet Cindy so he ate in a restaurant again for Monday's lunchtime. He decided not to talk to her again until things with Gabe and Juliana had settled down. At low heat, he stewed in his own grease, awaiting the result of the suggestion potion.

He went grocery shopping after work with a strange feeling in his stomach. It seemed like everyone in the super market, housewives mostly, was staring at him. Did one of them lead a double life like he did and was a governmental agent on his heels?

He drove straight home, watching out carefully. Nobody seemed to be following him. He sighed, the stress was getting to him and caused paranoia. And what would he do if Juliana didn't come to see him tonight?

chapter 29

REPORT No. 33 from Agent 9836B12
   Subject: Hagen Patterson (HP)
   Status: Change of customers.
   Next action: Further investigation.
   Details of current status:

1)   Alissa Caradine has not visited HP for two weeks. Instead, HP's high school love interest, Juliana Daniels, is now a frequent guest at his apartment. She has visited him for four days in a row and stayed with him for several hours each time, once overnight. On Sunday, Juliana's husband Gabriel visited while his wife was also in HP's apartment but left again half an hour later. Illegal substance transactions could not be confirmed.

2)   Courier movement is following the regular schedule reported earlier. No new couriers sighted.

3) No new customers since HP presumably received new potion formulas from his teacher.

4) HP seems astonishingly inactive. Recommendation is to wait for his next major move.

She Should Have Called Him Siegfried

Monday night, close to midnight, Juliana had not yet returned. Hagen paced his rooms, restless. He found that unbearable and during the twenty-minute drive to Juliana's house, horror scenarios chased each other in his head.

What if Gabe's potion had worked too well? What if he now despised her so much that he had beaten her or done something even worse? What if the potion hadn't worked? What if he loved her still and had chained her to the bed to prevent her from coming to see Hagen?

Lights shone through the bedroom window when he arrived at her house at a quarter past midnight. Hagen waited in his car for a while, unable to see anything except the lights. They went out at half past twelve.

He moaned. Only one day had passed. He'd have to give her and Gabe more time. It'd be stupid to sneak into the house now. The potion for Gabe had surely worked since no police had come to accuse him of capturing and drugging him.

With an utmost effort of self-discipline and self-conquest, Hagen restarted his car and drove home. He could hardly sleep that night. Instead, he tossed in his bed and prayed for morning.

Tuesday, 11th of January

Hagen again ate at a restaurant off the company grounds the next day, desperately avoiding Cindy. After work, he drove home and waited. He brewed a bit to distract himself and to fulfill his potion schedule for Sandra.

His doorbell rang. He sprinted upstairs. He threw open the door, without checking who it was.

"Hi, Hagen, can I come in?"

He frowned at his mother and stepped aside to let her enter. Emma walked into his living room.

"You're not calling me, visiting me, nothing. I was getting worried. We also haven't had our Sunday night dinner in a damn long while."

He hated the way she inspected his apartment. She scanned everything like a detective, no, worse, like a mother.

⇥⇤

You shouldn't have come here, Emma. Important things are going on; I can feel it. He needs to finish them. Then you, that means I, can take care of him, Alberich said in her head.

He's my son. I can visit him and talk to him whenever I want to. Shut up.

She sat down on Hagen's old-fashioned sofa.

"Want something to drink?" Hagen asked.

"Thanks, a soda, if you have any."

He left her in the living room, which looked as it always did, although it could've used a round of dusting.

Hagen returned with two glasses of Coke and gave her one.

"I haven't noticed Alissa's car lately."

Her son frowned even more. "We split up."

"Oh really? That's too bad. Are you okay?"

"Yeah, we parted amicably."

She tried not to hear the mockery in his voice. "I noticed another car parked in front of the house pretty often and I can hardly believe it but it looks like Juliana's car. What's going on, Hagen?"

You're so blunt, Emma, so blunt, Alberich said and sighed deeply.

"Mom, sorry to be so rude and frank, but that's none of your business. And so that you know, I'll be moving out in the not too distant future."

Emma gasped.

Oh…Things are getting interesting around here.

"Where to?" Emma asked. "And what about your job?"

"I don't know yet, haven't decided, and I'll find another job. Chemists are usually well sought after."

"Why do you want to go away? Because of me?"

"No, Mom. The world doesn't revolve around you, you know."

"Don't be so nasty."

"Sorry, Mom." He seemed to be struggling whether to tell her something or not.

"Hagen, please, tell me what's going on."

You're begging, Emma.

I don't fucking care, she thought back and Alberich snickered.

Hagen opened his mouth to speak but the ringing of the doorbell cut him short. He jumped to his feet as if electrified.

"Excuse me," he said and ran for the door.

Something's awfully wrong, Emma thought.

Are you addressing me?

Emma only moaned. The front door opened and closed, no conversation, nothing. She got up and walked slowly towards the hallway.

Emma, stop that, that's one of the reasons why he wants to leave, because he's sick of you spying on him.

Emma ignored Alberich and peeked around the corner. Her lower jaw dropped and her limbs froze. Hagen was kissing Juliana. Emma jerked her head away from the corner.

"What the hell…" she whispered.

Oh, oh…wonderful! Fantastic. This isn't natural. Emma, my dear, the boy not only brews but finally he is using his potions, Alberich said with triumph in his voice.

Hagen led Juliana into the living room with his arm around her.

"Hello, Emma," Juliana said and smiled bashfully.

"Juliana…what…"

"Could you please leave, Mom? We'd like to spend the rest of the evening undisturbed." Hagen grinned broadly at his mother.

Emma stared blankly and in shock. He looked so happy with his arm around Juliana and pride glowed in his entire posture. His was the face of a victor. And she knew that this wasn't natural.

No, it isn't. Alberich sighed with great satisfaction.

"What have you done?" Emma whispered in fear and naked terror.

"Mother, not now."

Emma, leave, Alberich ordered.

Stunned, Emma walked past Hagen and Juliana. His front door slammed shut behind her and she stood

318

outside on the porch in the chilly night air. Snow covered the lawn. She turned and walked to the stairs on the side of the house that led up to her apartment. She let herself in and stood bedazzled behind her entrance door.

"Juliana…she has been here every day since last Thursday."

That's one of the reasons why he doesn't want to involve you in his life. You even keep a record of how often he's moving his bowels.

Emma staggered into her kitchen.

Rejoice, Emma, the boy has finally discovered his potential. He's taking things into his own hands. He's acting now, not just reacting. He's reaching out, using his powers to change the world. He is finally becoming worthy of and ready for his father, Alberich's voice swelled to a crescendo in her head.

Emma grabbed her phone.

Emma, what are you doing?

She dialed a number.

You can't be serious. Not that girl! Why? For Christ's sake, why?

"Hello?"

"Cindy? It's me. I know it's late, but can you come over? Something happened."

"Are you okay?" Cindy asked, the good girl.

"Yes, it's about Hagen."

"I'm on my way."

Emma, that's grossly stupid. You cannot tell that girl about Hagen and Juliana. Why? What for? If he finds out, he'll hate you even more than he already does.

Emma grunted and stomped her right foot onto the floor. "Alberich, shut the fuck up!" she shouted. "This is my life and my decision. I can call and talk to whomever I want. Leave me the hell alone and stop with your fucking comments. I don't want them. I don't want you. I hate you. And you won't get Hagen! I'd rather kill myself." And she hated that evil laughter she heard in her head more than anything.

Half an hour later, Cindy sat with her at the kitchen table and Emma told her the outlines of the relationship between Hagen and Juliana and that…well, that he brewed potions and that now he had presumably gone too far.

Cindy stared flabbergasted at her. "Emma, I'm shocked to hear that Hagen has his own little lab in the cellar and that he's apparently doing dangerous experiments down there, but an evil love potion? Please… there is nothing like that."

"You're a chemist yourself, Cindy. You know that there's a hell of a lot of stuff a capable chemist could do with certain ingredients."

"If you had told me Hagen is cooking meth or anything like that, fine, but a love potion? That sounds like something from a gothic novel."

"Honey, Juliana is not here by her free will."

"You said she comes by every day now. That means she also leaves every day, sounds pretty free to me."

"You don't understand, Cindy. She comes here because she must, the potion forces her to."

"Emma, please…" Cindy said, her voice soothing and full of pity.

She Should Have Called Him Siegfried

The girl is more reasonable than I thought. I'm starting to like her, Alberich said.

Emma moaned. "I'm afraid Hagen also did something to Gabe, Juliana's husband...he'd never put up with Juliana suddenly being in love with Hagen otherwise."

"Emma, I think you should rest."

Emma stared at the girl. Yes, she was right; what Emma said had to sound like the phantasms of a madwoman.

Oh, if she knew what phantasms you carry around with you, Alberich said and chuckled.

✦

"How is Gabe?" Hagen asked Juliana after Emma had left, not even trying to suppress the quiver in his voice.

"He's fine," she said, as she stared at his living room carpet.

"Juliana, tell me more." He put his hand under her chin and raised it gently to make her look at him. Her deep brown eyes were sad but also sobered and they had a tiny bit of a mean glint in them.

"We had a big fight last night. He accused me of leaving him because he could not give me a child, which, of course, is true in a way. He spoke of killing you and me too but then he crumbled and started to beg. We had a round of charity sex, and at the end of it, I despised him.

"Congratulations, Hagen, you managed it. You successfully separated me from my husband and I despise you too. Gabe threw me out. I have some stuff in the trunk. I have to move in here with you. Help me to get it inside before we fuck." She stared up at him, fire sparkling in her eyes, desire and love mixed with hatred.

"Wow, you leave me speechless. All right, let's get your stuff," he said.

They needed three round trips from the car to his house to empty her trunk and her backseats. The cold January air cut into Hagen's lungs but cleared his head. He wondered if she would soften up once he had gotten her pregnant. He hoped she would, he liked her to be more ladylike and not using the "f" word.

As they brought in the last load of her stuff, Hagen thought he saw Cindy's car approaching, but quickly closed the door. They stored Juliana's clothes in a corner of his bedroom for the moment and after they were finished, she turned to the bed and, without a word, started to undress. He quickly followed her example.

⚜

Wednesday, 12th of January

Hagen had barely arrived at work the next day when Cindy dropped by his lab. She nodded to the left and right at Hagen's co-workers, smiling falsely, and stepped close to him.

"We have to talk about your mother," she said in a low voice.

"Fine, see you at lunch."

She nodded and left. Hagen grunted in anger as he turned to his experiments. He'd bet that Emma had talked to the girl about Juliana. Damn her. It was time to leave and to get away from that woman.

She Should Have Called Him Siegfried

At lunch, Cindy leaned over the table towards him and whispered. "I'm very worried about Emma, Hagen, she says that you have a secret lab in your cellar and that you're an old school alchemist who brews potions. She also said that you have bewitched your high school girlfriend Juliana with a love potion. Man, where does she get such crazy stuff from?"

"Too much Wagner, I guess," Hagen said dryly, condemning his mother to hell's worst tortures.

"Hagen, this is sick and she needs help. She's delusional."

"I'm glad you finally noticed, took you long enough."

Cindy moaned. "We have to help her."

"How? It'd be no use to drag her to a shrink. The first step must come from her."

"But…" Cindy trailed off.

"Cindy, for reasons that have nothing to do with my mother, I'm going away. I am moving to another town soon. And I think that will also be good for Emma. I'm her only son and she's too fixated on me. It'll be good for her when we get a little physical distance between us."

"Oh," she said and nothing else.

As Hagen had expected, she couldn't hide that the news shocked her. He continued, "I'd appreciate it if you could keep an eye on her. I don't think she'll do anything stupid, but it'll be hard for her when I'm gone, at least in the beginning. She'll get used to it quickly though, I'm sure."

"Yes, I can do that."

"Thanks." Hagen sipped his juice. "Love potion, wow, mom's getting better." He shook his head and smiled.

Cindy's face contorted into a grimace of embarrassment, as she nodded. He eyed her carefully. People were not what they seemed. What if there was more to Cindy than he had ever imagined? If he suspected housewives in the supermarket to lead double lives, then why not Cindy, too? What if every word she said and did was a show? What if she was a governmental agent? Hagen stared into the rest of his juice and found the world without guarantees that unfolded before him to be extremely scary.

⪤⪥

When Hagen returned home, Emma and Juliana sat in his living room, talking. Damn, he really had to get away from his mother as soon as possible.

"Whew, what elements of conspiracy against me did I miss?" he asked as he looked at the two women: the perfect mother/daughter-in-law duo, teaming up against him whenever possible.

"Hagen, you must stop this," Emma said.

"I can't, what's done is done. Potions of such potency are not reversible. I have no time for discussions now. I have to brew Helena's potion and bring it to her. And Mom, I want you to leave and stop pouring poison into Juliana's ear."

"You don't even know what we talked about," Juliana said.

He didn't like Juliana's cocky undertone or the way she looked at him, the fire of rebellion in her eyes.

Maybe he should slip another dosage of love potion into her drink.

"Not about the weather, I presume," Hagen said. Then he turned and descended into his cellar. He quickly brewed another batch of love potion. He cut into his thumb for a third time so that Juliana wouldn't get suspicious from too many cut fingers. It hurt badly. He grimly watched his blood turning the black fluid into gold for a few moments before it made the liquid transparent. He stored the love potion in his fridge and moved on to Helena's potion.

It'd be too dangerous to leave Juliana alone, so he phoned George once he was finished.

"Hagen, how are you? Are you okay?" George asked.

"Yes, I am, how are you and Helena?"

"She hasn't had a waking moment yet since last week's big one."

"But no negative side effects either, I hope?"

"No, not that I can tell."

"Good. George, I'm awfully busy at the moment so could you drop by and pick up her potion? I also can't ask you in, I'm afraid, things are a little crazy around here."

"Of course, I can come by. I'll ask the neighbor to stay with Helena for an hour. Have you talked to your mother about what Helena said?"

"No, not yet. But I'll do so soon."

"Understood. I'll be there in half an hour or so."

"Thank you and sorry."

"Oh, you have nothing to be sorry for, Hagen, nothing at all."

They both hung up and Hagen stared at his phone. Yes, damn it, George was right; no need to be sorry for anything. Gabe had never deserved Juliana.

With Helena's potion in his hands, Hagen went back upstairs. He found Juliana sitting alone in his living room. She had switched on the TV, but she was reading a book.

"What did you and my mother talk about?" he asked.

"We discussed the things you did to me, of course," she said, looking up at him.

"And what did I do to you?"

"You ruined my marriage, tore me away from my husband, made him indifferent towards me, and bound me to you against my will."

The calmness of her voice sliced worse than the knife with which he had cut his thumb. She was acid, cauterizing everything she touched, burning away his love.

"Then why are you still sitting here?" he asked.

"I have nowhere else to go. And you're right; the game that you play interests me. I want to see more of it. And, ah, yes, I want to get pregnant."

"What is my mother going to do?"

"Nothing much, I suppose. She loves you for reasons inexplicable to me. Can you believe it? She asked me to keep an eye on you and try to prevent you from doing something really stupid."

She Should Have Called Him Siegfried

Hagen chuckled and Juliana laughed too, loud and hard, too loud. Her vicious laughter etched into his heart, lashed at him like a whip.

He turned away from her and that laughter and went into the kitchen. He suddenly felt sick. He had made her into the ideal woman and had worshipped her at his shrine of pictures. To admit that the real Juliana was different from the one he had dreamed about….

He pushed that awful thought aside. She would calm down. She had drunk the potion only six days ago, and he had just brewed another batch. She would become softer when she drank it a second time.

Did Alissa have similar problems with Benjamin? He hadn't even told her about his success yet, and he had received no e-mail from her in a week. He took out his cell phone and messaged her.

"How are you?" he wrote. "Everything fine? Things working out? Trouble? Juliana is mine now, but she's being nasty at times. I don't know how to deal with that yet."

He pressed the send button at the same moment that the doorbell rang. Oh, that would be George. He walked to the door and peered into the living room as he passed it. Juliana sat bent over her book again.

George smiled up warmly at him. Hagen squirmed. George was the only person who really cared for him.

"Hi, Hagen."

"Hi, George, come in for a second, it's so cold."

"Oh, thanks."

George stepped into the small hallway and closed the door behind him. Hagen gave the potion bottle to George who transferred it into a bag he had brought.

"Sorry for asking you to come here."

"Hagen, please, Helena and I are in your debt, not the other way round."

"Give her a big kiss from me and thank her for what she told me next time she wakes up."

"I will. Be careful about Emma."

"I will be, thank you."

"I better leave you then. I can pick up the potion or you can come to my house, whatever is more convenient for you, Hagen."

"Let's see what happens until next week." Hagen smiled at the old man.

George nodded and turned towards the door again. "See you soon, Hagen, and thank you."

"You're most welcome, George, take care."

George patted Hagen's arm and was gone.

Hagen waited for a moment in his hallway, steeling his nerves for Juliana, before he returned into the living room.

She looked up from her book. "Who was that?"

"George, picking up a potion for Helena."

"I thought you wanted to bring it to her?"

"I decided that I'd rather stay here with you tonight."

"I see. Seems you're also doing good with some of your potions."

"Sometimes."

"Duties done for tonight?" she asked.

"Yes."

"Fine, then let's try to make babies," she said and got up.

"Sure."

She walked past him towards the bedroom. "By the way, I'm going to my gymnastics class tomorrow night."

"Of course, why shouldn't you?"

"Just informing you."

"Well, thanks."

They had reached his bedroom and they both started to undress. He hadn't expected her matter-of-factness to hurt almost as much as rejection.

⌦⌫

Thursday, 13th of January

Sometime during the night, Alissa sent Hagen a message. He read it the next morning when he sat in his car in his garage about to go to work.

"You did it!" he read. "I'm proud of you. Everything's fine, but yes, our idols are a little different in the flesh than we imagined them to be, aren't they? Benjamin isn't nasty and I love him still, but he needs his ego schmoozed big time. Hadn't expected that but I'm coping. If she's mean, give her another dosage. All the best and thank you again so much for everything."

Hagen smiled at her message, Alissa and Benjamin hadn't stayed in seventh heaven either. His muscles relaxed a bit. He noticed, damn, he was so tense. Her suggestion to administer a second time reassured him even more. Yes, he would. And tonight, while Juliana was at her gymnastics class, he'd administer the suggestion potion to Emma and finally find out, after thirty-one years, who his father was. He had the odd feeling that he wouldn't be the grim, bearded German sorcerer he had imagined him to be since his childhood.

chapter 30

JULIANA LEFT AT half past seven, after promising to return before midnight, which was later than normal. The ladies of her gymnastics class were planning to go for a drink after their training to celebrate the New Year.

With the bottle of suggestion potion in his pocket, Hagen climbed the stairs to his mother's rooms after Juliana had left. So pathetically delighted to see him, Emma led him into the kitchen where she sat down. He preferred to stand.

"Mom, don't tell Cindy one more word. I mean it. I'm very pissed that you told her what you did."

Emma looked at the floor.

"Luckily, Cindy seems to think that you're nuts and belong in psychiatric care. Leave it at that. Stop telling her about potions."

"I'm only trying to protect you from yourself. What you did with Juliana and Gabe was wrong. You're not even aware of having committed a crime but that's what you've done."

Hagen bowed threateningly over her. "I know damn well what I've done and what I'm doing. I need to use my potions for one more personal thing, but after that, when things are sorted out the way I want them, I'll return to my profession and brew for the big picture and not for myself."

Emma stared back up at him. "And what is that one more personal thing?"

Hagen took the bottle for Emma out of his pocket. "Drink this, it won't hurt."

Baffled, Emma stared at the bottle in his hand. "Hagen, I—"

"You will drink this, Mom, whether you want to or not. Don't make me use force. I will do it. I'm stronger than you. I'll win. I don't want to hurt you, Mom, but I will if I have to. You will drink this."

He held out the bottle to her.

Emma looked from the bottle up at her son. Strength in his posture, determination. He wouldn't take no for an answer. He'd really force her.

Oh, this is exciting, Alberich said.

She ignored him and took the bottle. "What is this, Hagen? Something to make me 'unlove' you?"

"No, drink it and you'll see."

Emma, this is about me. I'm sure. I don't mind, of course, but I think you do, don't you? Alberich said and never had his voice been more wicked.

Emma's hand, which had been about to unscrew the cap, stopped in midair. "This isn't about your father, Hagen, is it?"

"Drink it, Mom."

She looked him in the eye. Neither of them wavered.

"No."

She jerked as Hagen tore the bottle from her hand. He unscrewed the bottle and threw the cap behind him. Then he grabbed her by the neck and tilted her head backwards.

"Don't touch me! Get your hands off me, now!"

Alberich laughed. *The moment has come, Emma.*

Hagen, still holding the bottle, released her and staggered backwards, his face as pale as a bleached wall. A rasping sob rose in Emma's chest and she buried her face in her hands. He had heard that, he had heard Al.

"Mom, what—"

"Step back and don't touch me," she ordered. "I'll tell you everything."

Emma, what are you doing? Alberich asked, not laughing anymore.

Hagen made another step backwards.

"You must never touch me again, Hagen, never," Emma said a little calmer.

"Why? What's going on? I heard a man's voice, I—"

"Sit down."

He didn't move, only stared flabbergasted at her, the open bottle still in hand.

"Sit down!" she shouted.

"Mom—"

"Do what I say! And don't touch me!"

Emma, what—Alberich started.

"And you shut the fuck up, Al."

"Al? Who's Al?" Hagen asked, his voice a mere squeak.

"Sit down and I'll tell you."

Her heart sank. What she had kept secret for some 32 years would finally come to light. Fatigue wanted to pull her to the ground.

Now I get it, that's how you think you can protect him from me, Alberich said, anger in his voice.

The world swayed around her, she felt detached from it, as if she stood beside herself. Her son still stood in arm's reach in front of her. Her son—the product of an unholy union. A strange peace settled over her, she would tell him now…everything. Why had she waited so long for that?

"Mom, who is he?"

"Sit down."

He grunted but finally sat down opposite her at the kitchen table and fingered the potion bottle.

"I have heard him in my head since the night you were conceived. I've had his fucking voice in my head for nearly thirty-two years…I hate him with all my heart," she muttered.

"Who is he, Mom?"

The pleading, wanting, urging tone in his voice made her cringe.

"I don't know." She giggled helplessly. "I don't know his name, nothing. I met this man in Germany, an Englishman, another fan. He sat next to me during the *Twilight of the Gods*. He was every bit the gentleman, handsome, cute. We flirted and he took me out, but we didn't have sex yet.

She Should Have Called Him Siegfried

"The next day he drove me to a lonely house in the countryside, telling me that he was housesitting for a friend. I was so excited. I wanted him. I did. We went to that house, we had dinner, and it was so romantic. But he slipped something into my drink, some drug, or potion, I don't know what it was. I stayed conscious, but…I knew what was happening and what I was doing, but I had no control over it. He brought me to the bed-room—"

Oh, Emma is telling my son, that I live to see the day… Alberich said and his voice dripped with mockery. *And after that, you'll touch him so that I can leave you. Rejoice, Emma, you'll finally be rid of me.*

"Shut the fuck up, Al," Emma said and Hagen jumped. "He undressed me," she continued. "I let it happen, I wanted it to happen. He undressed too. But suddenly, we weren't alone anymore. Another five men entered the room, two of them young, but three of them were over fifty for sure. All of them were stark naked except for Venetian carnival masks.

"The Englishman, he had told me his name was Robert, though I'm sure that was a lie, started paint-ing something onto my body. It looked and smelled like blood. He had hid the jar of blood and a brush under the bed. While he did that, the five men were chanting something in a language that I didn't understand. It was some ritual.

"And then…then, they all fucked me, all of them, all six of them, one after the other, with the other five watching and chanting and cheering, and it felt good… it felt so good. I came for each and every one of them.

It felt so fucking good...I don't know why it felt so good, because of the drugs, I suppose."

Alberich snickered in her head. *Ah, my last moments inside you.*

"I must've fallen asleep at some point. The next morning when I woke up, the five men were gone and only Robert was left, still asleep. My body was covered with blood and semen and then I heard a voice in my head, the voice of your father, much deeper than Robert's voice. He said that they had impregnated me the previous night and that the baby would be theirs, not mine.

"I panicked. I tried to sneak away but the door was locked and my clothes were nowhere to be found. I tried to escape through the window but Robert woke up and struggled to hold me back. He was shouting something about the fruit of last night belonging to him. We fought by the window and I don't know what happened. I tripped and fell against him. He must have lost his balance. He fell out of the window. It was an accident, I swear. It snapped his neck when he hit bottom."

Alberich giggled. *Yes, Robert dying wasn't quite planned, but never mind; now things will finally be corrected.*

"I climbed naked out of the window and could manage to reach an adjoining room. I was in a sheer panic. It's a miracle that I didn't fall. Luckily, there was no one else in the house.

"I found my clothes, washed myself, and then I fled. I couldn't find the car keys and I walked for miles until I found a decent road. I hitchhiked a ride and the horny sucker of a driver almost raped me. I managed somehow to get back to my hotel, packed up my stuff, and fled Germany pregnant, doubly pregnant, with you and Al.

"He never told me his name. So I gave him one, Alberich. I don't know what ritual they were doing there or to which cult they belonged. I don't know why they wanted a baby. I don't know anything, except that since that dreadful day, I have this idiot in my head who's commenting endlessly on every stupid thought that I have. For a while, I thought he was the devil himself, but he's not, he's just a pathetic idiot, some demon I suppose, and a weak one at that."

Alberich laughed out loud.

"I told my parents about that night…begged them to allow me to have an abortion, but they're devout catholics. They forbade an abortion. They locked me in my room and called an exorcist instead. Didn't help. I was going mad from the cursed voice in my head.

"When I was past the safe abortion period, my parents said that they'd either put me into a monastery until the baby'd be born and would give the child to foster care or I should leave the house and never come back. I chose the never-come-back. I had hoped the voice would go away once you were born. But it didn't. It stayed.

"I hate him so much…Who am I not to believe in magic? I've had this evil thing inside me for thirty something years. He's evil, Hagen, Al is evil.

"And he wants to take you over. He wants to slip from me into you. I don't know how…maybe he can transfer when we touch each other. You must never touch me again. I don't want him to take over your life. He's evil and you are too if you don't let Juliana go…"

Finally, she looked at her son and tears shot to her eyes when she saw his expression of terror and the horror.

"Why did you never tell me? Why?"

"What's there to tell? I can't tell you anything. I don't know who the hell he is. I don't know what any of this shit is about!" she shouted.

⋙∗⋘

Hagen jumped to his feet, towering over Emma, but not touching her. He didn't know yet what to think of what he had just heard and that he indeed had been conceived during an orgy. He only knew one thing: he wanted to know more. However, that voice still echoed in the very marrow of his bones, an awful voice, cold and wicked, the evil spirit that Helena had seen.

"Why didn't you try to get rid of him?" he shouted.

"Of course, I tried! I took drugs, I've tried to will him away, I prayed, I bought books on black magic, looking for a clue. I've tried to be rid of him, Hagen, goddamn it, I've tried. But nothing worked. He's still there."

"You should've gone back to Germany and found out more!"

"How?" her voice rose to a shrieking. "I don't know where that house was. Robert drove me there in the dark and I didn't pay attention to the road signs, I was too young and flirting and excited. When I left in a panic, I ran through the woods for miles, not exactly paying attention to landmarks then either. Robert was dead and I was responsible for his death!

She Should Have Called Him Siegfried

"I've never even seen the faces of the five other men. I don't know their names, not even their nationalities. They were all white, that's all I know. Al talks in plain English, if I were German he'd talk to me in plain German, I'm sure, he's a demon, he speaks any language.

"I had nothing, no lead, nothing. And I was afraid. I have this cursed voice in my head, Hagen!"

"Let me talk to him," Hagen said and grabbed her arm.

He heard a terrible roar the moment he touched her, like a moan reaching his ears from a deep cave. Emma shrieked and getting up, tried to rip her arm free of him. The roar turned into laughter. A second face appeared behind Emma's terror stricken one. A face made of gray smoke with bottomless hollows for eyes and a huge, evil smile. Emma saw something and shrieked even louder. Hagen followed her eyes and that same gray smoke seemed to rise from Hagen's hand, shapeless smoke in contrast to Alberich's face. Hagen stared incredulously at his hand.

An edge of his smoke mingled with a bit of Emma's and Hagen moaned. The outskirts of a powerful will touched him but Emma finally jerked her arm free of him and staggered backwards. The two smoke bits ripped apart, Hagen's slipped back into his hand and the second face behind Emma's disappeared. The roaring laughter in Hagen's head stopped.

"No!" Emma shouted.

Hagen swallowed air.

Tears poured down Emma's cheeks. "I won't let him have you! He wants to act, work, and live through you. Don't touch me! I don't want him to be in your head. I wouldn't wish that kind of fate on my worst enemy and most certainly not on you. I love you, Hagen, I do, you're my son too, not only his."

Hagen shuddered. "Mom, as you've seen he's already with me, at least a part of him. Helena saw him too, his spirit, aura, whatever. She's seen him around both of us. What can he do? What can he not do? I need to know!"

Emma flinched and squirmed.

"What's he saying now?" Hagen asked when she didn't answer his questions.

"He is telling me to touch you, but I won't, I won't." Emma's voice was drowning in tears. Her muscles jerked spastically, as if the thing inside her was trying to force her to move.

"Mom, this is crazy, who or what is he?"

Emma sobbed. "I don't know."

"Mom…" He made a step towards her.

Emma screamed and jumped backwards. "No, no, no! Don't touch me. You don't know how vicious he is. You don't know what he has been saying to me all this time."

"What, Mom?"

Emma sobbed. "I don't know what he wants, Hagen. He's just there, talking to me, commenting on everything that I think and do and say…it's hell, Hagen, hell on earth…never alone, never myself. I don't want to do that to you. Don't touch me. I'm so tired, so tired. I want this to stop, I want to die…"

She sank to the floor where she stood, her muscles still jerking. Her sitting down at all looked like a struggle of will. Her limbs tweaked spastically.

Hagen stared at her in horror. "What's his agenda, Mom? What does he want? What does he want with me? What can he do?"

"I don't know…I asked him a thousand times what he and his friends had wanted to do with the baby, with you…he never told me. He never tells me anything. He laughed at the books on black magic that I had read. The only thing I ever wanted, that kept me alive, was to protect you from him. His agenda is to take you over, but to what end, I don't know. I swear."

"What's he saying right now, Mom?"

"That the time has come, that I can be rid of him if I touch you. That he'll join you now. But I can't and I won't let him do that. It's hell, Hagen, to live without knowing, without understanding, only knowing that you'll never find out the truth. That it'll be denied you, forever.

"No love either, nothing…and all this because I had wanted to have an affair with that Englishman. So much punishment for one night of weakness, I don't deserve that much punishment! I don't want this anymore. Why? Why has this happened to me? Why?"

Her voice grew thick with tears and Hagen stared down at her, not at Emma, but at an old broken woman who had suffered too much and too long. Was it true? Could the thing in her head take over his mind? Would he lose his free will? Would he become Alberich's instrument? He didn't feel like wanting to risk it.

Emma looked up at him. "Let Juliana go, Hagen. Go away and leave me. I fear that Al will find some way to take you over now that you know…we must never touch again. Leave, but without her, leave Juliana behind. Go away and start from scratch, without me, without her…I can do only that, Hagen, set you free, I can do nothing else. But you must let her go. You must…" she said.

Hagen stared down at her and shuddered. "I'll think about it," he said.

"Leave me now, go…go!"

He nodded, turned on his heel, and left the room. He could hear her bursting into another round of tears behind him.

⌖

Emma! What are you doing, you stupid bitch? You can be rid of me. Touch him! Let me join him. It's his destiny. You cannot stand in the way of destiny, you stupid broad, Alberich shouted in her head.

She had never heard him like that, his voice transformed into a deep growling. Finally, he showed his true nature. He wanted her to move, to get up, but she didn't. How stupid of him. He had waited too long; he had become too comfortable inside her. He hadn't thought that she'd sacrifice herself.

Bitch! Bitch! What you're doing is useless. Sacrifice? Ha! I'll get him. I'll get him in the end, Emma, I'll get him!

"No, you won't," she said aloud. Then she stood and straightened her clothes and hair.

⌖

She Should Have Called Him Siegfried

Hagen sat down on his sofa one floor below Emma and stared at his distorted image in the empty TV screen, overwhelmed by the madness of it all. He barely realized that he still held the bottle with the unused suggestion potion in his hand. He hadn't needed it after all.

He would never know who his father was unless he allowed his voice, spirit, or whatever, to take him over. Well, the little he had heard and felt hadn't sounded or looked very inviting. His biological father had been a presumably British dude with black magic ambitions. He had either been the carrier of the demon and had passed him on to Emma while having sex with her, or the ritual these men had performed had somehow freshly evoked the demon. He had no experience with demons and chuckled to himself helplessly.

Emma was astonishingly sane for someone who has been hearing a voice in her head for more than thirty years. He pitied Emma, but then he frowned. Her choice of names for him and his father had a foul taste to it. How cynical to choose those names. He had never thought of Emma as a cynical person.

But…it was befitting somehow, wasn't it? He, Hagen, brewed potions, he didn't forge swords like Siegfried had, and this demon, whoever he or it was, resembled an ugly wicked dwarf much more than a god.

Hagen sighed and leaned the back of his head against the sofa. A little bit of peace spread inside him. At least he now knew Emma's secret.

He'd go away and leave Emma to her misery. What if she killed herself? What if she was just too tired of her unwanted guest?

What about Emma's plea for him to leave Juliana alone? No, he couldn't and he wouldn't. He was now responsible for her. They had sex every day; he had probably already gotten her pregnant. He couldn't abandon her now.

He got up and stored the bottle with suggestion potion in the cellar fridge. Then he went to his office and checked for houses on the Internet. He'd go house hunting with Juliana over the next weekend.

⚞⚟

Hagen made them lemonade and poured the second batch of love potion into Juliana's glass.

She returned at a quarter to twelve. She didn't have a key to his apartment yet so she rang the doorbell. It had been a week now since she had drunk her first batch of the potion. Her cheeks were rosy from the gymnastics and she smiled at him as she entered.

"Hi, how was it?"

"Nice and relaxing. You should do some sports too," she said.

"Yeah, maybe, once we've moved. Come to my office, I selected a few houses. I'd like you to take a look at them. We could go house hunting next weekend."

"Oh," she said. "Sure."

"I made lemonade, there's a glass for you in the fridge."

"Ah, thanks."

She went to the kitchen while he walked to the cellar. She joined him a moment later and he noticed that she had already drunk half her glass of lemonade. They looked at houses together while they both drank the rest of their lemonades. They decided on four candidates.

"I'll phone the real estate companies tomorrow."

"I can't move before spring though," Juliana said. "School."

"Oh…Can't you quit earlier?"

"I could, but I don't want to."

"I see." He didn't insist any further. He hoped she'd change her opinion once the second batch of love potion took effect.

He thought it did when she begged for more while they made love an hour later.

⌖

Emma lay in her bed and stared at the ceiling. The walls of her house were thick, but, nevertheless, she heard Hagen and Juliana making love below her because they were both so damned loud. They moaned and screamed, both of them.

Emma, I don't like the fatalism that you are radiating, Alberich said, calm again.

What do you expect, you bastard?

Doesn't sound to me as if he'll give up on her. Good boy, he's my son after all.

Tears crept into her eyes. Tears of loss, anger, of her life wasted.

I wouldn't call it wasted. You gave birth to the potion master downstairs. And he's working on procreating himself. I'll live forever. From you to him, from him to one of his children…

"If I die before you've switched, what's going to happen to you, Al?" she asked, not expecting a truthful answer but she asked anyway.

I'll choose when to join him, not you, Emma.
Silent tears poured down Emma's cheeks.

⚶

Friday, 14th of January
When Hagen woke up, Juliana lay awake next to him. Her face was that of a suffering Madonna.

"What's wrong?" he asked.

"I don't feel so well."

"Why, what is it?"

"I don't know. Hold me."

He took her into his arms. Oh yes, heavens, the second batch was working.

"Are you in any pain?" he asked.

"No, I just feel lousy. I don't want to go to school today and I don't want you to go to the lab either. Please stay with me."

"Sure, let's call in sick. I haven't had a sick day in a long while anyway."

"Okay."

She huddled closer to him and he caressed her long brown hair.

"Make love to me," she said after a while and his heart bounced with joy. She called it making love, not fucking.

She cried after they had made love. He caressed her face. "Why are you crying?"

"I don't know, I really don't…I feel so miserable…"

She sobbed; he held her tightly and let her cry. What a relief, now she would cry out all the acid. She'd be softer from now on, his holy nun who'd be begging for his attention.

He called the lab, she called the school, and they both reported in sick. Hagen took a shower first and then prepared breakfast while she showered. She shuffled into the kitchen, listless, sad, tired, broken somehow. That would pass, that was just the first reaction to the second batch.

She sat down in front of him. "Hagen…have you given me something again? Did you put something into the lemonade last night?" she asked in a quivering voice.

He looked her in the eye and nodded. "The same love potion. You were so acidy, so vile, I—" he stopped as she burst into tears.

He got up and embraced her; she let it happen.

"Hey, it's all right. You're mine now and I'll do anything for you. I'll make you happy. You'll soon get pregnant. We'll go away from here and we'll live in a fine house and you can raise our kids and we'll be happy, Juliana, we will be."

She just cried and he caressed her. Her cell phone rang; it lay in the living room on the table. She got up to take the call, trying to dry her tears. He walked after her, anxiously watching.

"Yes?" she answered the phone and listened. "What?"

She grew pale. "No…no…oh no…" she said and collapsed to the floor in tears. The phone slipped from her fingers.

Worry stung Hagen. Now what? "What happened?"

She didn't answer, only cried.

He took the phone and held it to his ear. "Hello?"

No answer, the other end had hung up.

"Juliana, what happened?"

"You monster!" she suddenly shouted. "You monster! Gabe is dead! He's dead! He cut off his own dick and bled to death!"

For a moment, she became the old acidic Juliana and her voice distorted to a shriek. Hagen held his breath and tried to fight the fear that crept into his guts.

chapter 31

REPORT NO. 34 from Agent 9836B12
Subject: Hagen Patterson (HP)
Status: Gabriel Daniels committed suicide
Next action: Further investigation.
Details of current status:

1)   Dramatic developments in the HP case. The husband of Juliana Daniels was found dead in his apartment on Friday morning. Gabriel Daniels left a farewell letter behind in what is an apparent suicide. He cut off his own genitals with a kitchen knife. I haven't seen the letter myself. However, I heard from the officer who is handling the case that Gabriel wrote something to the effect that he thinks his wife, who had moved out last Tuesday, left him because he is infertile. He didn't want to live on with his shame and without her so he ended it all. Since the letter doesn't even mention HP or any involvement of illegal substances, it'll

be difficult to prove anything even if HP should be related to the incident.

2) Since it's in our utmost interest to get to the people behind HP, my recommendation remains to continue watching HP and not to intervene at this point.

She Should Have Called Him Siegfried

Juliana cried through most of Friday. Hagen didn't know whether she cried because of the second batch of love potion or because of Gabe.

"This is not my fault," Hagen told her a thousand times. "The suggestion potion that I gave him had nothing to do with what he did. If anything, the potion didn't really work. I suggested that he never loved you and to not go to the police. He didn't go to the police—the potion works for concrete actions. But something as general as loving someone is apparently hard to suggest away.

"He cut off his genitals, for Christ's sake. He was having inferiority complexes about his infertility. That has nothing to do with my potion. And hell, what kind of man is he that he cuts off his own dick? He was nuts. You should be happy that you're rid of him."

Juliana only shook her head and cried and cried.

In the afternoon, two police officers stood on Hagen's doorstep and wanted to interview Juliana. Fear clogged up Hagen's throat so badly that he could hardly speak. What if Juliana told those police officers to search his cellar?

Hagen led the two men into his living room where Juliana sat on the sofa crying. Hagen could hardly move. Fear could paralyze you; he learned that first hand.

Nearly unconscious with fear, Hagen stood in the doorway to the living room and watched the police officers interviewing her.

"I shouldn't have left him," she wailed over and over. "I wanted a baby but I shouldn't have left him. I never thought that he'd do a thing like that…what kind of man does a thing like that? Cut off his own cock!" she wailed and the police officers, along with Hagen, winced.

Hope tried to push the fear aside—she wasn't accusing him. She said nothing to implicate Hagen in any way. Was that the potion too? Amazing stuff. How good that he had given her the second batch.

Except for tears and self-accusations, the police officers got nothing much out of her and left again quite soon. One of them even gave Hagen a pat on the shoulder as Hagen brought them to the door.

"That was the grossest suicide I've come across in my career so far. Poor girl, tell her not to take it so hard."

"I'll try." Hagen lifted the corners of his mouth in an attempted smile and the police officers nodded and left.

Hagen hurried back into the living room and hugged the crying Juliana. She leaned towards him and sobbed at his chest.

"I'm so sorry, my love. So sorry," Hagen told her. "I love you, Juliana, with all my heart and soul. It'll pass, darling, it'll pass."

He tried to soothe her but she just kept crying. The amount of tears that she shed was staggering.

⊸≍⊱

At seven in the evening, Emma stood on his doorstep.

"I've heard about Gabe. Is this your doing?" she hissed.

"Come in, Mom, and no, damn it, it's not. I suggested to him not to go to the police and that he never loved Juliana. I didn't tell him to cut off his dick."

Emma closed the door behind her. To his relief, she looked like the old Emma again and far from suicide.

"Juliana has been crying the whole time. Could you console her a bit?"

"I'll try."

Emma walked to the living room and sat down next to Juliana. She was still sitting on the sofa and wept sometimes more, sometimes less. Hagen could not believe that any human being could cry that long and so much. Emma hugged her, while Hagen stood in the doorway again, watching and listening.

"Why did he do that, Emma? Cut off his dick! What kinda man would do that?" Juliana wailed. "I should've stayed with him."

"It's not your fault, honey, stop blaming yourself."

"But I am to blame!" she suddenly shouted. "I told him to his face that he was only half a man if he couldn't get me pregnant!"

Hagen gasped and Emma too.

"I told him that it was useless to have sex with him if he couldn't get me pregnant...I humiliated him every day. I've been so mean and vicious. I feel so bad. I'm so sorry! Oh, God, forgive me!" she howled and burst into a new round of tears. Emma patted her back, looked at Hagen, and then she nodded.

He understood the meaning of that nod. She was giving her blessing for him to take Juliana for himself.

He nodded back and smiled, Emma did as well. How odd, he and his mother had just made their peace with each other.

※

Fine, Emma, fine, now that you've made your peace with him, fulfill the rest of your destiny and be rid of me.

No, Al, and as of now, I'll never talk to you again. You won't get what you want.

Ridiculous, Emma, you have no chance against me.

Peace washed over Emma, and knowing that she'd be victorious.

Ha, dream on, Emma, dream on.

She smiled to herself and let Juliana cry in her arms.

※

Sunday, 16th of January

It had been a weekend of horror. All of the acidity, but also all of the joy and all of her life energy seemed drained out of Juliana. She would just lie in Hagen's bed or on the sofa in the living room, sometimes crying, other times just staring into space.

Hagen escaped the gloom she radiated and worked on Sandra's potion schedule in his cellar.

※

Monday, 17th of January

On Monday, Hagen and Juliana took another day off from work for Gabe's funeral. Hagen reveled in Juliana's sight. She looked breathtaking in that black formal dress, despite the puffy and red face that she hid behind a black veil attached to her hat.

She Should Have Called Him Siegfried

Covered in patches of snow, Hagen found the cemetery to look wonderfully gothic with its black trees bare of leaves. The morbidity of how Gabe had left this world had the mourners in its grip. Their bodies seemed hunched in embarrassment; shamed at the mere thought of how he had died.

Gabe's parents and other friends and relatives eyed Hagen accusingly while he supported Juliana. After a while, he realized that those accusing glares didn't target him, but her....

Emma stood next to Hagen, sovereign again, quite herself, but careful not to touch him. Almost against his will, Hagen started to admire her. She was a strong person. Her parents had discarded her, she had boxed her way through as a single mother, and on top of everything else, she had been hearing Alberich's voice in her head all this time. Hell, what a strong woman she was.

⌦⌫

Emma, touch him.

Emma looked stoically at the open grave, her gloved hands folded in front of her.

Emma, not talking to me anymore is ridiculous. How long do you think you can keep that up?

Juliana sobbed beside her.

The time has come, Emma, touch him.

Emma shivered a bit. Her feet were getting cold. She should've worn warmer shoes.

Emma! I mean it! I'll join him now. Take off your gloves and touch him!

Gosh, would this funeral never end? Emma stifled a yawn.

Alberich screamed in her head. She scratched her ear.

Emma! You cannot resist me, you can't!

Emma stepped from one foot onto the other and wiggled her toes, trying to get them warm.

Alberich hollered and shouted while Emma smiled.

⸎

Juliana sobbed in Hagen's arms. She seemed to shrink and shrink under the glares of friends and relatives. Hagen didn't mind; he stood proud and tall and stared right back at them. People took their eyes off him quickly and glowered at Juliana instead.

Hagen tried not to look too satisfied. Finally, things were working out the way he had wanted. He had made his peace with Emma, he knew as much about his father as she knew, Juliana was his, and Gabe was out of the way, permanently. He had purged Juliana of acid and he'd soon give her a new life in a new town. What had threatened to become a disaster for him had turned into one for her.

Hagen looked down at the coffin that contained the penis-less corpse of Gabe. He felt sorry for the bastard. Hagen had gotten his fair share of her acid too; he knew what Gabe had gone through. He had envied Gabe ferociously. No need for that. She had made his life hell, humiliated him, had hurt him where it hurt a guy most of all, at his manhood.

When the funeral was over and the crowd dispersed in the cold and black winter day, Gabe's mother approached Hagen and Juliana. Her husband tried to hold her back, but she shook him off.

She Should Have Called Him Siegfried

"My son didn't kill himself, you killed him, you bitch," Mrs. Daniels hissed and Juliana shivered in Hagen's arms. Mrs. Daniels looked up at Hagen, tears shone from behind her own black veil. "I can't understand why you're willing to take her in. She'll kill you too, Patterson, she's poison!" Without waiting for an answer, Mrs. Daniels turned on her heel and strode away.

Juliana clung closer to Hagen, crying again.

"And so the tables turn," Hagen said and she shrunk even further. He relished the warm simmer of satisfaction in his stomach.

Finally back at home, he stripped her naked and fucked her for hours.

⚜

Tuesday, 18th of January

Tuesday, Hagen returned to his lab and had lunch in the cafeteria where Cindy joined him.

"I've heard about the Gabriel story from Emma, wow, man, that's tough stuff."

"Yes, it is," Hagen said with his mouth full.

"Emma apologized for the love potion story. She said her imagination had gone wild because she hadn't known why this Juliana woman had turned to you. Now she knows. Although she finds it amazing, and I do too, I must say, that you still want that woman after what she has done to her former husband."

"She won't do that to me, I'm not infertile, and I also learned one thing during this whole disaster, that Juliana and I are one of a kind. I can handle her. Gabe couldn't."

Cindy shook her head. "You have strange taste in women, Hagen."

"Says Cindy, who has never even met my women." Hagen grinned at her.

Cindy smirked. "Sorry. However, I'm glad you put your house in order. Emma said that she talked important things over with you and that you made your peace with each other. She was very relaxed and herself on Sunday. I'm glad. Did you talk about your father with her? Emma wouldn't say anything; she only smiled…like that."

Cindy pointed at Hagen's face.

"Yes, we have made our peace with each other, Cindy."

"Oh, come on, tell me more," she begged.

"Nope."

Cindy sighed and Hagen chuckled. No, she wasn't a governmental agent. If she were, he'd call himself Siegfried.

As Hagen returned home on Tuesday night, Juliana sat on his couch in casual wear. She looked up at him, not crying, but her face was a pale mask of misery.

"We can move any time," she said. "The school fired me. The director called me to his office and told me that he cannot have someone as amoral and low as me teaching the kids."

Hagen cleared his throat. "Good, then we will go house hunting next weekend and I'll quit at the end of the month."

She nodded and looked back at her hands in her lap.

Hagen grinned broadly at her. Finally, his world was what he wanted it to be.

chapter 32

WEDNESDAY, 19TH OF January

The healer is happy. Hagen sits across from me again on our sofa with George beside him. They are talking. He has brought my potion. I haven't been awake in a while. The long waking moment during which I talked to Hagen about the shadow around him had exhausted me.

I feel peace coming from Hagen. Today the shadow around him is small; he shines through it with satisfaction. Good. I'm happy when the healer is happy. And yet, something is odd, something is missing. It's Colleen…heavens! I know what is wrong….

Hagen sat next to George on his sofa. The bottle containing Helena's potion stood on the table. George held a piece of paper in his hand and stared at it in awe.

"It's actually not so difficult to brew this potion, George. You can do it. I'll send you the weekly ration whenever I can, but there might be a week when I cannot manage to brew the potion, pack it properly, and bring it to the post office to send it to you in time. It could also happen that a blizzard or whatever disrupts postal service. I would feel safer if I knew that you have a copy of the formula as a backup and that you could brew the potion yourself in case something happens. None of the ingredients is illegal or that difficult to get, you can do it yourself. But please follow the instructions to the detail and don't show this copy to anybody, never, ever. Okay?"

George looked up at Hagen, smiled broadly at him and nodded. "I promise you that nobody will ever see this copy, only over my dead body. And I'm highly honored that you trust me with this."

"Not a problem, George."

"I wish you all the best of luck, Hagen."

"Thank you. I'll come by and visit from time to time, I promise. I'm not moving out of the world, you know."

"Good. Really, I cannot thank you enough, I—"

"Hagen?" Helena whispered.

George and Hagen both stared at her. Like two weeks ago, both men jumped to their feet and rushed to Helena's side.

"Helena, thank you so much for what you said the last time," Hagen said. "It helped. I sorted things out with my mother, at least as far as possible."

"Oh, that's good. I'm so glad to hear that. Hagen, there is one other thing. Colleen Hardwood…"

Hagen raised a brow. "What about her?"

"We know how she died, in a house fire, but do we know why that fire happened?"

"Um, no."

"I feel that is was no accident. She was murdered and you must find out why. It's important…that's all I know," she said and closed her eyes.

For a moment, Hagen and George stared at her, speechless.

"Murder? Why would anyone want to murder Colleen?" Hagen said.

"I still don't understand what this is about."

"Me neither, not really, but I'll try to find out."

George nodded. He gently felt Helena's pulse at her wrist.

"Is she all right?" Hagen asked.

"Yes, she is. Calm and steady."

"Good."

Their farewells went on forever. When George and Hagen finally ran out of things to say, they hugged each other for a while.

Yes, I would've liked you to have been my father, George, Hagen thought and damn, why not tell the old man?

"George, I've never known my father, but I've always wished he was like you."

"Oh, thank you, Hagen. I…take care of yourself, son," the old man said with tears in his eyes.

"You too." Hagen hugged him once more, and finally left.

⸎

Back at home, Hagen found Juliana in her now usual pose, sitting on the sofa. She had switched on the TV and stared at it, but she wasn't really watching. Her empty eyes looked dull and infinitely sad, defeated.

He squeezed a kiss onto her cheek. "I'll be back in a moment. I have to check something on the Internet."

She nodded absentmindedly, not even saying a word.

With a sigh, he left her and went to the cellar. He Googled Colleen's name again and saved all he could find about her on his computer. He skimmed through her blog, but he had already done that and found nothing special this time either. Her life had been happy and free of enemies, at least according to her blog entries.

Hagen searched through the online archive of the local newspapers and finally found a tiny article on the house fire. It said that an "astonishingly fierce" gas explosion had caused the fire. Explosion…if someone had murdered Colleen, as Helena said, then this someone had blown up her house? But how and why?

Well, if someone set fire to Hagen's cellar, there'd be a big explosion as well, considering all the chemicals….

Hagen held his breath. What had Helena said? Colleen feared that her hand would burn twice? Did that mean more than him owning her hand? Could it be that…?

He stared at the formaldehyde bin with Colleen's hand in it that stood next to his computer screen.

Hagen turned back to his computer and wrote Sandra an e-mail that consisted of only one sentence.

"One odd question, do you know someone named Colleen Hardwood?"

Only moments later, he got a reply, Sandra was online too.

"Yes. Why do you know her name? Write me a letter about this issue."

Hagen yelped and jumped to his feet. "Holy fuck!"

Colleen had been an alchemist!

She had been discovered. They had taken her out. They had murdered her.

An "astonishingly fierce" gas explosion—fueled by the many volatile ingredients in her cellar—had killed her and almost her entire family. Hagen's hands and feet turned to ice. Were they on his heels as well? No, no, no, not now! Not when he finally had what he wanted! Who the hell were these people?

With trembling fingers, Hagen wrote Sandra a letter. He could hardly hold a pen.

Oh, bless Helena for that warning that she didn't understand herself. Burning twice...once for real and once because they'd find Hagen too and blow up his house with everything and everyone in it! Those bastards hadn't even had mercy on Colleen's children. Damn, this was bad, bad, bad!

He finished the letter to Sandra, sealed it, and paced his office. If they wanted him to stop brewing, they wouldn't arrest him, they'd kill him. Simple as that.

Juliana was right, if someone found a way to slip, for example, a suggestion potion into the President's drink, they could suggest anything to him, anything.

Magic wasn't natural in this world; the old world order had died after the *Twilight of the Gods*. He and his art were relics from an ancient time and realm that should have no place in the modern world. And yet, they were here...still....

What an incredible coincidence that Ivan had given him Colleen's hand…or maybe not a coincidence? Ivan knew what and who he was…Oh, my God! It was Ivan, it had to be! Not Cindy or someone bunkered down in an empty house but Ivan! Ivan had sold him out long ago and as a last twisted act of friendship had given him Colleen's hand as a warning?

Why were they waiting? Why hadn't they taken him out yet? Oh, God! They wanted him to lead them to Sandra. Shit, of course! He was only a tiny fish in the pond. Sandra was a much bigger one. They wouldn't burn her house down, surely not, or, more correctly, only after they had gotten their hands on the secret formulas in her safe.

He tore open the letter again and added a few more lines.

"Don't send me any formulas at the moment. Don't send the couriers. Freeze everything, I think I'm compromised! I'll move ASAP and I'll contact you again when I'm sure they've lost my trail."

He stuffed the letter into another envelope, sealed it, and scribbled Sandra's address onto it.

"Calm down, Hagen, calm down…" he whispered to himself and took a few deep breaths. He'd go to work tomorrow as usual and start packing up in the evening. He'd find a new house that weekend. He had told nobody to which town he wanted to move.

But, oh shit…they probably already had his social security number. As soon as he had a new job and was processed by the system, they'd have his trail again. There were a thousand ways to locate somebody these days, but that couldn't be helped. They surely knew where he lived now. He'd have to leave. He'd have to stop brewing for a while, maybe forever…a short raspy sob escaped from his throat. Stop brewing? What a terrible thought. He couldn't grasp yet what that would mean and didn't want to either.

So good that he had gotten his affairs in order before he had found out that he was compromised, all except Ivan. He'd confront Ivan, the bastard. Damn him, they had been friends for so many years.

Hagen hurried upstairs and found Juliana in the same pose as hours before, sitting apathetically in front of the TV. She reminded him to a frightening degree of Helena…Oh, God bless Helena. Without her hint, he never would've found out what was happening.

He took Juliana by the hand, brought her into his bedroom, and made love to her desperately. He didn't care that she cried afterwards. He had too much on his mind.

Damn, he'd make Ivan pay, that bastard.

Would moving be any good? If he didn't lead them to Sandra, he'd become worthless but too dangerous to keep alive. They'd kill him and blow up his house if Ivan told them that Hagen knew about them. Fuck! He'd have to think this through…calmly, not now.

He tried to sleep—impossible with Juliana silently crying into her pillow.

Thursday 20th of January

Restlessly, Hagen went to work and took the letter to Sandra to the post office during his lunch break.

He knew of no way how he could disappear, he was an alchemist, not a criminal. He had no idea how to cheat the system into forgetting him. Ridiculous! He could make someone do what he wanted, he could give someone second sight, but he couldn't fight his enemies. As soon as the enemy became an institution, not a person, all of his potions became useless.

And Ivan…Ivan was the spy, the guy with the double life. Damn, if he could take Ivan out…would that help? He now had an amnesia potion. Sandra had given him the formula. He was brewing it for someone. Sam, the twenty-eight cities guy, delivered that potion. He'd have to study it in more detail. If he could apply it to Ivan and make him forget…but forget what? Ivan would have to forget everything. They knew each other for twenty years. They had been friends for twenty years.

Tears welled up in Hagen's chest. How could Ivan have betrayed him like this? How could he dare! Yes, he'd wipe out Ivan's memory. Even if that didn't help Hagen, Ivan deserved it for betraying him like this.

⚔

He went home and the sight of Juliana's listless heap of misery on the sofa made him squirm. Alissa was twelve years older than Juliana but now looked younger than Juliana did. Juliana sprawled there, not a lady anymore, but a slut. In his mind's eye, Hagen saw Juliana ten years from now: fat, with greasy hair, common, and commanding their six kids around, all beauty and edge gone. Hagen shuddered and went into the kitchen.

She Should Have Called Him Siegfried

Gabe's suicide had surely also contributed to her current state, but it had been too much love potion. Hagen moaned. He should've stayed with Alissa.

Things would get better once he had settled into a new place with Juliana, once she was pregnant. And for this purpose, he had to get rid of Ivan.

How damned convenient that Ivan had told him about his new girlfriend and that their friendship cooled off at the same time. Had Ivan lied? What if Amanda wasn't his new girlfriend after all? What if Ivan only used her as an excuse to end their friendship so that he wouldn't have to look into Hagen's eyes once the shit of betrayal hit the fan? Amnesia potion for Ivan it was.

Hagen had a quick dinner of instant food and went into his cellar. He studied the amnesia potion and read all instructions until he knew them by heart. Given in small dosages, as he brewed them for Sandra, the potion caused gradual memory loss. The affected person showed symptoms resembling Alzheimer's disease so that nobody noticed that the memory loss was unnatural. If administered in one massive dose, the potion's effect would resemble that of total amnesia, depending on the strength of the dosage. Just what Hagen needed.

He brewed a batch for Ivan, the strongest that the potion instructions allowed. He poured the potion into one of his screw cap bottles and jogged upstairs.

Juliana was lounging on the sofa. Things would get better once they had moved and once she was pregnant. They'd get better.

"I have to drop by Ivan's place. I'll be back as soon as I can," he said and she nodded absentmindedly.

Hagen left the house and drove by a liquor store to buy a six-pack of beer. Then he drove to Ivan's apartment.

chapter 33

Luckily, Ivan was at home.

"Oh, hey, man, nice surprise. Come on in," Ivan said as if nothing had ever happened. However, Hagen thought he saw a hint of terror in Ivan's eyes, well hidden by Ivan the actor, the beautiful boy whom everyone trusted, whom nobody expected to be evil and treacherous.

Hagen looked around Ivan's apartment. That Amanda had moved in seemed to be true. Additional lamps, small tables, and African sculptures that didn't quite fit into the furniture-shop show-room cluttered Ivan's apartment. A couple of yet unopened boxes stood in a corner of the living room. Clothes, women's clothes among them, lay spread over the sofa.

"Brought a six-pack," Hagen said and walked on into the kitchen.

"Where are you going?"

"To get glasses, in your noble place, I have to drink the beer out of glasses."

Ivan chuckled. "I'll clear off the sofa."

In the kitchen, Hagen got two glasses from a cupboard. He hastily poured the amnesia potion into Ivan's glass and filled it up with beer. Then he poured himself a glass.

Was this really the right decision? Ivan would forget who he was with that potion...fuck it. Ivan might have even set fire to Colleen Hardwood's house himself.

Hagen took the two beer glasses and returned into Ivan's living room. "I don't know if you've heard. Gabe has killed himself." Hagen offered Ivan the beer glass that contained the potion.

"I'm glad you mention it first. I've seen him...at the hospital's morgue, you know. So gross."

"Yes. Why didn't you call me?"

Ivan shrugged and drank from his beer.

"Because you think I had something to do with that?"

"Did you?" Ivan asked.

Damn it, now it all made sense...Ivan's growing warnings about how Hagen should give up on Juliana. Ivan's bad conscience had motivated all that. He surely had instructions from above to take Hagen out when he crossed a certain line, and he had with the love potion. Ivan had severed their friendship at that point. He had retreated and marked Hagen for the kill.

"No, I didn't. Juliana, with her unique charm, frequently told Gabe that he was only half a man if he couldn't get her pregnant, that he wasn't worth the fuck, and so forth. After years of humiliating him and then leaving him, it was too much for his gentle soul and he cut off his dick in a last desperate act."

She Should Have Called Him Siegfried

"Really…" Ivan said, doubt in his voice as he sipped his beer.

"Yeah, really. I had nothing to do with his passing."

"How're you getting along with Julie?"

"Quite well. I'm in control now. That thing with Gabe put me in charge."

"Are you in control?"

"I am, Ivan. How's Amanda? Where is she?"

"Oh, we're doing well, thanks. She has the night shift today at the hospital…this beer tastes weird."

The same moment Ivan spoke, knowing flashed over his face.

"Fuck…what's in there, Hagen?"

Hagen let his glass of beer drop. Its content splashed onto the floor and the glass shattered into a thousand pieces. With his left hand, Hagen grabbed the glass Ivan held and didn't even spill a drop. With his right, he hit Ivan into the stomach at almost the same time.

With an "Ugh," Ivan let go of the glass and stumbled backwards. Hagen quickly put down the glass with its precious content, jumped forward, and hit Ivan square in the face. Shit, he should've brought the chloroform and rope. Ivan moaned and tumbled to the floor. Hagen jumped on top of him and hit him once more across the jaw. Then he turned over Ivan's body and twisted his right arm behind his back.

"Fuck! Hagen! What are you doing?" Ivan shouted. He yelped as Hagen almost tore his arm out of its socket.

"Don't shout and don't struggle," Hagen hissed.

"What the hell?"

"I know about Colleen. I know what you did to her. I know that you sold me out. You only haven't taken me down yet because you want me to lead you to Sandra."

"What the hell are you talking about? I don't understand one word of it. Let me go! What was in that beer?" Ivan moaned from the pain in his arm and shoulder.

"Fuck you, man, we were friends! For twenty years. I trusted you! How could you sell me out like this? Did you start the fire yourself? Damn it, asshole, two children burned, too!"

"I don't know what the hell you're talking about!"

"You can't fool me any longer, man, not me."

Still pinning Ivan's arm behind his back, Hagen forced him to his feet.

"I don't know what's going on. I swear! I didn't sell you out. For what? To whom? I didn't start any fire. What the fuck? I feel dizzy; what did you put into that beer?"

Hagen dragged Ivan with him to the front door. He had seen a scarf there that he could use to tie him up. Ivan struggled against him, if only half-heartedly. Hagen had a good grip on him, but not only that, Ivan had already drunk quite a lot of the amnesia potion and his strength was leaving him.

"Hagen, stop it, what are you doing? Shit, I'm dizzy...what's in that fucking potion?"

With the scarf in one hand and twisting Ivan's arm with the other, Hagen steered him into the kitchen. There he sat him down onto a chair and bound his hands behind his back with the scarf.

"What did you say about selling out? I didn't sell anyone out. Colleen? I don't know a Colleen...What... Hagen, what the hell..." Ivan said in confusion as blood dripped from the corner of his mouth.

Hagen hurried to where he had left the half-drunken beer/amnesia potion. He rushed back to Ivan and held the beer under his nose.

"Drink it, Ivan. If you drink only half of it, the effect will be even worse."

Ivan's eyes focused and unfocused. "What? Hagen, what are you doing?" His speech was slurry and slow.

"Who set fire to Colleen's house?"

"I don't know a Colleen," Ivan prattled. He was already gone.

"Drink, Ivan, and thanks, you've been a good friend...most the time."

Ivan didn't resist as Hagen put the glass to his lips. He drank it, all of it.

"What? Ow..." Ivan said and licked his split lip.

Hagen got a tissue out of his pocket and dabbed at the blood on Ivan's lip. He untied the scarf from his friend's hands and hung it back over the wardrobe. Ivan remained seated, his body hanging awkwardly in the chair.

Hagen got several paper towels from under the sink in the kitchen and cleaned up the mess his dropped beer glass had caused, so terribly aware of the parallels to that Thursday evening some four months ago when Juliana had asked him for the fertility potion for Gabe... when she had started all of this.

He wiped away the beer, gathered the glass splinters, and suddenly he started to cry. Yes, he had crossed the line; he was forfeit. He had just erased the memories of his best friend. He had lost Alissa, and Juliana…he had lost her too, he had never really had her in the first place. But he had done good with his potions, too. He helped Helena, he had helped Alissa, and he had made his peace with Emma thanks to potions.

Damn it, he had to focus and he had to stop using potions for personal stuff. He had saved some money, not much, but it would keep him going for a while. He'd move, stop brewing, live with Juliana, and become a father. Yes, he had to focus on that.

He finished cleaning up and dried his tears. When he was done in the living room, Hagen returned to the kitchen.

Ivan still sat in his chair, awkwardly bent half over the kitchen table.

"Ivan?"

He didn't react. Hagen supported him under the arm and dragged him to his feet. He steered Ivan into his bedroom.

Ivan looked up at him. "Who're you? Where am I? I feel weird…" Saliva drooled out of the corner of his mouth.

"Try to sleep, you'll feel better after that. Close your eyes and try to sleep."

Ivan did as told and closed his eyes. Hagen covered him with a blanket.

"Good bye, Ivan."

She Should Have Called Him Siegfried

Hagen got up and checked the apartment. Except for the stench of beer, he had cleaned up the mess. Hagen looked one last time around Ivan's place, knowing he'd never come back here. Grimly, he left and pulled the door shut behind him.

When Hagen returned home, Juliana was still sitting on the sofa, as if she hadn't even moved an inch in the meantime. Hagen sat down next to her. She kept staring with her empty eyes at the TV. He took her left hand into his and massaged it, she didn't react.

"Honey, you can't sit on the sofa all day long and watch TV..." he said.

"What else am I supposed to do? I have no job anymore, no husband, no life, nothing...the only idea I have is going into your cellar and brewing poison for you."

Her words didn't even shock him. "Why don't you?" he asked.

"You're the only thing I have left."

Hagen nodded. "Let's go to bed, Juliana."

"Sure, Hagen," she said and they both stood and headed for the bedroom.

Hagen cuffed her hands to the bed above her head, but even that failed to distract him from the agony of having to stop to mix and to stir. Juliana cried herself to sleep next to him and he lay there and stared at the ceiling thinking about Ivan and all the good times they had had together.

Suddenly, clicking noises disturbed his bleak thoughts. Hagen held his breath and listened. Yes, someone fumbled at the door between kitchen and garage. Odd, he hadn't heard the garage door opening. They were here. Ivan's colleagues had found him incapacitated and had decided to blow up Hagen's house.

Hagen sneaked out of bed, careful not to wake Juliana, threw over a bathrobe and rushed to his kitchen. They were still fumbling with the lock. Barefoot, he hurried into his cellar. If he had to go down, he'd do so fighting.

Hagen quickly filled a spray flacon with sulfuric acid, got out the cholorform, and readied a gas cassette and a lighter to make a flamethrower. There was no time for more. Someone came down the stairs. Hagen rushed to his cellar entrance door and hid behind it, the spray flacon and the chloroform in his bathrobe's pockets, gas cassette and lighter in his hands.

The door opened, Hagen lit the lighter, pressed the button of the gas cassette and sprayed fire at whoever entered the cellar. A woman screamed as her hair caught fire and she let herself drop to the floor. A much taller person jumped into the cellar over her and towards him. Hagen dropped the gas cassette and flung out the spray flacon instead and just when he felt an electric shock jolting him, he sprayed acid into his attacker's face.

Both of them hollered. Hagen fell backwards onto his butt and writhed on the floor. Incredible that electricity could hurt that much. Sure, they didn't want to get holes in him or anything, so that a coroner who'd examine his scorched body wouldn't get suspicious and tell the police it was murder.

She Should Have Called Him Siegfried

Hagen tried to ignore the pain that rattled his every nerve and to focus on his attackers. The man he had sprayed with acid lay howling on the floor, the woman had managed to kill the flames but they had singed her hair and skin and she moaned and groaned. Hagen squirmed still but the pain slowly waned, at least it allowed him to breathe again in painful rasping gasps. He groaned as he caught a full glimpse of the woman's face. Amanda...Ivan's new girlfriend.

"You bitch!" Hagen shouted. "You fucking bitch! How did you turn Ivan around? How did you turn him against me?"

"I didn't," Amanda said and stood up. She motioned to a third person behind her. A man entered the cellar and started to pour a fine powder around Hagen's workbench, while Amanda took the yelling man with acid in his eyes under his armpits and dragged him towards the stairs. They were all dressed in black jumpsuits and the men were tall, clean-shaven and slick. They looked as if Amanda had hired them for their muscle.

Hagen tried to move, but the pain still didn't let him, he only jerked spastically.

"What do you mean?" Hagen grunted towards Amanda.

"Ivan was innocent. He knew nothing of who I am."

"What?"

"You wiped his mind for nothing, Hagen. Poor Ivan."

Her voice sounded indifferent, a bit pitiful.

"Goddamn it! He loved you!" Hagen shouted.

"Well, he had his moments."

Hagen yelled out loud. Heaven and hell, he should've known that Ivan wouldn't betray him. He should've known him better.

"I'm sorry, Ivan, I'm so sorry," he whispered.

Amanda had dragged her partner around the corner and Hagen couldn't see her anymore. Groaning, he tried to get up. Impossible. His limbs refused to do what he wanted.

"Hagen?" Juliana called from upstairs. He could barely hear her.

Amanda came back and poured tab water from the sink next to his workbench into a glass.

"I'm wondering whether to warn Juliana. I'm inclined not to, considering how her former husband died."

Hagen moaned. Amanda left the room again to wash out her partner's eyes with the water, Hagen presumed.

He tried once more to get to his feet, as the second man, who poured the powder in a line around his workbench, came past him and gave him another electro shock with a monstrous little machine. Hagen yelled on top of his lungs and writhed next to the man on the floor, while the guy continued working as if nothing had happened.

The pain took Hagen's breath away. Nothing had ever hurt that much. He feared his head would explode, that he'd lose consciousness, but he didn't. The electricity condemned him to lie there, unable to do anything and to have to watch how Amanda and her men prepared his death.

She Should Have Called Him Siegfried

Amanda returned and stepped over Hagen towards the door to his study. Her cheek was badly burned, that'd leave a nice scar. The man with the acid in his eyes still hollered, but not so badly anymore.

"Where are your formulas and what's the combination of your safe?" Amanda asked.

"Why the hell should I tell you?" Hagen said between moans. He noticed that the man in the corridor was suddenly very quiet.

The third man had finished pouring powder around Hagen's workbench and, kneeling next to it, lit a cigarette. Hagen's eyes widened as Emma sneaked into the cellar, a big kitchen knife, blood dripping from it, in one hand, a wine bottle in the other.

Emma sneaked up on the kneeling man. He noticed something, whirled around, but too late, Emma flung the wine bottle over his head full force. With a dull thud, bottle and skull connected and the man fell to the floor. The bottle didn't break. The man's burning cigarette fell onto the powder band, which caught fire immediately. Fire started to race around the workbench. Emma sprinted towards the door to Hagen's study and threw it shut just when Amanda noticed something was wrong and wanted to return. Emma leaned against the door while Amanda banged at it from the other side.

"Hey! What the hell! Hey!" she shouted.

"Key," Emma said.

"There is none," Hagen said and robbed over the floor towards the door, taking one of his stools with him. He reached Emma and she understood. While holding the door shut with her backside, she wedged the chair between the workbench and the door. Flames were shooting up around the workbench, licking at the cabinet with the ingredients and starting to spread.

"Get up!" Emma shouted.

"Let me out!" Amanda shouted.

Grunting, Hagen tried to get up, impossible.

"Go," he said to Emma.

"Oh, damn," she said and reached down to help him.

The moment she touched him, roaring laughter sounded in Hagen's head. Something inside him sucked and something from outside pushed.

"Oh no!" Emma said, but did not release him. She dragged him towards the door to the stairs instead.

Hagen yelped as something seemed to spread inside his body, taking root in every muscle, bone and cell, firmly anchoring itself.

Ah, finally. Hello, Hagen, my son! Alberich said. *It's good to finally be where I belong.*

"Holy fuck," Hagen mumbled.

"Hagen, get up!" Emma said.

The first vials were popping with plopping sounds on Hagen's workbench. Something shot to the ceiling and crashed there, sending a shower of glass and smoke through the cellar.

They had reached the corridor. The man with the acid in his eyes lay there, sliced throat, in a growing pool of blood. Hagen gasped. Emma had killed him. Well, no, not Emma.

Ah, ah, it's too easy to blame everything on me.

Who are you? Hagen thought.

Not now. Get up.

And indeed Hagen managed to get up and to stumble upstairs alongside Emma.

"Juliana…" he whispered.

On Emma's hand, Hagen staggered to his bedroom, while more and more vials exploded in his cellar.

"Quick!" Emma said.

Juliana stared at them with terror in her eyes.

"What the hell is going on?" she asked.

"Government trying to take me out," Hagen answered, stumbled to the bedside, got the keys for the handcuffs out of his nightstand and fumbled to open Juliana's handcuffs.

"Hurry!" Emma shouted. The explosions from below started to rock the building.

"Mom, bathrobe!"

Juliana was naked after all. Emma understood and ran towards the bathroom.

Hagen managed to free Juliana and pulled her to her feet. When they reached the door, Emma was there and threw Hagen's second bathrobe over Juliana. Hagen dragged her into the kitchen and his garage. Emma opened the garage's door, while Hagen opened the car, pushed Juliana inside, jumped in himself and started the engine. Emma joined them as Hagen hit the gas and dashed out of his garage the moment the house exploded.

⌁

Regina Glei

1) Due to the demise of agent 9836B12 and two of her friendlies, many open points remain in the HP case. It is unknown what kind of conclusions HP has drawn or why he believed that Ivan Fuller was acting against him. The last message from 9836B12 that I received says that she found Mr. Fuller in his bedroom when she returned home, apathetic and unresponsive. She brought him to his hospital and they diagnosed him with amnesia. He doesn't even remember his own name and is barely functional. 9836B12 was sure that a potion had caused Mr. Fuller's condition. Since HP had rendered Mr. Fuller innocuous, 9836B12 concluded that her surveillance had been compromised and decided to take HP out, arguing that he wouldn't lead us to his teacher.

2) Three bodies have been found in the remains of HP's house. I initiated necessary measures to make the authorities etc. believe that the three bodies are those of HP, his mother and Juliana Daniels.

3) HP's trail has been lost and I consider it unrecoverable. He probably called on his teacher and the inner circle is now providing for him.

4) Thanks to the surveillance of HP's couriers, we have located another two potential alchemists though, and I will personally follow up on one of those cases.

꘡꘡꘡

Tuesday, 25th of January

George is inconsolable. He thinks the healer is dead. I know better, but I believe it's unwise to tell George. I am not at all sure whether it's good that Hagen survived. I can feel him, somewhere, out there. Although he is physically far away, I can feel his presence. The shadow around him and Emma has merged into one. The creature that dwelled with Emma now dwells with Hagen and is much stronger than before. That makes me wonder why. Are women more resilient to evil than men? It seems so, at least to this kind of evil.

George told me Hagen's house exploded. I don't understand why, but I know that Colleen Hardwood, whoever she was, suffered the same fate twice. Her hand burned twice. It's almost as if her hand had been in Hagen's house, though I find that very disturbing. How could a part of a dead woman end up in Hagen's house? The mystery bothers me greatly I must say. However, I admit that pondering the Colleen mystery helps to distract me from the fear of the new entity that Hagen has become.

George is devastated. I feel so sorry for him. He loved that boy. He had projected his wishes of fatherhood onto him. George told me that Hagen had confessed that he would've liked George for a father. I have to be strong for him now and be by his side. I cannot let George know that Hagen is still alive for his own good. So, now I have two secrets before my husband, taking the pill after Carl's death, and the knowledge that Hagen lives.

Hagen left me a great gift: the formula for the potion that keeps the tumor inside my head at bay. I'm grateful for this. It means that I can stay with George for a little while longer.

George insists that somebody murdered Hagen. He says that Hagen was too careful and too diligent to let an accident like that happen. If George only knew how right he is. It will be hard to keep my secret, but I must be strong.

George now brews my potion. He talks about picking up Hagen's trade. I hope that urge will pass, once he has come to terms with Hagen's death.

I, for my part, am looking towards the future—in many ways. I see things about people. I want to see more people. I want George to take me places. For this purpose, I have to get better. In the spring, I want to go outside and see a little bit more of the world. Be quiet, poodle in my head, be a good dog and be quiet. George is in the room. I open my eyes and look at him.

"George?"

"Oh, you're awake, my dear," he says and kisses my cheek.

"George, is there still snow?"

"Yes, it's snowing right now, too."

"I have a bold plan, George. I want you to take me outside when the weather is fine. Do you think you could do that?"

Regina Glei

His eyes are glowing with happiness. It's the first time they have done that since he thinks Hagen has died.

"Of course, honey, of course," he says and kisses my lips.

To be continued…

About the author

Regina Glei was born in Germany but nourished a fascination for the Far East ever since she was a little girl. A graduate in Japanese Studies, she has resided and worked in Japan for more than ten years. Living far away from her home country has been a powerful influence on her fiction, which she describes as speculative and sometimes weird...

Regina's SF adventure novel "Dome Child" was selected Runner-Up at the 2012 New York Book Festival, SF category and also received an "Honorable Mention" at the 2012 San Francisco Book Festival, SF category.

You can find more information about Regina and her writing on her homepage http://www.juka-productions.com